Lost in a World
That Began and Ended
with His Kiss . . .

For a moment in the starred dark, Gabrielle and Neill stood still against each other, balanced against the pitch and yaw of the ship, and then his mouth grew more insistent, gently forcing her lips to part against the bold demand of his tongue. A shiver of desire spun through her, quivered within her . . . One of his hands moved slowly, sensuously, to cradle her head and caress the silken darkness of her hair . . . She trembled again, and as he drew her closer she felt as if she were being sucked into the hard power of him . . .

Dear Reader,

We, the editors of Tapestry Romances, are committed to bringing you two outstanding original romantic historical novels each and every month.

From Kentucky in the 1850s to the court of Louis XIII, from the deck of a pirate ship within sight of Gibraltar to a mining camp high in the Sierra Nevadas, our heroines experience life and love, romance and adventure.

Our aim is to give you the kind of historical romances that you want to read. We would enjoy hearing your thoughts about this book and all future Tapestry Romances. Please write to us at the address below.

The Editors
Tapestry Romances
POCKET BOOKS
1230 Avenue of the Americas
Box TAP
New York, N.Y. 10020

Journey To Love

Cynthia Sinclair

A TAPESTRY BOOK
PUBLISHED BY POCKET BOOKS NEW YORK

Books by Cynthia Sinclair

Beloved Enemy
Journey to Love
Promise of Paradise
Winter Blossom

Published by TAPESTRY BOOKS

An *Original* publication of TAPESTRY BOOKS

 A Tapestry Book published by
POCKET BOOKS, a division of Simon & Schuster, Inc.
1230 Avenue of the Americas, New York, N.Y. 10020

ISBN: 0-671-54605-8

First Tapestry Books printing October, 1985

10 9 8 7 6 5 4 3 2 1

POCKET and colophon are registered trademarks
of Simon & Schuster, Inc.

TAPESTRY is a registered trademark of Simon & Schuster, Inc.

Printed in the U.S.A.

Chapter One

THE AIR WAS COOL AND SO CRYSTAL-CLEAR THAT it hurt Gabrielle's lungs to run, and she paused on the crest of Monsieur Chauvin's hill to catch her breath. Late afternoon sunlight caught blue highlights in her long, thick black hair, glinted over lashes that shaded worried dark eyes. Simon, she thought. Where in God's name was Simon?

At the foot of the hill lay the village of Laforet, but she could see no sign of her brother in the streets between the simple stone houses. Nor was he walking over the pine-furred headlands that swept away from the village and out to sea. Hopefully, she looked next toward the woods that bordered Laforet on two sides, but the only sign of life there was a golden eagle that soared high above the pines and white birches, yellowing now with the onset of Acadian autumn.

1

The imperious grace of the big bird caught her attention, and as she watched it ride the wind, she was touched with a longing and an old loneliness. She lifted a hand to shade her eyes and thought: Papa, Maman, you should have lived to see this day.

"*Sacré nom, petite*, what are you doing here?" Startled, Gabrielle saw that the women of Laforet had gathered at the foot of the hill and that her neighbor, plump Marthe Richaud, had climbed halfway up the slope toward her. "You should be at home, waiting for us to escort you to church," Marthe added.

Gabrielle went to meet her. "I'm sorry. I've been terribly worried about Simon. He went out early with Jean, and he's not back, even though he promised to be here for the ceremony." She lowered her voice. "Simon and Jean have been talking against the English ever since Fort Beau Séjour fell. You don't think that they've gotten into trouble?"

"You mean, have they slipped over to the Micmacs and joined the Indians in a raid on the English settlements?" Marthe sniffed. "Don't worry. Those two are all talk." She put a motherly arm about Gabrielle and began to lead her down the hillside path toward the waiting women. "Don't let that brother of yours spoil your betrothal day, Gabrielle. Simon's nearly sixteen and can take care of himself."

An old woman standing at the foot of the hill interrupted. "Gabrielle's nervous and that's natural. Every woman is on her betrothal day. It is now forty years since I was engaged to my late husband, and don't you think I remember how worried I was when I walked to the church? My heart was pounding so hard I thought it would break through my ribs."

Marthe's daughter, pretty teenaged Thérèse Richaud, groaned in exasperation. "Tante Nicole, you tell that old story every time somebody gets betrothed."

"But why not?" Another woman chuckled. "I remember that I, too, was frightened. At least you needn't be afraid of Monsieur Chauvin, Gabrielle. He's been so kind to you."

There were nods and murmurs of agreement from the others. Gabrielle knew that many in the village shook their heads over this match, envious that a dowerless young orphan should be chosen to marry one of the richest and most powerful men in Acadia. And not only that, Monsieur Chauvin was the head of the successful Company Chauvin and the owner of the grand house on the hill.

"He's always had an eye for you," old Nicole said, somewhat sourly. "Why else would he have helped your sick mother and your young brother? And the fuss he's made over you." In a high voice she mimicked, "Gabrielle must have lessons with her brother. She must learn English as well as French. She must be taught to ride like a fine lady . . ."

"Well who can blame him?" Marthe interrupted, loyally. "Look, *mes amies,* at the hair like jet, the black eyes like soft velvet. And that figure—*hélas,* the poor man didn't have a chance!"

A burst of laughter was cut short as the bells of the village church began to ring. "Come,"

Marthe said, importantly threading her arm through Gabrielle's, "it's time to go."

Gabrielle carefully smoothed the folds of her new dark linen skirt and straightened her embroidered bodice. As she walked with the laughing, chattering women, she told herself that today was her betrothal day and should be one of the happiest days of her life, but all she could feel was worry over Simon. And there was another anxiety that gnawed at her as she came within sight of the church and the waiting men. Was she elegant enough to do credit to Monsieur Chauvin?

"Ah, my dear child, how pretty you look."

Old Father Maboeuf, Monsieur Chauvin beside him, was beaming down at her from the high top step of the church, and curtseying, she glanced shyly at the man who would soon be her betrothed. Today Monsieur Chauvin was dressed in an embroidered suit of imported velvet that fitted his erect, slender figure to perfection. He was smiling and fingering the birthmark on his cheek, as he always did when he was pleased, and her heart lifted. He approved of the way she looked.

So did the other men of the village. They were all standing near the church steps, and she could see them smiling and nodding to each other as Monsieur Chauvin walked down the church steps toward her. Hoping that perhaps Simon was among the men, she glanced about her. Closest to her stood pudgy Guy Richaud, Marthe's husband, and beside him . . . Gabrielle's eyes widened in surprise.

4

A tall, well-dressed stranger with the broadest shoulders she had ever seen stood next to Guy. The late afternoon sun gleamed against tawny-gold hair, etched the fine, bold lines of his face and drew attention to thick-lashed eyes, the color of sun-warmed topaz. Eyes, Gabrielle noted, which studied her with a keen interest.

For a moment, their glances locked, and then white teeth flashed in a smile. He bowed, and his deep voice was richly and warmly resonant. "Mademoiselle," he said.

There was a twitter of surprise from the women, and the men around the stranger looked at him in disapproval. Guy Richaud turned to whisper something, no doubt an explanation that here in Laforet it wasn't customary to address young women without an official introduction. Gabrielle saw awareness come into those tawny eyes and felt an instinctive sympathy. How was a stranger to know the customs of the village?

Sinking into another deep curtsey, she smiled reassuringly at him. "Monsieur," she replied and saw his white smile widen.

Behind her, the buzz of surprise rose again, but now Monsieur Chauvin was taking her arm and leading her up the steps of the church to where the old priest waited.

"It is a great pleasure to welcome you to this church, Gabrielle," Father Mabouef said. "I greeted you and your mother on the seashore sixteen years ago when you arrived at Laforet. I baptized Simon four months later and then consoled your mother on the sad occasion of the death of your father, the Chevalier de Mont-fleuri. With much sadness I gave your dear mother the last rites only last year. Now, how I rejoice to see you betrothed to a good man."

Gabrielle tried to keep her mind on what the priest was saying. It wasn't easy with the man with the golden eyes standing a scant few feet away. With an effort, she kept her eyes straight ahead as Chauvin escorted her into the church and then left her at her place on the wooden pew, but as the women filed in behind her and the men followed, she couldn't help glancing back at the tall stranger. She had only time to note that he walked with the swift, easy gait of a mountain cat, before she realized that he had caught her watching him. Tawny eyes met hers, an interested eyebrow quirked upward. When she turned away, she found that her pulse was jumping erratically.

Thérèse Richaud nudged her mother. "Who is he, Maman?" she hissed.

"I've heard that someone was visiting Mon-sieur Chauvin on business. Something about furs, I believe." Marthe frowned at her daughter. "You stay away from him, Thérèse. Anybody can see that that one has a way with women."

A way with women—was that why the stranger disturbed her? On this day of all days, she should not even want to look at any man other than her betrothed. Gabrielle forced her attention back to the church with its candles and incense and the armfuls of wildflowers she and Thérèse had gathered this morning. But before she could compose herself, the door of the church was thrust open and a lanky youth hurried in. Simon had arrived in time for his sister's betrothal ceremony.

He looked unhurt and was dressed in his Sunday clothes, and for one moment Gabrielle felt pure relief. This faded when she saw that Simon was scowling, black brows drawn across the bridge of his proud nose. What had he been up to? she wondered, torn between concern and exasperation.

"Simon," she called softly.

But he'd stopped stock still and was staring at the broad-shouldered stranger who sat next to Monsieur Chauvin. Then, making a very rude noise, he stalked away to take another seat at the back of the church.

Before Simon's behavior drew comment, Father Maboeuf began the ceremony. It was a simple service. Chauvin and Gabrielle stood in front of the altar while the priest linked their hands and blessed their betrothal. Then, still holding hands, they led the congregation down the aisle and outdoors.

"Are you tired, Gabrielle?" Chauvin bent to murmur.

"No, Monsieur." Try as she would, she couldn't make herself think of the dignified gentleman beside her as "Louis," much less call him by his given name. At forty, he was nineteen years older than she was, and there was also something grand and aloof about him that kept her from such familiarity. "I'm not at all tired," she added.

He squeezed her hand. "Well, we are now betrothed. Tonight at the feast you must act like the mistress of my house, for soon you will be my wife." Then, as they descended the church steps, he added, "Wait a moment. There's someone I want you to meet."

She turned obediently and found herself looking up into golden eyes. At close quarters the stranger was bigger than she had thought, and his eyes were so clear that she could see herself reflected in them. And though she remembered the whiteness of his smile, she was still unprepared for its effect on her. She realized that she was holding her breath and let it out very slowly as Monsieur Chauvin introduced them.

"Gabrielle de Montfleuri, my betrothed—Mr. Neill Craddock, a businessman from Boston. Mr. Craddock is a partner in the well-known C. and C. Company and honors me by doing business with my firm."

From Boston? But Boston was a British colony, and so Neill Craddock must be English. No wonder Simon had acted so rudely. "Monsieur," she murmured and added in the careful English that Chauvin had insisted she learn, "I am glad to make your acquaintance."

"And I am honored to have been invited to your betrothal ceremony." His answer came in ready French, and he did not shake her hand in the English way but bent over it with all the grace of a French courtier. "I'm grateful that my business with Monsieur Chauvin brought me to Acadia at this time."

The touch of his hand on hers was light yet somehow hinted at the man's strength. She drew a steadying breath and found that it was scented with a blend of leather and faint cologne and the clean, vibrant scent of the man himself.

She felt unaccountably unbalanced and she struggled to find her poise again.

"You deal in furs, Monsieur?" she hazarded.

Chauvin explained. "Mr. Craddock wishes to buy furs through Company Chauvin."

"It's common knowledge that Company Chauvin deals in the finest furs in Canada," Neill Craddock added, smoothly, "and Louis Chauvin's hospitality is also legendary."

"It's time for more of that hospitality, my good sir." Beaming, Chauvin slipped his arm through Gabrielle's. "Tonight I am hosting a betrothal feast at my home. The entire village will be there, of course, and you will be my honored guest."

"The honor is mine." Looking about him at the villagers, who were all apparently waiting for Chauvin to lead the way up the hill, Neill considered drily that wealth and power always induced respect. Then, glancing down at the sable-haired woman beside Chauvin, he reflected that respect wasn't the best thing that wealth got a man.

His thoughts were interrupted by a hissing noise close by, and turning, Neill saw the youth who'd stared so rudely at him in church. Well, he reminded himself, it was natural for the Acadians to feel some resentment toward the English. Originally of French extraction, these people lived in a portion of Canada that had been ceded to England only a score or so years ago. It was scant wonder their sympathies were with the French during the current war between France and England.

Not that there was anything warlike about

Laforet. Here were forests of pine and birch, broad, peaceful farms that disappeared into the headlands which jutted into the sea. Long-necked herons winged far above the high-peaked, low-sloping stone houses of the village, and the twilight was scented with woodsmoke and pine and fresh-turned earth: good, solid smells that made him think of his own land near Boston. He drew an appreciative whiff but found now that his senses registered something new, new, the delicate fragrance of wild roses and lavender, which came from the slender young woman who walked between him and Louis Chauvin.

"You approve of our village, Monsieur?" she was asking. Her voice had a low, shy sweetness, and remembering how quickly she had championed him back at the church, he hastened to nod.

"Very lovely," he said and was surprised to realize that he was not thinking of the village but of her.

"I hope you'll enjoy this evening's fete," she said. "It is the custom of our country to hold parties whenever possible, and a betrothal is a good excuse." She glanced at Louis Chauvin and saw that he was nodding approvingly. Well, she told herself, she would have to learn to talk to all kinds of people, among them Englishmen, as Madame Chauvin. And yet this man beside her puzzled her. She had met merchants and traders before, and once she had even met a French lord on his way to the north fur country. Neill Craddock was like no one she had met before.

They had finished climbing Chauvin Hill now, and the grand house came into view. Like most of the other houses in the village, it was made of stone, but Gabrielle glanced at the Englishman to see if he appreciated how the grounds around the house were decorated with flowers and trees brought at great expense from Europe and even from San Domingo, where Chauvin owned property.

A well-swept pathway led to the front door, which had been thrown wide to show the polished wooden floors of M. Chauvin's sitting room —something unheard of in the village, where houses consisted of one large room in which the family ate, slept and entertained—and at one end of this room stood a table loaded with food.

"Ah, regard, what a feast," Guy Richaud exclaimed rapturously. "Marthe never makes such wonderful stuff for me at home."

Everyone laughed and gazed at the food in delight. There were tureens of chowder, filets of fish, scallops heaped high on elegant china plates, pies made with game and seafood, mountains of crabs and lobsters, mounds of vegetables steamed or cooked in succulent sauces. There was even an entire roast pig, which held an apple in its jaws. Flagons of wine stood next to pewter goblets and plates, and Chauvin's servants hovered about, ready to assist their master's guests.

At first the villagers hung back shyly, but at Louis Chauvin's urging they soon clustered about the table to drink to the couple's health. Then, as if the wine had liberated them from embarrassment, the party became lively. Children pelted each other with orange peels, wives commented loudly about the excellence of the food, and the men gathered in groups to drink and eat and tell jokes about their own betrothals.

Standing a little apart, Neill found himself watching Gabrielle move among her fiancé's guests. Though she laughed and talked like the other women, she carried herself with an unconscious grace that made her stand out from all the others. Her beauty was obvious, and the slender young figure with its high, proud breasts and long legs showed promise, even in her simple dress. Chauvin, he thought, was a lucky dog to have captured this one's heart.

Then he was astonished at his own reactions. Gabrielle was a beauty, but there was no percentage in becoming attracted to Chauvin's woman. The world was full of beauties, and more than a few awaited his return to Boston. Suddenly, he felt anxious to be gone from this backwoods village and was thankful that his business with Chauvin would soon be concluded. He'd already paid the man a handsome sum against shipment of furs, after all . . .

"Goddamned English—they're bloodsuckers, every last one of them." The fierce young voice, cracking with adolescent anger, broke into Neill's thoughts. "Their government stinks of corruption. They seek to have our support in Acadia, but I for one will never sign an oath of fealty to England. Never!"

Talk died away at Simon's outburst, and Gabrielle, who had been accepting congratulations at her fiancé's side, turned swiftly to see her brother facing the tall Englishman. Simon had apparently drunk too much and was spoiling for a fight.

"The new British governor Lawrence is worse than all the rest," Simon was snarling. His voice cracked and broke into a stripling's quaver as he added, "I spit on England!"

"I, too, would fight for France any time," Simon's best friend, Jean Dumont, now added. "The English are liars. At first, after Utrecht, they promised us that we could be neutrals, and then they forced our fathers to sign a treaty swearing that they would not bear arms against England. Now Governor Lawrence wants us to swear to fight *for* England. Would a man fight for his tyrant? Never."

An angry mutter arose from the other men in the room, and Simon shoved his face close to Neill's. "What do you say, Englishman?" he sneered.

Gabrielle wasn't aware that she had made a sound, but she must have, for Neill's eyes met hers across the room. The tawny eyes were reassuring, but she still held her breath as he began to speak.

"I never discuss politics at parties," he said in his perfect French. "It's bad for the digestion."

For a moment everyone was speechless. Then Guy Richaud laughed. *"Sacré nom,"* he shouted, "sacred name—the Englishman has a sense of humor." Then, turning to Jean and Simon, he added, "It's time you hotheads shut up and let us enjoy the party, *hein?"*

Sullenly, Jean turned back to the table and poured himself more wine, but Simon paled and stormed toward the door. Gabrielle was about to follow when Chauvin spoke. "Gabrielle, it's time for dancing," he said. "Perhaps you could teach Mr. Craddock a few of our Laforet steps, eh?"

His eyes carried a message which Gabrielle understood at once. To compensate for Simon's inexcusable behavior, she must now pay special attention to the Englishman.

"I would be pleased to try," she said.

Chauvin gave a signal and the musicians began to tune their fiddles. As the villagers cheerfully formed a circle for the first dance, Gabrielle saw Neill Craddock's eyebrows quirk upward. "I'm not much of a dancer, Mademoiselle."

"The dances are not at all difficult. You will see." The dark eyes that sought his were anxious, and Neill felt immediate sympathy. Both the young firebrand and Chauvin had put the poor girl in an awkward position. "You're going to regret this," he warned, as he bowed and offered her his arm. "My last dancing partner complained that I stepped on her toes."

Her laugh was husky, unexpectedly mischievous. "Then we are even. When we danced last, Simon said that I kicked his shins . . ." Her words died away uneasily.

"You needn't worry. I can understand how he feels," he told her gently, and was rewarded by a grateful look. Then, as he drew her into the circle of dancers, he added, "I can also sympathize with his love for France. Were you two born there?"

"I was born in France, but he's Acadian-

14

born." She knew that this was just a dance, and yet as his arm went about her waist, she felt unaccountably breathless and even a little dizzy. She spoke swiftly to counter her feelings. "Your French is excellent, Monsieur Neill. Have you lived in France?"

"I had a French nurse who taught me the language," he explained, "and I studied languages at the University. Later, I spent a great deal of time in that country."

"How Simon would envy you that." Worry filled Gabrielle's voice as she added, "My brother is not yet sixteen—five years younger than I, and so I feel responsible for him. He hates the English because Governor Lawrence captured the French fort of Beau Séjour. Now he feels we will be invaded next."

Neill laughed. "There's room for everyone in this country—much more room than there is on this floor." As Gabrielle had said, the dancing wasn't hard, rather like a country measure in England. Dip and sway, link arms, cross arms, bow, retreat, then circle the room—that was all there was to it. And yet the nearness of this slender, dark-haired girl made the dance unlike any other. He was acutely conscious of her flower-fresh scent, the way the candles glinted blue highlights in her long, luxuriant black hair, most aware of the closeness of the graceful, lithe form.

As his arm settled about her waist, he felt her grow suddenly tense. "Did I step on your foot?" he asked.

She tried to laugh as she denied this, but she was troubled. She had not danced with any man save Simon before, only once or twice with Monsieur Chauvin, and perhaps that was why her pulse raced as she registered the hard muscle of his thigh pressed against hers, his whipcord-tough leanness and his strength. Involuntarily, the strange thought formed in her mind that such a man could offer a woman both safety and excitement . . .

Before she could complete that thought, the door of the great house slammed open and Simon hurtled into the room. His face was paper-white and his black eyes blazed.

"English soldiers are marching toward Laforet," he shouted. "Did I not warn you about the English? They are coming to invade our village. If we don't do something quickly, we're lost."

Chapter Two

FOR A MOMENT THERE WAS SILENCE, AND THEN Chauvin began to laugh. "Why should English soldiers invade a peaceful village? You have gone mad, Simon."

"Then why are they marching toward us?" Simon demanded heatedly. "Monsieur, it's no laughing matter. We must arm ourselves."

Gabrielle left Neill's side to take her brother's arm. "Are you sure you saw soldiers?" she asked, anxiously. "Couldn't you have made a mistake in the dark?"

The youth's ferocity left him, and he looked young and even afraid. "I wish I hadn't seen them, Gabrielle, but I did. You and the other women must go home and keep hidden, while we fight them off."

"Monsieur Chauvin, what shall we do?" Guy Richaud asked.

The thin Acadian thoughtfully rubbed the

birthmark on his cheek. "First, let's see if Simon's news is true. Guy, you and Jean make your way to the other side of the hill and take a look."

As the two hurried off, Simon spoke in a hurt tone. "I really did see the soldiers."

Affectionately, Chauvin put an arm around the boy's shoulders. "Fighting is in your blood, my dear boy, just as it was in the blood of your father, the Chevalier de Montfleuri. I, however, think it's always wisest to check one's facts. Do you not agree, Mr. Craddock?"

Gabrielle saw how the attention of the villagers turned from Simon to the tall Englishman, who shrugged. "Of course."

"As you were for many years an officer in King George's army, you might also know what these soldiers are up to," Chauvin continued.

Neill saw the sudden hostility in the many pairs of Acadian eyes trained on him and realized what Chauvin was up to. To prevent a panic he was diverting the villagers' attention. Since he had no desire to be used as a scapegoat, he answered quietly, "I was in the army only briefly when I was a young fellow of twenty-one. For the last six years I've been a simple landowner and businessman."

Simon said, bitterly, "If I had known you had been a British soldier, I would never have allowed you near my sister's betrothal. The daughter of a French knight should not be bothered by Englishmen."

"Simon, you forget yourself." Gabrielle's black eyes flashed as she glared at her brother. "You will apologize at once." As Simon shook his head, she added contemptuously, "It's a good thing that our parents are not alive. They would be ashamed at your lack of manners."

Simon flushed, but before he could reply, Guy Richaud came hurrying up the walk. "It's as Simon says," he reported in a scared tone. "An entire troop of English soldiers has surrounded your hill, Monsieur Chauvin."

"Didn't I tell you?" Simon began, but Guy hadn't finished.

"Jean thinks he's spotted a ship sailing into our harbor, and we fear that it's an English ship. He slipped down to see."

Neill walked to the doorway and looked out. The hill on which Louis Chauvin had built his home was indeed ringed with torches. Behind him there was a gasp of consternation from the women as the news spread, and some of the men pushed past him to get out of doors.

"Where are you going?" Chauvin demanded.

"To arm ourselves, as Simon suggested. We're not going to be like lambs led to the slaughter," was the grim reply.

But now Father Mabouef intervened. "They that shall live by the sword shall die by the sword—that is what the Bible tells us. No, *mes enfants*. We will meet with the English commander of these troops and ask what he wants of us. They cannot mean to hurt us, since we have done nothing at all to them." He turned to Neill. "Isn't that so, Monsieur Craddock? Your countrymen are fair and law-abiding men, aren't they?"

For a moment Neill hesitated. "Perhaps these troops are only marching through Laforet in order to engage with French soldiers further north. If you wish, I can talk to the English commander when he gets here and find out what's going on."

"Thank you, my son." The old priest now spread arms wide. *"Mes enfants,* let us pray for guidance and safety." He looked sternly at Simon and the other young men. "And let us pray for peace."

"Amen." As the heartfelt word echoed from the assembled villagers, Gabrielle heard the dogs in the village begin to howl. On the heels of the barking came a distant shout.

"To arms! There are English ships in our harbor."

"That's Jean," Marthe Richaud gasped.

Simon sprang through the door and into the darkness beyond. As he did so, a nasal voice snapped in English, "You there—stop, or I fire."

"Christ, that young fool—" With an oath, Neill followed Simon through the doorway. "Don't shoot, dammit," he shouted into the darkness. "The boy isn't armed. No one is armed here."

There was no immediate answer. The torches had come much closer, and now the shadowy shapes of men could be discerned coming up the hill. There was the sound of a scuffle and then a yelp from Simon. "They've captured me," he shouted in French.

Gabrielle would have run out of the doorway but Neill held her back. "Simon? Where are you, Simon?" she cried in terror. There was no answer. "What have they done to him?"

"We'll soon see." Neill let go of her and strode

down the pathway, a massive form in the torch-light. As he did so, the same nasal voice came out of the night.

"You. Don't come any closer."

Neill halted and spoke with cold deliberation. "My name is Neill Craddock, late Major in his Britannic Majesty's service. I demand to know what is the meaning of this disturbance, and I want to see your commanding officer. Immediately."

"You a Major?" An English soldier with a lieutenant's insignia stepped into the light. He was a large, fat fellow with the flat face of a flounder. "I don't believe you. What's more, I . . ."

"Immediately." The fat Lieutenant jumped at the underlying hardness in the big man's voice. He muttered something to a trooper, who hurried off. "Good," Neill said in the same hard voice. "Now let the young man go."

"You don't give orders here," the flat-faced soldier blustered, but Neill simply repeated his request, and Gabrielle felt herself bathed in a tension that was almost electric. "He came flying out at us in the dark—what were we supposed to do?" the Lieutenant whined.

"He's done you no harm. He's a civilian, unarmed, a mere boy." Neill looked about at the glowing ring of torches. "Let him rejoin his friends."

"Let him go, Lieutenant Dray." The order was given in a high, affected voice, and a round-faced man in full military regalia now minced his horse up the slope of Chauvin's hill. As

21

Simon shook himself free and ran back toward the house, the man on horseback added, "You're far from home, Major Craddock."

"And so are you." Straining to follow the rapid English dialogue, Gabrielle noted that the round-faced officer smirked at Neill's retort.

"Perhaps not." He dismounted, tossing his reins to the flat-faced soldier. "I'm Major Lampert on a mission of great importance to His Excellency, Governor Lawrence. Perhaps you can guess what that mission might be?"

Neill was in no mood for games. "Suppose you tell me," he suggested.

"Oh, come, Major. Certainly, you've followed the uncertain politics of this area." Once on the ground, Major Lampert was seen to be a very short man, with fat, booted legs. He teetered back and forth on those legs as he added, "You know very well, don't you, that these Acadians are suspected to be allies of France and traitors to England?"

Neill did not know when he had disliked a man more. Major Lampert typified everything that was wrong with the British army, but it wouldn't do any good to make an enemy of him—not now, anyway. "It would be folly to suspect these villagers of anything," he protested. "They're simple farmers and fishermen, except for Louis Chauvin, who owns the Company Chauvin."

He'd hoped that the name of the well-known Acadian's name would take some of the wind from the fat Major's sails, but Lampert only smirked his maddening little smile as he turned his attention to Chauvin.

Chauvin was at his most dignified. Speaking in his accented English, he began, "Major Lampert, it would be good of you to tell us why you have come to Laforet." Chauvin ignored a stifled sound from Simon to add, "As Mr. Craddock says, we are peaceful people, and we are neutrals in your war with France."

"You'll be told in good time." Loftily, Lampert waved Chauvin away and turned to Neill again. "Can you speak their ridiculous language enough to tell these people to congregate at their church so that I can read them Governor Lawrence's proclamation?"

"No need to go to church," Neill cut in. "Everyone in the village is here under Monsieur Chauvin's roof."

Lampert's eyes narrowed. "A military gathering?" he accused.

"No—my betrothal party." Chauvin caught Gabrielle by the hand and drew her toward him. "There was no talk of fighting here."

Gabrielle felt the fat English officer's eyes slide over her and bristled with insult. The insinuation in his eyes made her feel as if something unclean had crawled over her. Resisting an inclination to shrink back, she lifted her delicate chin to stare defiantly into the man's insolent eyes.

"By Jove, a wedding," Lampert was saying. He lowered his voice and added, "A pretty wench, eh, Craddock? Do these damned Frogs believe in the *droit du seigneur*? A night with this one would be almost worth the time I've spent getting to this Godforsaken spot."

Looking down into the Major's florid face,

Neill found that his fingers were itching to close around the man's fat throat. He said coldly, "Perhaps it were best to read the Governor's proclamation now. I've no doubt that after a long ride you want to waste no time finding quarters for your officers and men."

"You're right." Lampert signaled to the waiting Lieutenant Dray. "Order your men forward so that they completely circle this house. Make sure that nobody runs." He then gestured toward Chauvin. "You, Monsieu, get everybody inside your house. Men with men, women with their children. And tell them to be quiet, because you'll have to translate what I read."

Neill saw that Gabrielle was already leading the women to one side of the grand sitting room. Even at such a time, her grace and poise did not leave her. As the women called hastily to their children and gathered about Gabrielle, Chauvin instructed the men to group together at the other side of the room.

Lampert swaggered forward on his short legs and drew a sealed letter from his breast pocket. He did not open it immediately but looked about him with dramatic deliberation, and Neill realized with disgust that the man was enjoying the situation.

"We are ready, Major," Chauvin said. In spite of his courteous tone, there was a brittle tension as he added, "Please begin."

Lampert let them wait another few moments and then said, "My name is Major Lampert and I represent His Excellency, Governor Lawrence in Halifax. I have been sent here with a special letter from him as regards Laforet's future."

24

Chauvin translated quickly, and Simon snapped, "What does he mean, our future? What does that damned Lawrence know about our future?"

Lampert now began to read. His Excellency, he said, had long studied the position of Acadia in England's war with France. Though technically ceded to Britain by the Treaty of Utrecht, Acadia retained strong French sympathies. Many Acadians had gone into French-held Canada to fight on the French side. Others, dressed up as Indians, had attacked English troops. Acadians moreover refused to sign a vow to fight on Britain's side. It was a situation that could no longer be tolerated.

"His Excellency thus feels," he concluded, "that you must be removed from Acadia and resettled elsewhere. I have come for the purpose of conducting this deportation in a peaceful way. Our ships, *The Lovely Lady* and *The Royal Princess*, stand in your harbors ready to take you to your new homes."

Deported! Gabrielle wanted to cry out against that harsh word, but she could not find breath to breathe, let alone speak. She could only stare at Lampert while her thoughts skittered like trapped animals.

"You can't be serious," Neill was protesting. "This is the most ridiculous idea I've ever heard of and the most inhumane."

Lampert frowned. He obviously hadn't expected a fellow Englishman to take this line. "His Excellency feels—" he began.

"His Excellency," Neill interrupted, "must have been drunk when he drafted this order.

What in God's name does he fear from a group of farmers and fishermen?" He gestured to the frightened women in the corner of the room. "Is he afraid that the women of Laforet will attack his residence in Halifax?"

"Your humor is lamentable." Lampert withdrew a snuffbox from his vest, took a pinch and drew the powder into his nostrils. "Be careful, sir, or I'll have you incarcerated with your French friends."

"Is that the only reply you can give me?" In spite of himself, Neill's temper now blazed. "By Christ, sir, the British army has fallen on sad times if it has to rely on a jackass like yourself to carry out its orders." As Lampert began to turn a bright magenta, he added, "I want to look at that letter from Lawrence. I can't believe that a Governor could consider such folly."

Other voices now cried out in French. "They can't take us from our homes," Guy Richaud shouted, and one of the young men swore that he'd die rather than obey the British.

"Let's make a run for the forest," he shouted. "Quickly, before the British pig knows what we're up to. Simon, you and you, François, and you, Clément . . ."

"No, that's crazy!" But Gabrielle's cry of horror was interrupted as several young men lunged past Lampert and dashed out of the door. Their rush was so swift and unexpected that several of them managed to evade the soldiers who waited outside. Lampert, his face quivering with rage, stamped to the door.

"Fire, Goddamn you. Fire . . ."

Muskets cracked, and Gabrielle screamed Simon's name. As if in answer, Dray's voice shouted out of the darkness: "Some of them got away into the woods, sir, but we have the youngster who charged us earlier. Caught him a good clip on the head. He won't go anywhere."

With a despairing cry, Gabrielle tried to get to the door. Lampert barred her way. "Where are you going in such a hurry, Mam'selle?" he demanded, and his hand closed on her arm.

She cried out at the cruel grip and then heard a sound close by her, an almost feral growl full of menace. The next moment Lampert was being hurled back against the wall, and Neill had caught her up in his arms. Then they were outside and he was carrying her down the hill to the woods.

For a moment she was too stunned to do more than lie quiescent in his arms. Then she cried out in protest. "Let me down. Simon has been hurt . . ."

Neill did not answer. He was running as swiftly as an Indian, despite her weight, and she heard his grim laugh as a musket cracked and the ball passed them harmlessly. "They're damned poor shots," he commented.

It took only a few more minutes to gain the woods, and he now let her slide to the ground. "You know this area," he said crisply. "Which way would pursuit be least likely?"

For a moment Gabrielle hesitated, and then she tugged at his sleeve. "This way." In silence she led the way through the familiar woods until they came to a little glade. "No one will find this place," she said.

He was looking around him keenly. "It seems well hidden," he admitted.

"It was my favorite hiding place when I was a little girl playing hide-and-seek." With a small smile she pointed to the tall birch trees that grew nearby. "These trees are called the white ladies of the forest. They are very tall and their branches kept me from being discovered. You'll be safe here, Monsieur."

He caught her by the shoulder as she began to slip away. "And where do you think you're going, Mademoiselle?"

Her reply was urgent. "I must get back to Simon." Fear welled in her voice as she added, "He may be badly hurt."

"Your brother's got a hard head. He'll mend. It's Lawrence's order that should worry you." She didn't reply and he added grimly, "You understand that Lampert's men are going to take you away from Laforet?"

Her voice sank to a husky whisper. "I heard the English officer read the Governor's order. It's horrible."

"Then you know there's no returning to Laforet."

Neill had to admire the courage with which she forced herself to speak calmly. "Is there something that can be done?" She asked.

"Perhaps." Here in the woods the moon gave off but dim light, and in that half-light he looked strong, indomitable. She was suddenly reminded of the great golden eagle she had seen only that afternoon, and this memory somehow steadied her as she heard him say, "If the Governor can be reached before the actual evacuation of Laforet begins, perhaps he'll see reason."

She protested, "To reach Halifax takes many days Monsieur."

He calculated rapidly. An evacuation of some three hundred people would take several days, and a fool like Lampert would probably bungle everything and need a week or ten days—ample time to get to Halifax and back. "I have maps of the area, and I've been to Halifax before," he told her. "Laforet is south of Cobequid. By following a southwest course, it'd be possible to reach Governor Lawrence within two days—three at the outside." He stopped and asked sharply, "Can you ride?"

Surprised, she nodded. "It was something that Monsieur Chauvin insisted I learn to do."

"Thank God for the man's foresight." He glanced up at the sky. "It's not yet midnight, which is all to our good. We can go a great distance before the dawn."

"But I cannot go with you . . ."

He interrupted her impatiently. "Good Christ, girl, there's no time to waste in arguing over proprieties. I'm sure that your fiancé will see the need of us traveling together. If we're to reach the Governor, we must leave at once."

Her face was pale and strained but calm as she faced him. "I wasn't thinking about propriety but about sense. I can ride, yes, but you are trained as a soldier. You can go alone at twice the speed where I would only hold you down." She paused and added in a low voice, "Besides, I cannot leave Simon."

Any other woman would have been clinging to

him, wailing for him not to leave her. Admiration and exasperation warred in Neill, as he realized she was right. But he could not think of returning her to Lampert. "I can't let you go back to Laforet," he reasoned.

"But you must. I can say you seized me and carried me off against my will. My place is with my brother and with—with Monsieur Chauvin," she protested.

Neill frowned at the mention of Chauvin. She was right, of course. Gabrielle de Montfleuri was not a woman alone and unprotected—she had a fiancé who was one of the richest men in Acadia. She was no responsibility of his, and neither was her village. If he had any sense, Neill thought, he would turn around and keep going until he was back in Boston.

Just as the thought came to him, she said in a low voice, "Monsieur, if you were wise, you would forget about us. It is not your quarrel and you are not responsible for our problems. It may be wiser for you to leave now and not look back."

"Thanks for the suggestion." As he began to walk back the way they had come, she realized she had annoyed him and tried to explain.

"I do not mean to insult you. I am grateful to you for trying to help me. But Simon is the only family I have in the world, and Monsieur Chauvin is my betrothed. That is why I return to Laforet."

A question of loyalty and honor . . . he tried the words in his mind and thought, wryly, that he had begun to think as he had done seven years ago when he was a green lad of twenty-one and a new officer in his Britannic Majesty's army. He spoke more curtly than he'd intended. "You forget that I have been conducting business with your fiancé. I've handed over a great deal of money to him to buy furs for the C. and C. Company, money that my partner entrusted to me. That entire sum may be lost if he forfeits his land and his business." She was silent, and he added, "I'll see you safe and then go on to Halifax and see Lawrence myself."

Until he spoke the words, she had not even dared to hope that he would really go to Halifax alone. Now tears of relief filled her eyes and they blinded her for a moment, so that she stumbled against a root in her path. As she fought to regain her balance, she sensed rather than saw him turn, and the next moment she was in his arms.

In that moment the world seemed to stop and she could not find her breath. Something in her breast seemed to hurt, but the pain didn't come from the press of his hard male body against her softness. Now when she breathed, the air was full of his clean, distinctive male scent. His arms were like steel bands about her, holding her close, holding her safe.

"Are you all right?" His voice was tense, breaking the mood of the moment.

"It is nothing. I tripped and fell. Clumsy—" her tongue was what was clumsy, unable to find the right words. The sense of longing and loneliness she had felt earlier that day flooded through her, and for a moment her limbs went weak with it. Then, she pulled away. "I'm sorry," she murmured.

He didn't answer, but as he began to walk

again, he could still feel the imprint of her soft, sweetly scented body against his, and it irritated him that at such a dangerous moment he could think only of her. And yet, he could not help himself. When she had fallen forward against him, he had wanted nothing more than to hold her close to him and bury his lips in the dark silk of her hair.

He turned toward her as they approached the edge of the woods. "You must go slowly and carefully," he cautioned. "Don't wait for the sentries to challenge you, shout out that I carried you off and that you're making your way back to your fiancé and friends." She nodded. "They'll ask you where I am and you must say that I've gone off with the other men—gone to join some Micmac Indians who will give us shelter."

"I understand. I will not fail you," she said gravely. "And you must be careful. I pray that *le bon Dieu* goes with you."

She lifted her face to him as she spoke, and he caught his breath. In the pale moonlight her beauty was enough to tempt any man. Her generous, warm mouth invited his kiss, the dark eyes like pools of clear water.

"I'll wait till you get past the sentries," he told her. "While they're questioning you, I can get back into the woods." She hesitated, and he added, "Go on."

Obediently, she began to run out of the darkness, and he heard her calling out to the sentries as he had advised. In a moment, he heard a hoarse English voice exclaiming, "Good God—it's the girl that gave the Major the slip."

She would be all right, he told himself. Lampert might be a fool and an oaf, but he would not harm her. His eyes still on Gabrielle's slender form, he took a step backward into the woods.

"Move another step and you're a dead man."

There was no mistaking the hard press of a pistol at the back of his head. Neill stopped where he was.

"You try anything and I'll have to blow your head off, and that will distress Major Lampert," Dray continued in a gloating tone. "He's got great plans for you."

Chapter Three

"IT'S THE GIRL THAT GAVE THE MAJOR THE SLIP."
Gabrielle tensed at the sentry's exclamation
but, managing a look of mingled relief and distress, she looked entreatingly into the man's
face.

"Monsieur, I am Gabrielle de Montfleuri," she
said in her charmingly accented English, "I
have managed to just now escape from that
madman who tried to kidnap me away from my
fiancé."

The sentry looked startled. "Then you weren't
going with him out of your own free will?"
She shook her head. "Where is Craddock
now?"

"I don't know." Inwardly, she prayed that
Neill had already returned to the deep woods.
"He took me into the forest, but I know the
woods as he does not. It was easy to escape
him." She paused, letting her eyes express even

more helplessness. "Monsieur, can I please go back home? I want to see my brother . . ."

He looked uncomfortable. "Nobody's going to hurt you, lass," he said, "but you can't see your brother just yet." At the very real alarm that flared in Gabrielle's eyes, he shook his head. "He's not bad hurt. He's just in the church with the other men. Major's orders."

"I do not understand . . ." She broke off at a sudden noise in the woods behind her, and the sentry called a challenge. A familiar, nasal voice made reply.

"Don't just stand there, curse it. Arrest the woman, you fool."

The sentry's mouth hung agape as the under-brush crackled behind them, and two shadows emerged against the greater dark. Two—then, sacred name, they had caught Neill, Gabrielle thought in panic. She couldn't see the big man's face at this distance, but she could read the tension in the set of his broad shoulders. He walked ahead of the smaller Lieutenant Dray, who now shouted at the sentry again.

"What are you waiting for, you prize idiot? I told you to arrest that woman." Then, as the sentry still hesitated, he sneered, "Major Lam-pert knew that the wench would come sneaking back to take a look at her brother, and he figured he could trap the gallant Major Craddock then."

Smoky, sputtering torchlight lit Dray's flat, triumphant face. Neill remained still, but Gabrielle sensed that all his thoughts were concentrated on escape. Could she help him? She glanced at the woods not far away. Perhaps she could.

Throwing up her hands dramatically, she gave a theatrical gasp. "It is too much," she moaned.

Then she pitched forward in a pretended faint. She saw the sentry start toward her, saw Dray's attention waver momentarily. At the same time Neill lunged forward and Dray went sprawling, while another blow upended the sentry, and for the second time that day Gabrielle found her hand caught as he urged her to her feet. "Now. Quickly," he ordered.

"If you move, the girl dies." The new voice was high and affected, though somewhat indistinct, and Gabrielle saw Major Lampert standing some distance away. Behind him were a score of his men, every one of them aiming his musket at her breast.

Neill felt the small hand he held tense and grow cold. He had no doubt that Lampert meant what he said, and he spoke with bitter contempt. "Your quarrel is with me, Major. Is it customary for an officer of King George to take his anger out on women?"

"I should have you shot here and now." Lampert's voice quivered with fury, and as he took some steps forward Neill saw the discolored and swollen jaw. "I should have you hanged for a traitor."

"Why? Because as a partner in C. and C. Company I was doing business with Louis Chauvin?" Cynically, he saw that his emphasis on the wealthy Eastern company had made the Major pause. He followed up his advantage by adding, "A great number of colonial firms trade with the Company Chauvin and so do many wealthy Englishmen. If you don't know that, you've been badly misinformed."

It was plain that Lampert was itching to call out an order to execute Craddock, but instead he turned to Dray. "Lock him up in the church with the other men," he snarled. "Since he's so fond of the Frogs, he'll be shipped out with them when we carry out our orders."

"Orders that I can't believe Governor Lawrence ever authorized," Neil retorted.

Lampert looked smug. "His Excellency has authorized deportations all over Acadia."

"That can't be true," Gabrielle cried.

"Right now, Colonel Winslow is supervising a gathering of Acadians at Grand Pré, and other officers are being sent to Minas, Cobequid and Rivière aux Canards."

His words had the ring of truth. Gabrielle felt as if her bones had suddenly dissolved within her. She swayed a little, and felt Neill's arm go around her waist, anchoring her against him. She clung to him as the one stable thing in this world gone mad, while Lampert gestured toward her: "You'll come with me."

The same feeling of loathing that she had experienced before swept over her, and she drew back. "I will not," she cried defiantly. "I want to see my brother. I want to talk to Monsieur Chauvin . . ."

"Bring her along," Lampert snapped, and two of the men behind him moved forward.

"Stop where you are." Such was the ring of command in Neill's voice that the armed troops actually halted uncertainly. "Major Lampert," Neill continued in that same voice, "if you cause any distress to this woman, I will personally see to it that you are dishonored and disgraced before your brother officers." His voice dropped to a more personal snarl of menace. "And I will also take great pleasure in wringing your miserable neck."

For a few seconds there was absolute silence. A cool September wind blew across the woodlands and brought with it the scents of autumn and the clean, salty tang of the sea. Then Lampert snapped, "What's the matter with you, you damned fools? I said, bring the woman." He added, "Shoot him if he so much as moves a muscle."

In the smoky light Gabrielle saw Neill's eyes narrow. She had never seen so murderous a look in any man's eyes, and she was suddenly terrified for him. She put out a small hand and caught at his arm, felt the bunching of furious muscle under her palm. "Please," she whispered, "don't do anything. Please." More loudly, she added, "I will do as you ask, Major. What do you wish of me?"

Lampert licked his lips and then ran a hand over the swelling on his jaw. He sighed. "You speak English," he said at last. "I need you to come and translate my orders to the village women. They have to be told that they only have a few days in which to gather together what household goods they can carry." He shook a finger at her. "Mind, they're allowed only what they can carry. Livestock, houses, everything else will be left to become the property of the Crown."

She heard him, but even so she could not

believe all of what he said. "A few days?" she repeated dully, and Lampert nodded.

"All of you will leave Laforet within the week."

"This way, Craddock. Excuse me—I should have said, of course, *Major* Craddock."

Neill made no comment. Obviously, Dray was enjoying himself, and he wasn't about to add to that malicious pleasure. It was past midnight now, and the spire of the church stood inky black against the faint moon, but Neill was hardly aware of it nor of the barking of the village dogs. Nor was he consciously thinking of Gabrielle, though the memory of her courage and dignity as she confronted Lampert clung persistently to his thoughts.

Instead, he considered what Lampert had said. If the man was telling the truth, Lawrence had truly gone mad. To suspect Acadians of harboring friendly feelings for the French was one thing, to order the deportation of all Acadians was another. And since there was no use trying to appeal to a madman, a trip to Halifax would have been wasted. There seemed no way to stop this senseless evacuation of innocent people—an evacuation, moreover, that would cause great losses to everyone, including the C. and C. Company and its investors.

"Halt. Who goes there?" Three men with muskets were standing directly on the steps of the little church. When Dray replied, they sprang to attention. Their leader, a grizzled little man, answered the Lieutenant's questions in a loud, hoarse voice.

"The prisoners are behaving themselves, sir. They were a bit rambunctious when they were first brought here, but now they've settled down."

Dray nodded. "I've brought you another prisoner—the Englishman who likes Frogs, especially female Frogs." He paused expectantly, but as Neill said nothing, added, "Watch him. I'll flay the man who lets him get away."

The door of the church had been barred from the outside. Neill waited until the heavy beam was moved aside and then stepped into the building. A dull glow came from the candles on the altar, but now mingling with the scent of wax and incense and flowers, was the stench of sweat and fear. A lamp, set high on the wall, shed its smoky light on the crowd of men who sat or stood or leaned against the walls of the church. Neill's eyes swept them quickly, registering the fact that about two hundred men were in the church.

Chauvin's anxious voice cut through his observations. "Gabrielle. Where is she? What have you done to her?" he demanded.

"I've done nothing to her," Neill replied coldly. "I tried to get her away, but she wouldn't leave you or her brother."

A shadow that had been lying on one of the pews now rose up, and under the clumsy bandage that covered half its head Neill recognized Simon de Montfleuri. "Then it's my fault the British have her," he moaned. "My fault for trying to escape. I should have thought of her before I ran."

There was such despair in the boy's voice that

though Neill agreed with what he said, he felt a stir of pity. Before he could respond, the pudgy Guy Richaud spoke bravely. "At least Jean and François and one or two of the others got away. They'll join the Micmacs who will take care of them, the brave lads."

The faces around Neill cheered marginally and then were plunged back into gloom as Simon muttered, "They're the lucky ones. Look at what's going to happen to us." He shook his bandaged head. "I always hated the English, but I never dreamed even they could do such a thing."

"Neither did I." Realizing that the men around him were muttering angrily, Neill spoke quickly. A burly, bearded fisherman glared at him.

"You, an Englishman, say this? Perhaps you have been sent among us as a spy by that *canaille*, Lampert. Perhaps we should send him your head."

One against two hundred wasn't great odds. As he tensed his body to fight, Neill saw Father Maboeuf for the first time. The old priest had been kneeling in the shadows, but now he got to his feet and shouted angrily. "That's stupid talk, Gaspard, and you know it. He's a prisoner just like us."

"And all of us saw the way he knocked that English Major silly," Guy Richaud added, shooting Neill a friendly grin. "Name of God—I beg pardon, Father—but that was an excellent punch. I saw six teeth on the ground."

"Naturally, Mr. Craddock is no enemy." Everyone fell respectfully silent as Louis Chauvin turned to Neill. "Perhaps you can help us, sir. We've been told so little. We know that we are to be deported. We know that British ships will take us away from Laforet in a week's time, and that while we are locked up here the women must pack the few things that we are allowed to take with us. We know that we can't take our furniture or our livestock"—a groan from the men interrupted him, and he gestured for silence—"but we have no idea where we're going. Can you find out for us?"

"Perhaps we're being moved to parts of French Canada," someone called hopefully, "or to other parts of Acadia. I've got a cousin in Grand Pré . . ."

Should he tell what he'd learned? Neill hesitated, and then decided on honesty. The faces of the men around him turned white as he spoke. "It is not possible," Chauvin breathed. "They are removing everyone from Acadia. Everyone from the Northumberland Strait on one side to the Atlantic Ocean on the other. That involves thousands and thousands of people."

In the horrible silence that followed, Simon spoke again. "What I would like to know is why we were taken so easily." He got up and swayed unsteadily for a moment, before adding, "We could have fought if they had come during the day. We would have met them with musket fire and knives."

"Simon, haven't you caused enough trouble already?" Father Maboeuf scolded, but the young man wasn't finished.

"If you ask me, the English knew when to come because some traitor in Laforet told them." Simon looked about him vengefully. "They knew that Jean and I and some others would fight, and so they came by stealth at night during Gabrielle's betrothal feast. How would they have known when to come if someone hadn't told them?"

Neill frowned. There was something in what the boy said, and yet who among the men present would have brought the English into Laforet? Everyone had too much to lose.

"What you say is nonsense," Louis Chauvin said sternly. "How can you say that one of us would be such a swine as to be a traitor? Which of us would let wolves into his own pasture, Simon—me? Father Mabouef? Guy? Gaspard? Or you yourself, perhaps, may have done this thing? *Sacré nom*, boy, don't make a bad situation worse."

Everyone looked at Simon, and the boy dropped his head. "You are right," he muttered. Then, he rallied. "It's not too late, Monsieur Chauvin. We should not calmly do what these bloody English tell us to do. We can overpower the sentries and run for the woods like Jean and François. We can join the Micmacs and fight for the French."

His words caused a stir, but Father Maboeuf was shaking his head. "We couldn't leave the women and the children behind. The English know this. That's why you've been separated from your familes." He then appealed to Neill. "The only thing we can do now is obey, isn't that so, Monsieur? Surely, the English are not all like this Governor Lawrence. Surely, as an important man in Massachusetts you know someone with influence, someone we can appeal to for justice?"

Again, Neill hesitated. "I'm not one for politics," he began, and then was defeated by the hopeful look on the old priest's face. "I'll do what I can. Governor Shirley in Boston has investments with the C. and C. Perhaps he'll do something to help."

Louis Chauvin clapped him on the shoulder. "Sir, you have our grateful thanks," he said. And then he added, "But for now all we can do is wait."

Chapter Four

"THÉRÈSE—SWEET MOTHER MARY, WHERE ARE you?" Marthe Richaud wailed.

"Here, Maman, packing the plates and linen, as you told me to do." Thérèse's eyes were puffed with weeping, and new tears were streaming down her cheeks as she worked.

Marthe plumped down amidst the confusion in her house. Her usually cheerful face was pale, and she appeared to have aged in the last few days. "How can they say we must move today?" she demanded, then put her face in her hands and sobbed. "*Sacré nom,* I can't do it. I will die right here in my own home rather than let them take me away."

"Don't talk like that." Gabrielle fought a spasm of nausea, induced by grief and sleeplessness and the fact that she hadn't managed to force down much food in the past seven days. She put her arms about her friend. "If you give

45

up, Marthe, so will Thérèse and Guy. You must remain strong."

"I can't," Marthe moaned. "I don't have any strength left."

Gabrielle squeezed the plump shoulders. "Is this Marthe Richaud who is speaking to me? Impossible. Marthe Richaud is the kind, good woman who met my mother and me when we landed here in Laforet, and took us home with her because our home hadn't yet been built. You were so good to us then . . ."

"So was everyone else in the village," Marthe muttered.

"The others were kind mainly because my mother was wife to the Chevalier de Montfleuri, who was going to live in French Canada on lands deeded to him by King Louis." She paused as a backwash of old sadness superimposed itself on the misery of the here and now. "But when my father died and all his property and wealth were lost, when Mother and Simon and I had no money and no place to go, you and Guy and Thérèse were still our dear and kind friends."

Marthe began to wipe her eyes. "Monsieur Chauvin was the one who helped you," she pointed out.

"Who was it who taught me to bake and cook? Who helped Mother sell her fine embroidery in Grand Pré? To whom did Simon and I tell our problems and dreams?" She hugged Marthe. "You've always been a second mother to me, Marthe Richaud, and you are the strongest woman I know. If you fall apart, everyone else will collapse in front of the English soldiers."

She had said the right thing. Marthe jerked her chin angrily, and color flooded her cheeks. "I'll never let those *canailles* humble me," she exclaimed and then added to Thérèse, "hurry, girl. Your father's hoe and his rake—and of course, my spinning wheel. Then we are ready."

Gabrielle walked away from her friends to her small bundle of goods which she had left near the doorway, together with her own spinning wheel. The bundle she had packed and repacked a hundred times, weighing this and that useful or sentimental object, taking things out, putting things in. But she had never debated about her spinning wheel. She ran her hand lightly over its polished surface now, remembering how Guy Richaud had made it for her mother and how that beloved woman had taught her how to spin on it. Though it was large and could be cumbersome, she'd never dreamed of leaving it behind. Simon would have to carry it on his back.

But when would Simon be released? From the doorway she looked down the narrow village street toward the church. Lampert had promised to set the men free today, but though it was already past noon, there was yet no sign of them. The women were all waiting, calling to each other and shifting their bundles in their nervousness, and already the air was full of weeping.

Children were crying because they would have to leave their pets, women lamented the fact that they must part with a rocking chair carved by a great-grandfather, the bedstead that had been a cherished wedding gift. Others wept over the sheep, goats and cows which would now become the property of the English, and the beloved stone houses which they would have to leave. The sounds and the confusion and the misery made Gabrielle's unsteady stomach roil, and she looked again toward the barred doors of the church.

As she looked away in despair, her eye fell on the scores of English soldiers who had been posted all around the village. On this day of evacuation, Lampert was taking no chances, and his men lined the road that led down to the sea and the longboats that would ferry the Acadians to one of the two waiting vessels. Gabrielle hated to look at these ships even more than at the soldiers, but her eyes were drawn to them as they stood arrogantly at anchor near the fir-covered headlands. *The Lovely Lady* and *The Royal Princess*—she vowed that these were names that she would loathe forever.

"They're letting the men out. They're coming!"

At the shrill cry, Gabrielle snapped her attention away from the ships and back to the church. She forced herself to remain where she was as the first men were let out of the building in which they had been penned for the whole week, but her heart was hammering wildly, and she gave a stifled cry as she saw Louis Chauvin come out first.

He was bedraggled and somewhat thinner but still obviously a respected figure, and even the English soldiers on the church steps gave way as he stood blinking in the afternoon sunshine. Behind him came Simon, very pale and wearing a bandage around his head.

Gabrielle didn't realize that she was still searching for someone until she saw him. Neill stood head and shoulder above the others, and unlike them had managed to remain smooth-shaven and well-groomed. But there was a difference between this man and the smiling, tawny-eyed stranger who had bowed and greeted her in front of the church on the day of her bethrothal, and she sensed it even at this distance. There was a dangerous cock to his broad shoulders, a seething anger in his movements. Her hand went to her lips as she watched him, and as if aware of her thoughts, his eyes came unerringly to where she stood. Even at this distance the impact of that look was unsettling, intense.

Now Simon too had spotted her. "Gabrielle!" She heard him shout. "Gabrielle, here I am."

She started to move forward and then stopped. The instructions Lampert had given the women had been brutally clear. He had warned that no demonstrations of emotion would be tolerated, that the women were to remain near their bundles until their men reached them. Then they were to proceed slowly and in orderly fashion to the longboats that would ferry them to the waiting ships. Aching to embrace her brother but afraid to provoke the obviously nervous soldiers, she waved at Simon and forced herself to remain where she was.

Other women weren't as farsighted. Gabrielle heard a scream as one of them ran forward to embrace her husband. She was followed by other women and their children, who shouted the names of their loved ones and fought to get to them. "No!" Gabrielle cried, but her voice was swallowed in the storm of voices.

"You've got to stop them, *petite*. The soldiers will hurt them unless they stop." Beside her, plump Marthe was as pale as wax.

Gabrielle called to her neighbors, but they ran past her without listening. Hurrying into the middle of the street, she tried to get their attention. "Please stop this," she begged. "You know the English commander's orders. There's no telling what the English will do." Then, as a squad of English soldiers began to advance on the crowd, she added, "Please, neighbors, in the name of God, be calm."

Some of the women heard and obeyed her, but others only saw their husbands and fathers and sons, only knew that they had been separated for seven horrible days and would soon have to leave their homes. Weeping and sobbing, they tried to reach their men through a hurriedly formed barricade of troopers. One of the soldiers pushed a woman backward, and she fell. "That's my wife, you pig," a man yelled, and before any could stop him, he had launched himself at the Englishman.

As if this were some kind of signal, there was a roar from the village men, and Gabrielle saw Gaspard fling himself at the soldiers. She caught a glimpse of Louis Chauvin and heard Neill's deep voice over the roaring of the crowd.

"No, you damned fools," he was shouting in English. "Hold your fire!"

Even while he spoke, a shot rang out, and Gaspard clutched at his chest. He looked astonished as blood seeped through his fingers, and he slowly sank to his knees. "Name of God!" Marthe shrilled. "They've killed Gaspard! They'll kill us all . . ."

Terrified that Simon might hotheadedly follow Gaspard's lead, Gabrielle started to run forward. Her way was instantly blocked by a soldier who held a musket at the ready. "You move, and you're dead," he snarled. "Get back—get back, or I'll fire."

The ferocity in the man's eyes convinced Gabrielle that he was frightened enough to shoot. She stopped at once, holding her hands palm up to show she meant no harm. Other women followed her lead, but now more and more English soldiers were racing up to the scene of the trouble. They shoved and clubbed all the men who stood in their way, and groans and curses in English and French filled the air.

Now Lieutenant Dray came up the street at a run. "Get them down to the ships now," he bellowed.

What had been more or less an orderly evacuation became a scene from a nightmare as Acadians clutched their bleeding foreheads while soldiers kicked aside bundles of carefully packed goods in their effort to circle the terrified villagers.

One elderly trooper protested. "Sir, the men haven't had a chance to pair up with their families."

"Never mind that. They can sort themselves out on board the ships. Just get the Frogs down to the shore before we have another bloody riot," the flat-faced Lieutenant snarled.

Nobody had to translate his order. A keening wail rose from the women as soldiers advanced, their muskets raised threateningly. "But we must wait for our men," one of the women screamed. "Tell them, Gabrielle. You speak their language. You can make the soldiers understand why we can't go."

Mustering all her courage, Gabrielle forced her way toward Dray and caught him by the sleeve. "Please," she begged, "let us wait here. There will be no more trouble. Only let us wait for our men."

His only answer was a shove that sent her reeling backward against the side of a nearby house. The hard stone impacted against her back, knocking the air out of her. As she sank to her knees, she saw Dray following her, kicking aside her pitiful bundle. She tried to protest, but she had no breath left to speak.

Even so, she must have made some sound, for obviously he heard her. He turned, grinned. "Worried about trouble, eh? I'll give you trouble."

Still grinning, he seized her spinning wheel and threw it with all his force against the side of the house. It smashed into pieces. "Now, all of you," he yelled at the horrified women. "Get going or I'll smash every one of your lousy, stinking bundles. Get moving!"

Terrified, the women made no resistance as they were pushed and shoved down the road to the sea. They shrieked and called for their men, fought to retain their footing as they were forced to more and even greater speed. One woman screamed that she couldn't find her children, an old man was knocked down. Bundles were torn away from anxious hands and trampled underfoot.

"This is a scene from hell," Gabrielle whispered as she tried to balance her own bundle and help Marthe as well, while at the same time straining to catch a glimpse of Simon or Louis Chauvin. She couldn't even see Neill's tall form, for the evacuation was raising so much dust that it seemed that a curtain of mist hung across the afternoon. As she tried to pierce that mist, she lost her footing and stumbled painfully forward onto her knees. She tried to get to her feet, but she could not. She caught a glimpse of Marthe's frightened face whirling away from her and then she was knocked down, again in the dust.

The shock of this fall took her breath away for a moment, and then she found that her nostrils were full of grit and dust. As she struggled to pull air into her lungs, the crowd about her miraculously seemed to thin, and she found herself hauled to her feet by a strong hand. "Are you all right?" Neill Craddock demanded.

Dazed, trembling with the pain in her knees and bloodied hands, she nodded, but he seemed to know better and put an arm around her waist to steady her. The crowd eddied around them, but he stood above and against it. For a moment his strength reassured her, and then reality flooded through her numbed mind.

"Simon?" she begged. "Monsieur Chauvin?"

"Both Chauvin and I tried to stop the violence before Gaspard was shot. Afterwards, we were separated in the confusion." An English trooper, musket ready, urged them on. Neill's eyes were murderous, but all he said was, "Can you walk? It's not far to the sea."

She nodded, only half aware of what he had said. "But I must find Simon," she cried.

He looked about him. "In this mob? Impossible."

"You found me," she protested.

"I saw you go down." He was unwilling to admit that he had been trying to get to her even before that bastard Dray had smashed her loom. He hadn't been in time to prevent that, but he had been fighting his way to her side ever since. "I managed to save your bundle," he added.

As they started forward, she registered the hardness of his arm spanning her waist, but she felt too weak to do without that support. Now they could see the beach and the ships riding at anchor on a sea that had turned gold and crimson with sunset. Two long boats filled with evacuees were pulling off to one of the ships. Another two had been beached, and Gabrielle saw Marthe and Thérèse being pushed into one of them. There were several men on this longboat, but there was no sign of Guy or Simon or Louis Chauvin.

She tried to protest as she and Neill were prodded into the same craft. "Please, Neill, explain. I must wait to go with my brother and my fiancé."

The officer in charge of this phase of the evacuation was a thin, harassed-looking Lieutenant, and he interrupted Neill before he'd finished speaking. "Everyone's saying the same thing, but my orders are not to wait. You and this young woman must get on the boat, and quickly, too. Major Lampert has ordered us to shoot anyone who resists."

"Christ, man—you'd obey such orders?"

But the officer was already turning away. "Tell the woman with you that she'll be united with her brother on the ship. Nearly a hundred people have been taken aboard *The Lovely Lady* already. Now get going or the men will fire on you."

They had not much choice. Pushed and shoved like cattle, they were loaded onto the longboat, along with scores of other evacuees. Gabrielle tried to believe what the officer had said. It was clear that many others were in the same situation, and though some families had miraculously managed to find each other in the melee, there were husbands who called frantically for wives, women who searched the shore desperately for the faces of brothers, husbands, sweethearts. Elderly parents wept because they couldn't find their sons and daughters, and one poor woman sobbed that her little boy had been torn away from her during the rush to the shore.

"He is only ten, my André," she wept. "What will he do without me? But the soldiers won't let me go ashore and find him." She clutched Gabrielle's arm. "You can speak English. What did that man on the shore say?"

"That we'd find our families on the ship." Pressed close to Neill, Gabrielle watched *The Lovely Lady* coming closer. Please, she prayed, let Simon and Louis Chauvin and dear Guy Richaud be there.

She searched the faces that thronged the rail, but could not see either of them. Nor could she see Guy. "Perhaps we can't see them from the boat," she said to Marthe. "Let's get on board quickly."

Climbing the gangplank was painful, but not as painful as the reality on deck. The first thing she saw were people—so many people. Acadians clinging to their children and their pitiful bundles, Acadians pressed to the side of the vessel and straining their eyes to see their homes or their loved ones still on shore. So many—but though she saw many neighbors including sour old Nicole and the village blacksmith, Henri Royale, nowhere among these were the men Gabrielle or Marthe sought.

She turned her gaze to the longboats that were still shuttling from shore to ship. The nearest boat was still some distance away, but as she followed its progress in the gathering dusk her breath caught in her throat. Surely, she recognized the man in the prow of the ship?

"Simon," she gasped. "It is he—in the longboat coming now. And Guy is there also, and Monsieur Chauvin." Joyously, she turned to Neill, who stood beside her. "Thank God, they are coming. It doesn't matter what happens, as long as we're all together."

Marthe had seen Guy, too, and she was almost delirious with joy. Other families had spotted mothers, grandparents, sweethearts, and the deck of *The Lovely Lady* was alive with cries of greeting and relief.

Suddenly, Neill swore loudly. "That long boat is making for *The Royal Princess*."

"It can't be." Gabrielle's cry was lost in the wail that rose from the others on *The Lovely Lady* who had recognized loved ones in the boat. Such was the noise that only Neill heard the telltale flapping of the ship's sails filling with wind. They were setting sail.

Not content with merely tearing the Acadians from their homes, Lampert was callously splitting up families. Rage was a hard, tight knot in his chest, and he found it hard to think rationally. As he fought for control, some of the deportees now realized what was happening. "They are taking the ship out to sea—we are sailing," a woman shouted, and instantly there was pandemonium. Marthe, her face like ash, clawed her way to the ship's rail and screamed Guy's name, while behind her, Thérèse wept uncontrollably.

"Papa, where are they taking you?" She sobbed, and Neill's big hands balled into tight fists. His instinct was to take the nearest English soldier by the throat and pitch him overboard, but he held back. Nothing could come of violence. Wait, he urged himself.

"Monsieur Neill—" He looked down into Gabrielle's upraised face. It was tearstained and white, but she was fighting for calm. "Will you help us to find out if these ships are at least going to the same place? Will we see our families and friends when we land?"

"I'll try." As Neill pushed his way toward the nearest English soldier, Gabrielle heard the ship's sails sigh as they bellied with wind. Now the command was given to weigh anchor and, rocking against the gentle swells of the Bay of Fundy, *The Lovely Lady* began to sail away from her sister ship. Gabrielle registered the rolling of the vessel under her feet and tried to follow the longboat that had carried Simon and Louis Chauvin away from her. But she could see only the shadow of the hulking *Royal Princess* and the sea that spilled like a dark bolt of uneven silk under a sprinkle of still faint stars.

Marthe clutched her hand, weeping. "I can't see Guy any more, he's gone," she sobbed.

Gabrielle felt her own tears flood her eyes, but she dashed them away impatiently. She wanted to gaze for the last time on the headlands of Laforet. Though she could not see them very clearly in the dusk, she said goodbye to the pinkish rocks that ringed the beach, the lavender water of the inlet where the fish swam. She breathed deeply, willing herself to remember not ship's tar and the odor of packed bodies, but pine and woodsmoke carried on the clean salt air. "Goodbye," she whispered around the knot that blocked her throat.

Other villagers were also saying their farewells, and a hush descended on them all. Suddenly, one of the women screamed. *"Sacré nom,"* she shrilled. "Look—there is fire on shore. The English have set fire to our homes!"

An orange glow began to fan up against the darkness, and Gabrielle stared helplessly, her mind unable to take in this last cruelty.

"Lampert obviously wants to warn the villagers that they have nothing to come home to in Laforet." Neill had returned to her side, and there was cold fury in his deep voice.

She felt sick and dizzy. "And we can do nothing."

"Not yet." There was a grim purpose in the words, and she turned to look at him. "I've found out that this ship is headed for Boston. As soon as we reach there, I'll go straight to Governor Shirley and demand something be done."

She forced herself to speak steadily. "And the other ship, Monsieur? Does it go to Boston also?"

"I hope so." Neill had never felt such helpless frustration before, but Gabrielle's dark eyes demanded total honesty. "The officer I spoke to wasn't sure, and I couldn't get to the captain. I'm sorry. All we can do is hope that Lampert sends *The Royal Princess* to Boston as well."

He fell silent as the lurid orange flames spurted higher against the night. Several of the people at the deck rail were trying to jump overboard to swim ashore to their homes, but they were restrained by their friends. Thérèse was kneeling at her mother's feet, her face buried in Marthe's skirts, her body shaking with sobs. Another woman had begun to wail out a hymn. Against this background, he heard Gabrielle's heartbroken whisper.

"I may not see my brother or Monsieur Chauvin for a long time. And—and I did not even say goodbye."

He looked down at her worriedly. She had grown even whiter and was swaying on her feet, and he knew that the girl had been pushed to the limit of endurance. Acting instinctively, he caught her around the waist and half-carried, half-walked her away from the multitude by the rail to the deserted starboard deck. Here he made her sit on a coil of thick rope. She protested, but he forced her to remain seated.

"It's not going to do anybody any good if you faint, Gabrielle," he told her.

"I—won't faint." With effort, she squared her slender shoulders. "And I thank you. It's better here where I can't see the burning."

There was a moment's silence and then he spoke quietly. "Perhaps I know how you feel. When I was an officer in my King's army, I fought an engagement in the southern part of France, just outside a little village called Layons. Our colonel ordered it burned to the ground, and because I was one of the few officers who spoke French fluently, he put me in charge. I refused to carry out his orders."

Even at such a time she was conscious of the remembered anger in his voice. "Is that why you left the army?"

"Not directly. I had to stand by helpless while someone else commanded the burning of Layons, and later there was an inquiry at which I was exonerated. It seems that the Colonel had a private grudge against the village and had taken his anger out on every soul living there." She caught her breath and he added, grimly, "The Colonel was officially reprimanded, but I found I'd had enough of the military. I hadn't realized that the British army was riddled with politics and advancements made through money instead of ability." He checked himself, shrugged broad shoulders. "Sorry. I have no idea why I got started on the very boring subject of why I abhor politics and bureaucrats."

"You told Simon that . . ." For a second time, her voice trailed away, and then she whispered, "Monsieur Neill, help me."

He looked at her, surprised. "In what way?"

"To find Simon and Monsieur Chauvin," she explained. Speaking rapidly, she got up from her seat of coiled rope and caught at his arms. "You are a wealthy and influential man in Boston. You know how to ask, whom to ask, where I know no one."

He hesitated, and she continued earnestly. "There is also the question of money. I don't mean to insult you, but I know that Monsieur Chauvin owes your company much money. Is that not so?"

She was right, yet he still hesitated. Some instinct warned him to put distance between himself and this lovely woman, and yet his senses urged him closer to her as she clung to his arms under the star-filled sky. A sea breeze tugged at her long dark hair and framed her face with fragrant darkness, while her desperate black eyes pleaded with him.

"Please," she said. "We both wish to find Monsieur Chauvin and—and Simon is with him. I fear so much for him. He is my younger brother, and he is kind and good and noble in a hundred ways, but he is also hotheaded and so foolish. He will antagonize English soldiers or pick quarrels with his guards, and God alone knows what will happen to him. Perhaps they will shoot him as they shot Gaspard. I beg you, Monsieur, for his sake to help me."

He drew in a breath scented with sea air and the faint flower fragrance she wore. "All right," he heard himself say. "I'll do my best, but I'm not sure if I . . ."

His words were cut off by her glad cry, as she

61

impulsively threw her arms about his neck and kissed him fervently on both cheeks. "Thank you," she cried, "oh, thank you."

He felt the touch of her mouth, registered the warmth and softness of her arms around him. Then, before she could draw away, a swell caused the ship to pitch slightly. The movement impelled Gabrielle against Neill, and instinctively his arms went around her to steady her. For a second they stared at each other, surprised, and then astonishment eased away into a new emotion as his mouth came down on hers.

In the first moment of that kiss, it was not astonishment that left her shaken but the realization that she had somehow known how his lips would feel. The taste of the cool, sure lips on hers, the texture of his tender-tough cheek against hers—she had known, somehow, how all this would be and now welcomed him. Lost in a world that began and ended with his kiss, she registered the strong wall of his chest against her softness, the tension in the rock-hard arms that held her close, in the starred dark.

For a moment they stood still against each other, balanced against the pitch and yaw of the ship, and then his mouth grew more insistent, gently forcing her lips to part against the bold demand of his tongue. A shiver of desire spun through her, quivered within her like stretched-out notes of music as his tongue caressed hers and then explored the satin secrets of her mouth. She had never been kissed like this nor felt like this, and yet her mouth knew what to do.

Her own tongue circled the periphery of his lips, touched his in shy welcome.

"Sweeting," she heard him murmur, and even the unfamiliar English word sounded like music when heard within the sorcery of their kiss. One of his hands rose to cradle her head and caress the silken darkness of her hair, moved slowly, sensuously to stroke her cheek. She trembled at his touch, yet pressed her cheek against his hand. He ran his thumb across her chin, rubbed lightly down her smooth throat and then stroked downward to the sensitive nape of her neck. She trembled again, and as he drew her even closer, she felt as if she were being sucked into the hard power of him. She could no longer breathe, and she didn't care. What need did she have of mere breath when her senses were swimming wildly, her heart leaping and hammering against his chest? And when he moved his mouth from hers to kiss the pulse at her throat, it trembled against his lips.

"Gabrielle," she heard him say, "lovely lady . . ."

Lovely lady. *The Lovely Lady*—the name of the hated ship caused a spasm within her, and she tensed within his arms. *The Lovely Lady* was what was taking her away from brother and home and fiancé, and yet here she stood in another man's arms. An *Englishman's* arms. Forcing all her will to obey her, she placed the palms of her small hands against his chest.

"No," she whispered, "we mustn't."

Her protest did not reach him at first, but when he heard the fear in her voice, he loosened his arms about her. He was shaken by the fear in her eyes and also by the emotions that were coursing through him. Good Christ, he thought, she was Chauvin's woman, not his.

She was speaking in a hurried, scared tone. "It—it was my fault, Monsieur. I forgot that in England you do not kiss to express thanks. I was so grateful because you said you would help me find Simon and—and my fiancé."

Without another word and giving him no time to respond, she gathered herself together and hurried away from him toward the other, more crowded side of the deck. It had been gratitude that had brought her into his arms, she told herself, gratitude that had made her overemotional at the end of this terrible day. And it was gratitude that was making her heart pound like a drum, not the sweetness of his kisses—kisses that she knew she must forget.

Chapter Five

GABRIELLE STOOD ON TIPTOE AS *THE LOVELY Lady* slowly rounded Dorchester Heights. The first thing she saw was ships—so many ships anchored in the sparkling blue of the harbor that they seemed to enclose Boston on three sides. A little distance from the harbor, many three-storied, flat-roofed brick buildings clustered about the high steeple of a church.

"That's North Church." She hadn't been aware that Neill had come up to the rail to stand beside her. "Not far away is the building that C. and C. uses for a headquarters, and above everything are the bluffs. On a clear day you can see for miles from that vantage point."

Gabrielle was silent. His voice was glad with homecoming, and it emphasized her own sense of loss. She strained her eyes to see if she could recognize any of the anchored ships as *The*

Royal Princess but could not. Well, at least they were going to be on land, and then perhaps there would be news of Simon and Monsieur Chauvin.

It had been a long journey and a bitter one. At first the cold had driven the deportees below deck to the cramped and stench-ridden hold, but there they had become so violently ill that most had struggled back up on deck again. There, huddled in their cloaks, they had lived and slept and tried to force down the hard bread and salt pork that had been doled out by the crew. Only a hardy few could stomach this rough fare, and, to make things worse, the seas had been very rough. Many Acadians had been desperately seasick, and a few of the old people had become so ill that without Neill's help they might have died.

Neill—she glanced up at him as he stood beside her and experienced again the curious sense of unbalance that she always felt when he was near. She had meant to avoid him during the voyage, but that had not been possible, for Neill was the Acadians' one link with the Captain of the ship. Learning that the tall Englishman was a partner in the influential C. and C. Company, Captain Scott, the skipper of *The Lovely Lady*, had given him the freedom of the ship, and Neill had used this liberty to ease the misery of the deportees. He had bullied the Captain into giving him blankets for the sick, persuaded soldiers and seamen to part with fruit for the children. And though there was no doctor and no medicine aboard, Neill had sought the help of the Acadians who weren't seasick and managed a kind of battlefield nursing.

Since she had been among those who had helped him, they had seen much of each other. With Marthe Richaud and some of the others, she had tirelessly made the rounds of the refugee Acadians, soothing screaming babies and bathing fevered faces in seawater. They had worked hard, but Neill worked harder still, and more than once when Gabrielle sat up beside a feverish sufferer, Neill had insisted on relieving her so that she could get an hour of rest. He never said much to her, but she knew that he was as aware of her as she was of him, and once she had caught him watching her with an odd, shadowed look in those keen golden eyes.

He was watching her now. She did not need to look up to know that. Even with more and more people crowding the rails, she was deeply conscious of the strength in the arm that lay near her on the wooden ship's rail, and of the muscular, whipcord-lean body beside her. There was a raw energy about him today, a hard, male vitality that was both reassuring and disquieting.

To break the intensity of the moment she said, "Do you think it's possible that *The Royal Princess* has already docked in Boston Harbor?"

"Anything's possible," he replied. "As soon as we get ashore, I'll find Sam Culpepper, my partner. Sam and his friends know everything that goes on in the city."

"Sam is your friend, yes?" she questioned and saw him relax into a smile.

"A good friend, too. I first got to know him back in England where he was struggling to start a business while I was suffering through school. He and his wife, Abigail, were friends of my family, and when they came to the colonies to start the C. and C., they invited me to join them. Sam said that I'd enjoy the challenge of building up a company that would rival John Law's famous Company of the East Indies."

Sam seemed to be a safe subject of conversation, and she nodded her interest. "And have you done so?" she asked, and his smile turned thoughtful.

"Not yet, but there's a great deal of money to be made in trade and in developing backward areas of the colonies. We share expenses and profits—and duties, according to our abilities. I travel, looking out for new opportunities and visiting the concerns that already flourish for the C. and C., and Sam attends to the books, the details of production and distribution." He paused to add, "You'll enjoy the Culpeppers, for I have no doubt they will invite you to stay with them. Abigail would like to mother everyone she sees, even insists that I make a home with them when I leave my own house in Stoughtonham to do business in Boston."

The Lovely Lady was now preparing to drop anchor, and the deportees gathered together in nervous excitement. Marthe Richaud's daughter, Thérèse, plucked at Neill's sleeve. "Monsieur, please, what will happen to us now? Are we going to go ashore so that we can find Papa?"

Neill's answer was nearly drowned in the bosun's shouts to lower the anchor. "Here comes the Captain," he added. "No doubt he's going to explain."

Captain Scott had indeed appeared on the quarterdeck. His presence commanded an immediate hush, and he cleared his throat nervously. "Mr. Craddock, if you please," he said, and as Neill stepped forward, he began to speak so quickly that Gabrielle could not follow his words. Instead, she watched Neill's face, saw the astonishment and then the swift blaze of anger.

"Something's wrong," she whispered.

"Sacred name, what could go wrong now?" Marthe muttered. The other Acadians fell silent as Gabrielle tried in vain to follow what Captain Scott was saying. At last, Neill came back to stand among them.

"There's going to be a delay," he said.

Henri Royale, the blacksmith, cleared his throat. "What kind of delay?" he demanded.

Neill hesitated. A few days at sea had transformed these people. Happy, healthy fishermen and farmers had become gaunt shadows, and even the children had no energy to play. Inwardly cursing Scott, he said, "When the ship reaches Boston, we aren't going to be allowed ashore until the Captain has a chance to present the papers and letters he carries to the Governor. Then a decision will be made."

"A decision on what?" Gabrielle didn't like the look in Neill's eyes, and his reply confirmed her fears.

"On whether you'll be allowed to stay in Boston. The Captain's orders are to present letters from Governor Lawrence and Lampert to Governor Shirley."

No one said anything. Looking down into the blank, pale faces, Neill felt a roil of fury at the stupidity of men and governments. As he strove to control it, a little boy of about four began to cry. "But, Maman, you said we could go ashore and walk in the grass. You said we could find Papa . . ."

"Captain Scott!" Neill's voice wasn't pitched loudly, but it cracked like a whip and stopped the Captain, who was in the act of returning to his cabin. Reluctantly, he turned and faced the tall man who had crossed the deck to tower over him.

"I think you've made an error in your orders." Neill's eyes were as hard as his voice. "If you consider carefully, you'll agree with me that these people need to have some exercise. A few hours on dry land will do them good."

The Captain began to splutter. "But my orders . . ."

"Nonsense. You are the sole authority on *The Lovely Lady*, and as such can surely order your men to convey the Acadians ashore and escort them, say, to the Common. There they can rest and wait until you have seen Governor Shirley." As the Captain's face turned a mottled red, Neill paused and, bending closer, held the man's eyes with his own. "I am personally acquainted with the Governor, who is a humane man. I'm sure he would approve."

Watching, listening, Gabrielle held her breath and then saw *The Lovely Lady*'s skipper deflate like a pricked balloon. "Very well—I see no harm in it," he at last mumbled.

"You're very kind, sir." Neill's tone was triumphant as he turned to the waiting Acadians. Then his eyes met Gabrielle's, and the triumph faded. His small victory over the Captain meant very little after all. The Acadians' fate was still unsettled. "Come, my friends," he said as cheerfully as he could. "Soon you'll see what Boston is like."

But "soon" was too optimistic. Though all of the deportees were anxious to leave the ship, it took quite some time to transport the more than one hundred and fifty men, women and children to shore. The march to the Common was even slower, for after so many days at sea, muscles were stiff and sore. Neill and the other men all carried or supported those who could not walk, while women like Gabrielle and Marthe assisted those who had little children and many bundles. The soldiers who had guarded the deportees on board the ship walked beside them, glum because they didn't, as they told each other loudly, want to play nursemaid to the accursed French.

Gabrielle was frightened by this hostility, which seemed echoed by the crowds who had gathered on the pier and along the street that led to the Common. Though some simply seemed curious, there were many angry and hostile faces. She was alarmed when one man spat on the ground and called them "the stinking French," while a drunk loudly suggested that the Acadians all be hanged in the Common. And as if this weren't bad enough, a sharp-featured middle-aged man was actually pushing his way through all the others to get to them.

"Look," Marthe quavered, "that tall fellow's going to attack us." Involuntarily, Gabrielle stopped and shrank back against Neill, who walked behind her. She found that his big body was shaking and looked up at him in alarm, but

71

he was laughing. "By Christ, Sam, what kept you so long?" he demanded.

Gabrielle saw the newcomer's sharp face soften in greeting. "I heard that a ship from Acadia had come into port and thought you might be on it." He gestured to the streams of deportees still disembarking from *The Lovely Lady*. "What in the devil's name is going on?"

Neill turned to Gabrielle. "My partner, Sam Culpepper. Sam, this is Mademoiselle de Montfleuri. She and these others are Acadians from Laforet who were deported by order of Lawrence."

Gabrielle saw surprise fill Sam Culpepper's shrewd hazel eyes. "Chauvin, too?"

Gabrielle now spoke in her faintly accented English. "Monsieur, Louis Chauvin is my fiancé. In the confusion of the—the deportation, he and my brother were taken aboard another ship, *The Royal Princess*. Did such a ship stop in Boston?"

"No, I'm sorry to say." Sam's face darkened. "It's as I've said before, Neill. I know how much you think of my political leanings, but this should convince you that I'm right. England's home rule is becoming worse and worse."

"Try to convert me some other time." Neill shot a look at the still-grumbling soldiers, who were marching alongside the deportees. "Walk with us and I'll tell you what happened. Meanwhile," he added somewhat reluctantly to Gabrielle, "you'd better tell Marthe and the others that *The Royal Princess* did not dock here."

There were groans of disappointment as Gabrielle translated Sam's news, but these sounds

72

were drowned out by shouts from the children. They had reached the Common, and at sight of an expanse of green grass, the little ones couldn't hold back their joy. They started to run toward the tree-shaded grass, and though the soldiers grumbled at this, they allowed the children to scamper around while the adults dropped their bundles and breathed deeply of the sunny air.

"This is better—it's not as good as home, but it's better," Marthe declared. "Gabrielle, come help me find some candy which I have hidden for the children."

As Gabrielle turned to help her friend, Neill drew Sam aside. "I'd give a thousand pounds to know what the captain of *The Lovely Lady* is saying to Governor Shirley right now."

"What's to stop you?" Sam wanted to know. "Surely there are no constraints on you. Besides, you've every right to see Shirley. He's invested in C. and C.'s fur trade, too, and if Chauvin is truly penniless, he stands to lose money."

"You saw the crowd by the pier." Neill's eyes unconsciously sought out Gabrielle as she laughingly handed candy out to the children. "These people have been through hell, Sam, and I don't want to leave them in case that mob gets anti-French ideas. Besides," he added with a grin, "you're the one to deal with bureaucrats. At the moment I'm feeling short on tact."

Sam sighed. "If only we hadn't bothered with furs from Chauvin. There are so many other suppliers, Neill. I'm afraid that the C. and C. is going to be much poorer because of this lamentable affair."

Neill watched his partner walk away past the soldiers who stood at attention at the fringe of the group of deportees. They looked very much like the men he had commanded years ago, honorable men fighting for King and Country, and yet they had just cheerfully supervised a brutal evacuation of innocent people. He frowned as he watched them, and then a husky, mischievous laugh made him turn back to Gabrielle and the children. They were playing a game of tag, and she looked like a carefree child herself, with her long dark hair flowing free behind her and her dark eyes sparkling with pleasure. Yet there was something regal about her movements even now, a grace and poise that were her own.

"She's quite a woman, no?" He hadn't heard Marthe Richaud come up beside him. "*Petite* Gabrielle, she is like her mother, who was a great lady." She paused. "You know, don't you, that her father was a Chevalier?"

"The Chevalier de Montfleuri. Yes—I remember hearing as much at the betrothal feast."

Marthe's plump face sobered. "Monsieur Neill, Kings have short memories. All his life, the Chevalier served Louis XV. On his death, the King took all of the Chevalier's estates and wealth—and he had much wealth, believe me—and left Madame de Montfleuri and her children penniless. Ah, that was a terrible thing. They had come to Acadia, you understand, to build fine estates and live on lands that the King was going to give the Chevalier for valor and service. When he died, they didn't have a sou— not even passage back to France."

74

Neill was astonished. "I've never credited princes with much gratitude, and I hear that Louis XV's court is a hornet's nest of intrigue and bureaucracy. But why would everything the Chevalier have revert to the crown? How did he die, Marthe?"

Marthe didn't know. "If it hadn't been for Monsieur Chauvin helping them, they'd have starved," she said. And then she asked, "How long must we wait here, Monsieur? Will we spend the night in the open?"

The deportees waited for one, two, then three hours. The warm noon sun began to slide into the trees and the tired children clamored for food. Finally, Neill saw Sam striding back across the Common.

"What news?" he demanded.

"Not good." Sam's tone was grim. "The Governor has just put the matter of the Acadians into the hands of the general court of Boston. The court is meeting now. It's my feeling that the Acadians won't be allowed to stay."

Behind Neill, Gabrielle couldn't force down an exclamation of horror. "What does he say?" Marthe implored her, but she hesitated to translate such bad news. Sam continued with even worse news.

"I bribed one of the Governor's servants to tell me what he'd overheard Shirley say to the Captain. Apparently, this deportation has been planned for some time. The resettlement of the deportees has also been planned. They're to be scattered up and down the coast of North America, left in any of the colonies that will take them in."

Neill's voice was sharp with disbelief. "But why, in God's name? Why not take them to some set place and let them be?"

"Apparently, it's feared that if the Acadians get together in one place, they'll form an allied force for the French."

"Politics." Spitting out the word as though he loathed the taste of it, Neill turned to the slender, dark-eyed woman beside him, but she spoke before he could.

"If that happens," she cried, "Simon and Monsieur Chauvin and Guy may be taken anywhere. How would we find them again? How would we even know where they were?"

There was no possible answer, and behind the tense Acadians the English soldiers stirred fitfully, their hands clenched tightly about their muskets, as Marthe Richaud screamed that she would never see her husband again. Within seconds, the Acadians were either weeping or shaking their fists at the soldiers.

"Pigs of English," one young man shouted through the tears that streamed down his cheeks. "I hate you and your country. I'll never forgive you."

"That is precisely why the council has refused to let any of this riffraff remain in Boston." Neill turned sharply and saw that Captain Scott had come up to the edge of the Common. "March all the deportees back to the ship," he ordered the soldiers.

"Then the court has refused to let these people stay in Boston?" Neill asked.

Looking harassed, the Captain nodded. "Aye,

sir, it has. The Governor feels, and rightly, that an addition of two hundred people—people unfriendly to England, I might add—would cripple Boston's economy and bring the danger of crime and disease." He paused. "Of course you may go your way any time, Mr. Craddock."

Neill glanced at the soldiers, who were now forcing the bewildered Acadians to form lines. Followed by Sam, he strode over to the Captain.

"At least delay setting sail till I've had time to see Governor Shirley myself," he urged the Captain, who hesitated and then shook his head.

"Can't be done, Mr. Craddock. I've done you a favor already, and the Governor was not pleased. Not at all. Riffraff on the Common, he said."

Seeing that Neill was rapidly approaching the boiling point, Sam Culpepper interjected smoothly, "Captain, the C. and C. is a company in which many prominent Bostonians invest heavily. The Governor is among those investors. I'm sure that he'd like to see Mr. Craddock and talk to him about the furs which we all hoped to procure from Acadia. You see, the Governor might suffer losses if the matter isn't brought to his immediate attention. I'm sure you'd want to avoid that as much as we would."

The Captain looked alarmed. "In that case—"

Before he could conclude his sentence, a new voice spoke. "I, too, wish to see His Excellency, the Governor," Gabrielle said. The men stared at her, but though under the scarlet and gold of the sunset her cheeks were pale, she spoke bravely. "Someone from Laforet must be there when

77

His Excellency hears about what has happened. My friends wish me to represent them."

"Impossible," sputtered the Captain. "I'm already committing an irregularity by waiting to sail until Mr. Craddock sees His Excellency."

Neill caught Gabrielle's hand in his own, and she was grateful for the warmth of that hard grip. In spite of her brave words she was more afraid than she had ever been. The people—her people—trusted her to help them, and yet she was as terrified and as lost as they. Instinctively, she drew closer to the strength and support of the man beside her.

"Having gone so far, why not be hanged for a sheep as well as a lamb?" Neill was saying. "Captain, I'm not by nature a patient man. I've endured a great deal since Major Lampert arrived in Laforet, and I warn you that I will tolerate no more nonsense. This lady will come with me before the Governor." He took a step forward, and the skipper of *The Lovely Lady* involuntarily took several steps backward. "If you have no objections—sir?"

There was a long pause, during which Gabrielle held her breath. Then the Captain gestured surrender. "Very well, Mr. Craddock. Only, make sure that the Governor sees you before tomorrow night. I can't wait any longer, and *The Lovely Lady* will sail with the tide."

The Governor's mansion was ablaze with lights that almost eclipsed the evening's first stars. A faint sound of music and laughter was borne toward them on a night breeze scented with roasting meats and woodsmoke, and at least a score of carriages stood before and about the door. Neill drew in on the reins of Sam Culpepper's horse and spoke with dry humor.

"Well, at least we know the man's home."

Beside him in Neill's carriage, Gabrielle shivered. The evening air was chill now that the sun had gone down, and since her own heavy cloak was too salt-stained to be respectable, Sam's wife Abigail had insisted she take her own shawl of fine thin wool. "Will he see us?" she asked the man beside her.

He did not answer at once, and she looked up at him questioningly. His strong-planed face was etched sharply against the darkness, and he held his big body with a tension that was obvious in his curt reply. "He'd better."

Outwardly, they looked as if they were a pair on their way to a merry evening. Knowing that appearances meant a great deal to men like Governor Shirley, Neill had agreed to Sam's insistent demands that both he and Gabrielle return home with him to bathe and change their clothes. There Sam's gentle wife Abigail had taken Gabrielle in hand, giving her both warm support and fine clothing. Though the dress she wore was a little tight in the chest and a trifle short, it was a pretty gold color, with lace at the neck and sleeves. She glanced at Neill, who looked elegant in a fawn-colored coat and breeches buckled above the knee. Deceptively so, for there was nothing of the dandy in his hard eyes.

Her lips felt dry with nervousness as Neill

urged the horse forward again, stopping just in front of the Governor's door. "But we have no invitation to this party," she murmured.

"That doesn't matter. Act as if you own the place." Neill tossed the reins of the carriage to a waiting footman, got down and came around to assist her. "Remember that you're the daughter of the Chevalier de Montfleuri and the loveliest lady here."

He spoke to rally her, and yet it surprised him that he meant it. She had never looked so lovely, not even on her betrothal day, when she was surrounded by friends and admirers. The long and hard journey had made her glowing skin almost translucent, emphasized the beauty of her dark-lashed eyes. For a moment she looked at him uncertainly, and then she smiled.

"Where you lead I'll follow," she told him and gave him her hand.

Instead of helping her to dismount, he lifted the small hand to his lips and held it there a moment, until all her awareness was centered on the warmth of his mouth pressed against her chilled skin. That brief touch ignited memory within her, and for a second the Governor's mansion and even her desperate mission vanished, and she felt as though she were once again in his arms. She could imagine again the sweetness of his kisses, the strong, sure pressure of his body pressed against hers. His tawny gold eyes held her captive, and she thought she saw his lips form her name as, nerveless, unresisting, she slid forward into his arms.

For a moment he held her, and she almost

cried out in protest as he let her go and offered his arm for her to take. "Shall we?"

Recovering her poise, she rested her fingertips against his arm and walked forward with him until they were through the front doors, and stood in an elegant hallway. A magnificent crystal chandelier spilled candlelight over late summer flowers in tall vases and over mirrors that flanked one entire wall. Another chandelier lit the way to a larger room beyond the hall.

"The music's coming from that room—that's where they're having the party," Neill said.

This room was bright with the light of half a dozen crystal chandeliers, and the air was thick with bayberry candles. Rich cherry and oak furniture had been pushed toward the wall to accommodate dancing guests. Beyond this room, Gabrielle could glimpse a long table covered with silver and pewter and food. She realized that she hadn't heard music or laughter or seen good food since her interrupted betrothal party, and the thought of her friends on board *The Lovely Lady* made her desperate to see the one man who might help.

"Do you see the Governor?" she whispered.

"Not yet." Neill's eyes were busy roving over the roomful of guests. He scanned the musicians at the far corner of the room as well as the dancers, men bewigged and powdered, bowing before ladies in wide-hooped skirts, who smiled coquettishly from behind fluttering fans. Several of the women arched their brows at him, and he noted that several gallants had turned to survey Gabrielle, but he ignored them all to nod to a richly clad gentleman in a far corner. "Over there," he said.

She followed his gaze and realized that His Excellency was staring at Neill in surprise. He blinked, his eyebrows rising to the hairline of his wig. "Good Lord," he exclaimed. "Craddock."

"Your Excellency." Neill bowed, then moved forward, followed by Gabrielle. "May I present Mademoiselle de Montfleuri, lately of Laforet, Acadia?"

The Governor's lips twitched over the last word but did not actually say it. He cleared his throat. "I'd heard you were in that part of the world. When did you get back?"

"Today, sir. On board *The Lovely Lady*." Neill held the Governor's eyes with his own. "I beg a word with you."

The music had stopped, and it seemed to Gabrielle that everyone in the room was listening to what was being said. One elderly gentleman in a suit of sprigged velvet was actually hushing the lady on his arm so as to hear better. "Not now, Craddock," the Governor was saying testily. "See me tomorrow."

"What I have to say won't wait, sir." Amongst the glitter of the guests, Neill looked as uncompromising and as immovable as stone. "And, with all due respect, I suggest you listen. You have, as I recall, a great deal invested in C. and C. So do your friends. I doubt if they or you want to lose your investments."

Gabrielle stared at him in surprise. Why was he discussing profit and loss at a time like this? She wanted to cry out that the Governor must stop a terrible injustice, but with difficulty she

held her peace. Not now, she warned herself.
Wait.

The Governor hesitated and finally shrugged.
"Well, I suppose that I can spare a moment," he
rumbled finally. "Come this way, Craddock—
and, er, Miss. No need to throw cold water on the
party."

He led the way from the ballroom to the hallway and through a side door into what was
obviously a study. A fire had been laid in the
shallow, wide hearth, and a flicker of candlelight danced across the spines of leather-bound
books and mahogany furniture. There were several comfortable-looking chairs in the room, but
Governor Shirley did not sit, nor did he ask his
uninvited guests to do so. Instead, he turned to
face Neill. "Well?" he demanded.

"I do not wish to bore Your Excellency, so I'll
come to the point. The deportation of the Acadians has been a disaster for the C. and C. As you
must know, since you invested in our new line of
furs, I was to conduct business with Louis Chauvin, a supplier of quality fur. Since Chauvin has
been deported with the others, the money advanced to him was lost. That loss will be felt by
our investors."

"That's what you get doing business with the
French." Gabrielle bristled at this unsympathet-
ic response. Surely now Neill would stop talking
about lost finances and address the real problem? But he continued to talk about the C. and
C.'s monetary woes.

"Chauvin's not French, sir. He's an Acadian
and loyal to England. He should be—enough
Englishmen trade with him." He leaned forward

to add, "His losses will soon become our loss—yours as well as mine. Naturally, he can't pay back the C. and C. if he doesn't have any money."

The Governor drew a gold snuffbox from a pocket and took out a delicate pinch. "You needn't worry, Craddock. Chauvin has property abroad," he said.

"But that doesn't help when no one can locate the man," Neill protested. "This order to scatter the Acadians all over the colonies is going to play havoc with our finances. It would be much easier if you could . . ."

Unable to keep still any longer, Gabrielle interrupted Neill angrily. "Finances—money—is that all you can think about?" she cried. "People have been torn from their homes and from their loved ones. Mothers cry for the children who were lost in the confusion in Laforet. My best friend in Laforet was separated from her husband—I, from my brother and my fiancé."

"Gabrielle." She heard the warning in Neill's deep voice. Glaring at him, she turned back to the Governor, wanting to tell him of Laforet and what had happened there. But before she could even begin, Shirley waved her silent.

"What do you suggest I do about this matter? The council has already voted not to let any Acadians into Boston. I neither can nor wish to change that decision."

She cried, "But you are a man of honor—or do the English have honor?"

Before she could continue, she felt Neill's hand clamp down on her shoulder. "That's enough," he told her, brusquely.

The governor had turned brick-red. He snapped, "Dammit, we're at war with France."

"Is England also at war with women and children and innocent people?" Gabrielle retorted, beside herself.

It was a mistake, and yet she could not regret speaking as she had. At that moment she hated the Governor, and hated Neill even more. How could he speak as if he only cared about money? she asked herself passionately. Hadn't he been there and seen them bleed?

The Governor was angrily signaling his dismissal. "I've heard you out, Mr. Craddock, and far more patiently than I should have. Now, you and this Frenchwoman must leave," he said coldly.

"Sir." Gabrielle began to protest, but Neill's hand on her shoulder was now like a vise, jerking her back through the door and into the hallway. She had a glimpse of faces—curious, interested, amused, or hostile faces, some framed by powdered curls, some enhanced by black beauty patches or jewels. She thought that she saw the older man who had listened so intently in the ballroom and that he gave her a look of sympathy before she was whisked into the darkness and toward the carriage.

Here she whirled to face him. "Is that all you are going to do?" she cried at him.

"What else would you have me do? You certainly did more than enough," he shot back.

She turned her back to him and started to mount the carriage without his help, but his big hands clamped down on either side of her waist like bands of iron. She gasped at the bite of his fingers, and she could feel his anger burning through the thin stuff of her dress as he almost hurled her up into her seat and strode around to the other side. They drove for a few moments in a seething silence, but as they left the Governor's Mansion behind, she turned to him again.

"I only spoke the truth," she cried. "It was you who spoke of profit and of loss—as if my people meant nothing, as if money meant everything."

"Men like the Governor feel that money *is* everything," he retorted heatedly. "Had you kept your pretty mouth shut, he might have listened to me. I thought you came to help your people, not to ruin the one chance they had."

"How could I listen to you lamenting about your lost investments while my people are breaking their hearts?" She glared at him. "You have no honor, Monsieur. You are worse even than Major Lampert."

He jerked the reins of the horse to a violent stop and faced her. "That's what you think, is it?"

His voice had grown quiet with anger, and in the moonlight she could see that his eyes were like frozen stone. She was reminded of a great, tawny mountain cat gathering its muscles to spring at its prey.

"Yes." Her heart was beating in sudden fear of his leashed fury, and yet she could not hold back the words. "That is exactly what I think. No need to drive me anywhere, Monsieur. I can find the way back to the ship by myself."

Her hand was on the side of the carriage, preparatory to dismounting, when he caught her by the arm. "Not so fast, Mademoiselle Vixen," he snapped.

She cried out in protest at his restraining hand and lashed out with her own. She had never hit anyone in her life, and the blow was clumsy. Next moment, he had caught her hand and pulled her around to face him. "So," he was saying, "you show your teeth, do you?"

"Let me go." She jerked backward with all her strength, catching him by surprise and nearly falling from the carriage. With an oath, he pulled her back to safety and, off balance, she found herself in his arms.

Her whole body shuddered with the force of that impact, and for a moment she could do nothing but lie breathless in his savage clasp. "Have you done, you foolish woman?" he was demanding.

"No," she tried to say, but could not for want of air. She glared defiance at him instead, but when she met his fierce golden eyes, she caught her breath in real fear. "No," she managed to whisper, "don't . . ."

And then his lips were on hers.

Chapter Six

THERE WAS NO TENDERNESS IN THIS KISS. ALmost bruising in its intensity, his mouth seemed content to punish hers. When she tried to jerk her head away, one large hand clamped itself around the back of her head, anchoring it for his pleasure, and the rest of her was captive to his angry, iron grip.

Surely, someone would see them here in the Boston streets and come to her aid. But she heard no footsteps, could hear nothing at all except the thud of her heart. Again she tried to pull free, and he drew her closer to him, so close that she could not breathe. Her lips parted involuntarily to draw in oxygen and instead gave entry to the invasion of his tongue. Now her senses registered him everywhere. Her labored breath drew in the clean, vital scent of him, her softness was pressed against the heat of his maleness.

She hated him for what he had said and what he was doing, and yet she was being ignited with that same fire. She caught it from the rough caress of his tongue, the harsh passion of his mouth. She fought against this betrayal of her senses, and yet as he held her, she felt the changes in her body. No longer tense and rigid, it was now warm and heavy. And in the place of the fury that had coursed through her, she felt languorous waves, as warm and as sweet and as thick as honey, flowing with the beat of her blood.

As if he had sensed the change in her, his arms loosened their iron hold, and the cruel pressure of his mouth eased away from hers. She felt that if she tried to pull away now he would let her go, but she couldn't move. It was surrender, and she knew it even before her dark lashes swooped down over her eyes and his mouth recaptured hers.

This time she felt no anger but only the heat of his desire. His mouth no longer controlled and demanded but urged her response, his tongue courted hers. She drew breath from his lungs, and felt beneath her own palms the arrogant strength of his muscled arms and shoulders and back. Pearls of fire seemed to bead across her skin as his hands moved under the shawl and over her shoulders, traced the delicate line of her arms and then back again, to lightly caress the contours of her breasts. The shadow touch made her breasts feel heavy with the same hot honey that pulsed through the rest of her, and she leaned forward against his questing hands.

"Neill." She whispered it against his mouth,

and he both heard and tasted the eagerness with which she breathed his name. He was afire with a thick, drugging want that admitted no other thought except the taste and feel of her. He drew his lips away from hers to kiss her eyes, the white smoothness of her throat. She moved in his arms and he felt the touch of her hands caressing his jaw, his hair as she murmured a love word in French, and he drank in the scent of sunlight and flowers that was always about her and that went to his head like wine.

She whispered his name again as his mouth moved lower to the swell of her breast. Under the thin fabric her heart beat wildly, as his open mouth skirted the nipples that strained achingly against the cloth. Teasing, loving, his lips brought sweet torment until she drew his head closer to her, burrowing her fingers into the thick tawny hair. Then at last his mouth closed lightly over the still-covered peaks, first one, then the other.

His lips left her breast to seek her mouth again. Feeling as if she were shattering, melting away into the tidepool of warm honey with which her body was suffused, Gabrielle met his pleasure with her own. Dazed, giddy, she had yet never felt so alive. She was soaring with him high into the sun, like great golden eagles she had seen winging over Laforet.

Laforet. Like a lightning bolt sizzling across the sky, the word slashed through the muzziness in her mind. Her brain was clear again, working independently from her treacherous body. She'd spoken of wanting to help her

friends, and yet instead of thinking of her betrothed, she lay here in the arms of another
man. With a little gasp of shame, she struggled
to pull free.

"Please," she said. She wanted to shout it,
but but there was no force to her voice. "We must
stop."

He had felt her sudden rigidity as she lay in
his arms. In the white heat of his want for her,
he would have ignored this, but he could not
shut out the distress in her voice. For a moment
his arms tensed around her, and then he let her
go. She withdrew from him immediately, wrap-
ping her arms about herself, and the helpless gesture caused him an almost physical
hurt.

Her hands shook as she pushed back the long
masses of hair that shaded her face. "Please,"
she begged him, "just let me leave."

"Impossible." His effort at control made him
sound harsher than he intended. "It's not safe to
walk the streets of Boston alone. Nor will I take
you back to that ship. We're going back to the
Culpeppers." She looked at him in bewilderment, and he said, "Sam knows many people in
Boston. He may be able to find some other way of
getting the Governor to change his mind about
your friends."

She was conscious of a stunning relief. He was
still willing to help her. As he called to the horse
and set the carriage into motion again, she
whispered, "Thank you, Monsieur."

His tone was suddenly dry. "No need for
thanks. As you yourself said, I'm interested in
Louis Chauvin's whereabouts for my own rea-

sons. The sooner we find your fiancé, the sooner he'll pay the C. and C. what he owes."

Sam Culpepper did his best. For several days, while the anxious Acadians waited aboard *The Lovely Lady* and Captain Scott grumbled about the delay, he and Neill visited every influential Bostonian they knew. Sam's wife Abigail meanwhile took Gabrielle with her to visit their wives. Sam talked about money and Abigail of children torn from their parents, and though both persuaded many citizens that an injustice had been done, they could not convince the Governor or the general court. All that came of their efforts was permission for Acadians who could find work in Boston to remain.

Several farmers were dispatched to Neill's lands in Stoughtonham, and some fishermen—Henri Royale, Georges Carre—found employment as laborers on the dock. It was harder for the women to find work. Though they were good cooks and seamstresses, they could not speak English. Abigail Culpepper prevailed on her friends to take on several women and their children and took many others into her own household to teach and train. Old Nicole was given work in a prominent Boston banker's kitchen, but when Abigail offered Marthe like employment, she refused.

"No, *petite*," she told Gabrielle tearfully, "I must go on and try to find Guy. I feel in my heart that I will find him if Thérèse and I just keep looking." She paused. "And you?"

"I've decided to stay. Boston is the first port of call after Acadia, and I pray that Simon and

Monsieur Chauvin and Guy and the others come through here. If they come, I'll tell them that you have gone on." She embraced Marthe and stifled a sob as the older woman wiped her streaming eyes. "Will we ever meet again, Marthe?"

"*Certainement.*" Marthe even managed a little smile. Then she said, "I'm glad that Monsieur Neill is going to help you, even if he does so only because your betrothed owes his company money."

Gabrielle felt that her heart would break over the parting, and as *The Lovely Lady* and her abject cargo slowly sailed out of Boston harbor, she felt that nothing could ever hurt as much. She soon discovered that waiting was worse. She managed to fill her days with teaching English to the fortunate Acadians who had found work in Boston, but the nights were filled with dreams of those she had lost. Sometimes, she saw Monsieur Chauvin cast adrift on an endless sea, or Simon, his face bandaged and his face bloodied. Often, she heard the wailing of the deportees or saw the fires burning on the coast or heard Lieutenant Dray's cruel laughter as he smashed her spinning wheel against the wall. And always there was Neill. Neill carrying her to safety into the woods near Laforet or kissing her with slow, soul-stopping delight—Neill, who now avoided her as if he could not bear to be near her.

But that wasn't the case. Neill watched Gabrielle grow pale and quiet and was angry at himself because he could not help and because he was so concerned. Since the night of their confrontation with Governor Shirley, he had avoided being alone with Gabrielle, leaving her to Abigail's care, and he was thankful that he was soon to leave on a long-planned business trip to Philadelphia and to Virginia to oversee the C. and C.'s several ventures in trade and shipping there.

When Gabrielle heard of Neill's leaving, she was grateful. Though he seldom came to the Culpepper home these days, preferring to spend days on his land in Stoughtonham or at the C. and C. office in downtown Boston, she was always aware of him. She would find herself listening for his deep voice, or turning swiftly on the street when she caught sight of a tall man with dark gold hair. Now, she could concentrate fully on teaching and working with her Acadian friends.

She excused herself from attending a dinner party Abigail held for him on the eve of his departure, yet next morning when Abigail told her that he had gone, she felt an uncontrollable sense of loss. Angry at herself, she set to work at once, and drove Abigail's carriage to see old Nicole, who had the promise of a good position as a cook if she could only learn some English. But when she reached the house where Nicole was staying, she found the old woman had gone.

"You haven't heard? A ship from Acadia's just come in," one of the house servants told her. "Nicole left at a run, I can tell you, and the mistress is furious. Nicole left bread baking, and now it's burned to a cinder."

A ship from Acadia—merciful God, could it be

The Royal Princess? Gabrielle drove straight to the pier, where she found a small knot of Acadians standing together and staring toward a vessel that had just dropped anchor. "Is it *The Royal Princess*?" she called to them.

Her friends turned to meet her eagerly. "Thank God you're here," Nicole cried. "None of us can speak enough English to find out."

Gabrielle next questioned a dock hand, and her heart sank as he told her that the ship was called *The Galahad*. "He doesn't know from what part of Acadia it sailed," she told the others, "and he's heard that nobody from that ship is going to be allowed to land."

"Then we've come here for nothing." Gabrielle saw that tears were streaming down old Nicole's cheeks. "There's nothing any of us can do."

The sight of the usually caustic old woman in tears took away some of Gabrielle's own disappointment, and anger flared instead. Who were these English to hurt her and her people like this? Her chin went up, and her eyes flashed dark fire as she turned to one of the men in the group. "Henri, will you please see to the horses and the carriage? I'm going to find one of *The Galahad*'s officers. Even if nobody can come on shore, there's been no order against visiting the ship."

Anger kept her steady for the next half hour as she faced a boatload of *The Galahad*'s officers and requested permission to visit the deportees on board the ship. Confronted by a beauty with flashing dark eyes and imperious carriage, *The Galahad*'s Captain hesitated, and at mention of the C. and C. Company, he gave in and ordered his longboat to transport Gabrielle to the ship. His only stipulation was that Gabrielle make the trip alone.

The early October afternoon was blue and gold when Gabrielle hurried back to her friends with the news. Instantly, the meager coins that the Acadians had among them were pooled and plans were made. Henri Royale was sent to the bakery for fresh bread, and old Nicole rustled off to bargain for fruit from a nearby grocery store. By the time the longboat was ready for Gabrielle, she was laden with fresh food and even bottles of wine for the deportees on board *The Galahad.* And a message—"Tell them to have hope, tell them that we will pray they find their loved ones," Nicole called after the longboat.

Even though she knew that this ship wasn't the one she sought, Gabrielle's heart thumped painfully as she was rowed out toward it, and she stared hopefully at the refugees on deck. There were so many of them, and as soon as she was within hailing distance, they began to cry out to her. When she answered in French, the deportees were beside themselves, and voices entreated her across the water.

"Madame, have you seen my husband, Gustave Loren?" "Madame, my old father, his name is Beaupère Sandel; he and I were separated—" "Madame, do you know if we are to be allowed to stay?"

These deportees were from Port Royal, and they clustered about her as soon as she reached the deck. There had been trouble with the evacuation, and whole families had defied the English and escaped into the forest. But these stories didn't have a happy ending.

"Many of the families were recaptured," one haggard deportee told Gabrielle. "Those were the lucky ones. Some simply starved in the woods or were attacked by wild beasts. Others died of exposure and sickness." He sighed deeply. "At least, they died together as free people."

At least they were together—Gabrielle kept those bitter words in her mind as she distributed fruit and fresh bread and then settled down to the long business of taking down the names of loved ones whose ships might come through Boston. Since many of the deportees couldn't read or write, she also spent hours writing messages on the scraps of paper they held so hopefully out to her. She wasn't aware of the passage of time, until one of the officers interrupted her and said that she had better be getting back to land.

"It's getting to twilight, Miss, and there's fog coming in," he warned.

The fog was truly rolling across the sea, but Gabrielle couldn't leave *The Galahad* with the letter writing undone. When at last she was able to leave, the mist seemed to shroud her, and by the time she reached the dock, she found that only Henri remained with her carriage.

"Will you be all right, Gabrielle?" he asked her, worriedly. "This fog is worse than anything we had at home. It's so thick that I'm not sure where the sea ends and the land begins. Maybe I'd better see you home?"

She was tempted, but Henri looked tired and cold, and so she only thanked him and mounted the carriage alone. But as she called to the horse, she had the impression that the whole of the city was wrapped in gray smoke. She could see very little, and she started out very slowly, relying on memory and instinct to find her way back to the Culpeppers', but she had not gone very far before she realized she had lost her way. Wishing that she'd taken Henri's offer, she reined in the horse to take stock of her surroundings and then tensed. Had she heard footsteps?

She listened intently, and the sound of footsteps echoed loudly against the fog bank. Someone was very near her, but she couldn't tell where, and remembering Neill's warnings about venturing out alone in Boston, she called to the horse and set it in motion. But before the beast could move, the dark shadow of a man loomed up beside her.

Seizing her whip, she lifted it to strike, but before she could bring down a blow, a strong hand had seized the reins. "You seem to be both armed and dangerous," a familiar voice remarked.

Relief and astonishment made her weak. "Neill—why are you here?" she stammered. "You are supposed to be on the way to Philadelphia."

"As you can see, I'm not. And didn't I warn you about venturing out alone at night?" Neill soothed the horse, came around to the side of the carriage and got in. "Give me the reins," he said.

The fright that he had given her had turned to indignation. "I will not. I can drive, sir . . ."

"Only if you know where you're going," he said

reasonably. "You were lost in the fog, weren't you?"

He took the reins as he spoke, and his warm, strong fingers closed momentarily over her chilled ones. It was a small touch, but even after all this time it reawakened the memories that simmered just below the surface of her conscious thought. She pulled her hand quickly away. "Why did you return?" she asked.

He didn't answer immediately, and she had the uncanny sensation that the entire outer world had disappeared into white mist. Only his strong presence next to her in the narrow carriage was real, and in the swirl of fog he seemed larger and uncompromisingly male.

"I heard something on the road to Rhode Island that brought me back to Boston." His voice seemed even deeper tonight. He seemed to be looking for something in the fog as he spoke, and now he gave a grunt of satisfaction. "There it is."

In the fog she could see very little, but that little was unfamiliar. "We're not at the Culpeppers's," she charged.

"No. This is the Red Dragon Inn, where I promised to meet some friends of Sam's." As she turned to him in surprise, he added, "There's news."

Her heart spasmed so suddenly that she nearly cried out. "About *The Royal Princess*?"

He nodded. "I thought you'd want to know immediately."

A wave of gratitude brought tears to prickle her eyelids, and she smiled at him through those tears. "I can't thank you enough."

Her brave smile caught him like an unexpected blow to the heart. As he helped her down from the carriage, he was very much aware of the warm, soft slenderness in his arms, and he sighed inwardly as he let her go.

"Of course," he told her, "this could be a false lead."

"After what I saw today on *The Galahad*, I am grateful even for a false lead." She bit her lip. "I felt ashamed of my own selfishness in looking only for my brother and my fiancé and friends. I have been given so many names and so many letters—even if we find a few of these, I will be thankful."

Without further word, he ushered her into the inn's narrow common room, a rough but cheerful place where a huge fire burned on the hearth against the early October chill. A small boy was carefully turning a spit suspended over the flames, and he looked up to grin a welcome at these newest guests. Succulent smells of roasting pork filled the air with their own welcome, and bits of fat sizzled enticingly against the hot coals. Several travelers had gathered about the hearth to await their dinner, while others, sitting on a long, low bench, drank hard cider or warmed ale.

Nodding to the innkeeper, Neill guided Gabrielle through a door adjacent to the tap room. This door opened into a room so heavy with pipe smoke that it seemed as foggy as the outdoors. Through the smoke Gabrielle saw Sam Culpepper and another man seated at a narrow table, while a third man sat with his heels to the warmth of a shallow fireplace. All three rose as Gabrielle and Neill entered the room.

"Good evening, Mr. Craddock, Mademoiselle de Montfleuri." The man by the fireside spoke first, and Gabrielle recognized the elderly gentleman she had seen at Governor Shirley's party. His voice was as grave and as dry as his appearance, but his eyes were kind. "I'm Caleb Langsdon, editor of *The Boston Crier*. At your service."

She curtseyed to him, and again as Sam introduced his third companion. "Gabrielle, Neill—this is Paul Revere, the silversmith who has of late become a firm believer in home rule."

"I'm glad to meet you, sir and Madam." The young silversmith had an open, engaging face and a pleasant smile. His eyes were direct and very clear, and Gabrielle found herself warming to their honesty. "I'd hoped to speak with you, Mr. Craddock."

"To convert you, he means," Sam laughed. "However, that can wait another time. When you told me of what you'd heard on your travels, Neill, I quickly reached Mr. Langsdon. As the editor of the most controversial paper in Boston, he's privy to a lot of news."

Neill set a chair for Gabrielle and then went to stand with his back to the fire. "What have you unearthed, sir?" he asked.

Caleb Langsdon cleared his throat. "What you heard was true. Many Acadians have been accepted as residents in Philadelphia." As Gabrielle caught her breath, he raised a judicious finger. "Mind you, the English military has kept very bad records, but it's almost sure that *The Royal Princess* was one of the ships to have discharged its passengers in that city."

"*Sacré Dieu*, then they are there. They are found." Gabrielle clasped her hands in her lap and strove for control. "I must go to Philadelphia."

"A moment, Madam." Caleb Langsdon stopped and sighed. "Only a portion of the deportees aboard *The Royal Princess* are in Philadelphia. The city fathers were kind, but they could only take a certain amount of people. The others had to go on."

"You see," Sam added, "our information is not clear on this point. Neill learned that some Acadians were in Philadelphia, but nobody had any names. I'm sorry, Gabrielle. One can only hope that your brother and fiancé were among the lucky ones who were allowed to stay."

Gabrielle got to her feet, repeating, "I must go at once."

Caleb Langsdon shook his finger at her. He looked like a schoolmaster explaining a lesson. "I think you had better go armed with a few facts," he said. "For instance, did you realize that six thousand Acadians have been deported from your homeland?"

The numbers were staggering. How many villages, how many peaceful towns had been emptied of their people in the name of the English King? "How terrible," she heard herself murmuring.

Clearing his throat, the editor of *The Boston Crier* spoke sententiously. "I trust you know that Acadia has been a thorn in the side of

British politicians for some time? Governor Lawrence has been contemplating deportation for a long time, the only problem being that of resettling six thousand people."

Neill broke in somewhat impatiently. "This we already know."

"But you don't know the real reason behind the deportation. It's economic. There are English and Scottish settlers moving into Acadia, and Governor Shirley wanted the land on which the Acadians lived. His motive was expansion and profit."

"So for money my people have been uprooted, scattered—" again she could see the pitiful deportees aboard *The Galahad*. She clenched her small hand and rubbed it against her breastbone, as if this could still the ache within her. "Tell me, please, when and how I can go to Philadelphia."

Sam immediately began to protest. A lady could not travel alone, especially not a lady unused to the country and the language and the customs. Neill agreed. "The C. and C. has business in Philadelphia. When I get there, I'll find out about your brother and fiancé."

"Can you also deliver the messages given to me today?" she protested. He didn't look in the least convinced and she begged, "Monsieur, take me with you. I will be no trouble, believe me. I must find Simon."

"Inhuman." Paul Revere had spoken the word with such force that it cut through Gabrielle's misery. "Intolerable. A government that foists such misery on others doesn't deserve respect or loyalty." He paused and then added sternly, "In a few years, we'll feel the lash of this intolerable government ourselves. When that time comes, even apoliticals like you, Mr. Craddock, will have to choose sides."

Neill was not listening. "I'd meant to go on horseback along the lower post road. I suppose a carriage could manage the route as well." He paused, to think. "We'll leave from Dedham. It'll take four days to reach New Haven, another two at least to get to Philadelphia. Once there, we'll stay at Fishe's inn. Fishe will help us find out what we need to learn."

"Then you're taking her?" Sam wanted to know.

Neill turned to Gabrielle and saw that her lips had formed the word "Please." Aloud, she said, "I will be of use to you, I swear it."

Why could this woman make him feel so deeply? Exasperated at the conflict in his emotions, Neill turned to Sam. "She's right in a way. If Chauvin isn't there, she might be the one to find out from the other refugees where he's gone. She's one of them, and they'll trust her with things they might not tell me."

She didn't dare believe that he had actually agreed to take her along. She gazed up at him with joy and gratitude, then saw that there was no friendship or even warmth in his face. "Very well," he repeated. "We'll leave as soon as possible and hope it's no wild goose chase."

She thought: He does not go for me but to help himself and his company. He will not mind the goose chase as long as he finds the goose that lays the golden egg. For some reason this knowledge hurt her terribly, and she was angry with herself. What did it matter why he took her as long as she was going to those she loved?

"Monsieur," she said formally, "I thank you for agreeing to take me to my brother and my future husband."

She would have said more, except that into his tawny eyes came a look that she had seen before, a strange, unreadable, here-now-and-gone-again look that she had puzzled over on board the ship that had brought them to Boston. For a moment that look held her, drew her. It seemed to call to her across the room and she almost took a step toward him.

Then he turned abruptly away from her. "The pleasure will be mine," he said, and there was a definite chill in his voice. "You know how much Sam and I both want to find Louis Chauvin."

Chapter Seven

THE OCTOBER AFTERNOON WAS BLUE AND CLEAR, the autumn sun still golden and bright. Gabrielle leaned back in the sturdy open carriage and lifted her face to its welcome warmth. A flock of geese, winging away to warmer climates, reminded her of Laforet, and she thought: At last I am going to find them.

"Tired?" It was the first thing he had said to her for miles, and it startled her out of her thoughts.

"No, not at all. I'm just happy to be on my way."

He made no reply. He was sitting relaxed in the driver's seat, driving with an expert skill that urged the greatest speed from the horses. And yet something must have displeased him, for his eyebrows were pulled together over his bold nose, and there was a tightness to his lips. His hands were large on the reins, square-palmed and strong-fingered, tufted with tawny hair. Hands that could be ruthless in battle, tender in love.

He was saying, "It's time to take a brief rest. We've been riding for several hours. We need to reach Fayerton by evening, but we're making good time and the horses could do with some rest. And besides, Abigail will be hurt if we don't eat the fine lunch she packed for us."

Food was the farthest thing from her mind and she was impatient of any delay, but she recognized the sense in what he said. "Perhaps this is as good a place to stop. See, there is a small pond where the horses can be watered."

They were passing green meadowlands full of goldenrod and hardy blue Michaelmas daisies. Neill guided his horses off the road and to the lip of the pond, and in spite of her hurry, Gabrielle looked about her with pleasure. Fringing the pond were tall white birches that seemed to shake their golden leaves at her in welcome. "I see that here, too, you have the white ladies of the forest," she exclaimed.

"The Indians in these parts have a score of uses for birchbark." He got down from the carriage and led the horses to drink. As they did so, he came around to her side of the carriage and then leaned against its side to look about him. "Truly, it's a fair country."

"Fairer than England?" she asked, smiling a little, but he answered her seriously.

"It's as if everything here is on a bigger scale. There's a sense of grandeur and newness about America." He paused, searching for words, but she understood what he hadn't said.

"I felt that way about Laforet, even though I was born in France. It is strange," she added, "but I do not remember very much of my homeland. I recall that the Louvre was magnificent, and that once, when I was only four years old, I was taken to meet His Majesty the King. How my mother fussed and worried over my clothes, my manners. I was to curtsey like a big girl and I was not to fidget or do anything so horrible as to suck my thumb."

When she smiled, her eyes turned to velvet that caught the creamy afternoon sunlight. "I'm sure your meeting with King Louis went superbly," he commented.

She wrinkled her small nose. "It was horrible. He was a fat, rather foolish-looking man, and he didn't even notice the small girl who curtseyed so carefully. But alas, one of his dogs did. It bit the edge of my skirt and I began to cry. Maman had to take me away." She laughed her husky, mischievous laughter. "She said I had disgraced myself before the King."

"You'd be the ornament of any court." He was not laughing, and she caught her breath at the look in his tawny eyes. They were as deep as golden water, and gazing into them, she could see only the reflection of herself. The thought came to her that a woman could drown in such eyes.

He was holding his hands out to her. "Come," he said, and without thought she put her hands into his big ones. They clasped hers strongly and again the familiar thought came to her. This strength could give her both safety and excitement. And danger, too, for warnings flashed through her brain as he lifted her from the carriage and held her for a moment before letting her down to the safety of the ground.

But there was no sanctuary even on the ground. His arms still held hers prisoner, and she could not take her eyes away from his. Under her sturdy travel clothes, her heart was beating wildly. He leaned closer, and of its own volition, her head tipped back, lips parting for his kiss.

Near them, one of the horses lifted its head and whickered, shaking droplets of water over them. She pulled her hands away hastily while he laughed. "They're reminding us that water's good enough but that oats would be better," he said. "While I see to them, perhaps you could unpack Abigail's basket."

Glad to have something to do, she spread a blanket on the fragrant grass and arranged on it the contents of the large hamper. There were fresh-baked bread, chicken, savory meat pies, apples and pickles, as well as a flask of wine.

"She's sent enough food to feed a village," he commented. She didn't look up as he spoke, but all her senses were aware that he was watching her.

"Are you hungry?" she asked.

He nodded, and settling down some distance from her, he stretched out his long, booted legs. "You'd best eat well," he advised. "This is our only stop before the inn at Fayerton."

Now that food was before her, she suddenly realized that she was almost ravenously hungry. Everything tasted wonderful. She ate with more enjoyment than she had since leaving Laforet, and it was only when she couldn't eat any more that she was aware of his amusement.

"I'd say you did justice to Abigail's cooking," he commented.

"Didn't you?" she retorted, and he laughed assent. "Everything tastes so good outdoors. It is like a picnic, such as the ones Maman and Simon and I had in Laforet. Sometimes Monsieur Chauvin joined us."

"Of course—no picnic would have been complete without him." Neill sent a half-eaten apple sailing through the golden air and got to his feet. "It's time we were moving." He added, "The horses have rested enough, and we need to reach Fayerton by dusk."

They made good time during the next two hours, passing through more of the meadow country that rolled into low hills covered with maples and flaunting brilliant fall colors. Once a post rider, his bulging mailbags strapped to the sides of his horse, passed them. Farther along they came upon a peddler, trudging with his packs on his back toward Fayerton. "He'll have customers for both his wares and the news he's picked up along the way," Neill said.

Gabrielle returned the peddler's wave and then turned to hear what Neill was saying about the road over which they were traveling. It was near sunset, and as they drove past a crossroads, he pointed with his whip.

"We might be riding over a man's grave." She looked at him in surprise and he explained, "It's customary to bury suicides at crossroads.

Rumor has it that one such wretch was planted here with a stake through his heart."

"How cruel—but the dead do not feel, do they?" she asked slowly. "I wonder why he killed himself."

"Probably because he committed the one unforgivable sin and lost faith." Neill's voice was casual, but there was no doubt he meant what he said. "There is nothing so bad that it can't be endured. While there's life, there's hope."

She thought of all the six thousand wanderers who had been torn from their homes, and bit her lip. As if reading her thoughts, he reached out and took her hand. "It will come right, Gabrielle," he said gently.

The clasp of his hand on hers was electric. Magic. It seemed as if the drowsy gold of the late afternoon sun had suddenly warmed to fever heat and that his touch had reached deep into her heart. It cost her an effort to disengage her fingers. "I pray it will. I want to see Monsieur Chauvin and Simon soon."

He interrupted her. "Tell me something. You always refer to your fiancé as Monsieur Chauvin. Why not simply call him Louis?"

"That does not seem respectful," she protested. "He was always our family's benefactor. Simon and I have always revered him."

"But do you love him?" The question was asked almost angrily, and it took her aback. She found that she had clasped her hands, holding them tightly in her lap.

"Of course," she exclaimed. She was again aware of his tawny gaze, and she looked back at him defiantly. "Why else would I marry him?" she demanded.

As she spoke, they turned a corner in the road and came upon a strange scene. Before them in the bright sunset stretched another crossroads, and here a number of people were gathered together. There were men on horseback, several women, and a nervous-looking middle-aged man who kept looking up and down the road and rubbing his hands together.

"What are these people doing?" Gabrielle asked curiously.

Neill slowed his horse and called a question. The answer was incomprehensible to Gabrielle, but Neill only grinned and lifted his whip in greeting.

"Good luck, friend," he told the nervous man. "You'll need it." Then as they bowled along he explained, "They're getting ready to have a 'shift' wedding." She looked bewildered and he added, "The bride, who has not arrived yet, is a widow, and her husband left her saddled with many debts. She wants to marry again, but naturally the new bridegroom isn't happy about paying up another man's bills."

Gabrielle was still perplexed. "But why marry at a crossroads?"

"It's a custom of these parts. If a widow remarries at midnight at a crossroads and in her shift, all debts are cancelled. That's why it's called a 'shift' wedding. Sometimes it's a love match; other times it's a convenient way of getting out of debt."

Gabrielle began to laugh. "And that funny worried-looking man, he is the groom?"

"No, just one of the principal creditors. He's hoping that the wedding won't take place because he wants his money." Neill did not join her laughter. "You see," he said, "marriages are made in many ways—and for many reasons besides love."

Gabrielle was suddenly quiet, and Neill was sorry he had spoken. It was, after all, not his affair. He frowned as he recalled that the dignified Louis Chauvin, who could be charming, could play the grand host, had been the acknowledged leader of Laforet. Exile or no, the man had land and money and could provide well for Gabrielle and her brother. He glanced at her and saw that she sat as flushed and rigid as the hands clasped in her lap. He reached out, took one of those hands and squeezed it.

"I'm sorry," he said.

She knew that he meant it, but when his voice went deep like that, she felt herself tremble. Merciful God, she thought, why can he make me feel like this? Surely, surely she had felt this way with Monsieur Chauvin, but she could not remember. In panic she realized that she could not even remember what her fiancé looked like. All she could think of was the strong, uncompromisingly male presence next to her in the carriage.

Suddenly, a jolt of the carriage carried her across the seat to fetch up against his side. The lean hardness of him, the arm with which he steadied her, evoked other feelings, but before she could analyze them or pull free, the carriage jolted again.

Neill halted the horses. "Look ahead," he said

in answer to her anxious question. "Some fool has been careless with his firewood."

It was well past sunset, and indigo streaks crisscrossed the bright skies, casting shadows on the road. She had to strain her eyes to see that logs of several lengths and sizes seemed to have been tossed across the road. "But this is terrible," she exclaimed. "If you had not seen these, we might have had an accident."

He nodded. "It seems that those people over there didn't see the logs in time."

Some distance ahead of them, a four-wheeled carriage, pulled by four stout horses, stood by the side of the road. It sat at an awkward angle, and Gabrielle realized that it had lost one of its wheels. Four men stood about the detached wheel, obviously wondering what to do.

"Should we offer help?" Gabrielle asked, but Neill shook his head.

"There are four of them, all grown men. They'll manage."

He got down from the carriage to remove the logs directly in their path, and as he did so one of the stranded travelers came hurrying over to them.

"This is a terrible state of affairs," he began in an agitated voice. "Name's Bailey—Geoff Bailey. My brothers and I've been hoping and praying someone would come by to give us a hand with that wheel."

Neill straightened from his log carrying, but before he could speak, Geoff Bailey had jerked his thumb in the direction of the coach. "My wife's in that carriage, sir. She's been taken with bad stomach pains, and we were heading for old Dr. Barnes in Fayerton when this happened."

A muffled groan from the stranded coach now echoed faintly in the gathering dusk, and Gabrielle exclaimed in sympathy.

"All we need is a minute of your time," Geoff Bailey said. "We can almost but not quite hoist the coach up to slip on the wheel. We need another strong pair of shoulders."

"My shoulders are at your disposal, sir." Removing his coat Neill handed it to Gabrielle, adding as he followed Geoff Bailey to the damaged coach, "Four of us can hoist the coach, the other will slide the wheel in. Is that agreeable?"

"Anything you say." The traveler's voice was soft, but something in it made Neill turn quickly to face him and to see a flash of dying light move on the descending blade. There was no time to think, only to react. Driving forward with his shoulder, he cannoned into his attacker. The man grunted and fell as if poleaxed, and Neill landed on his shoulder, rolled over and regained his feet just as the three other men, swords upraised, charged him.

Unarmed and unprepared, he still had time for one shout. "Get out of here, drive out," he called to Gabrielle. Then he sidestepped one attacker, caught him a vicious blow at the side of the neck and tipped his inert body into the path of another. Then, he turned to face the fourth. "The odds seem better now," he said.

"Not for you." Sword held high, the man circled Neill warily. "We want you dead, friend."

"If it's blood you want, maybe I can oblige." If he kept the man talking, there was a chance he could reach the sword that one of the others had dropped.

Gabrielle saw Neill bend down and, with a movement that was so swift it seemed like a blur of light, snatch up a sword. "Now," she heard him say grimly, as he sprang to the attack.

Neill's adversary fell almost at once, screaming and pressing his hand to his side. As Neill faced the other three, Gabrielle heard a movement inside the disabled coach and remembered what she had forgotten till now—that there was yet another person inside that coach. But it was no suffering woman who had remained hidden there, for now a man's head and arms appeared —a man who was holding a pistol aimed at Neill's back.

Gabrielle acted instinctively. Screaming a warning, she whipped the horses and turned them sharply, so that they carried her and her carriage straight at the coach. She saw the man in the coach turn toward her, saw him aim the pistol directly at her and fire. Gritting her teeth, she bent low over the backs of the horses, as the ball went wide. And before the man in the coach could reload, Neill's sword had pierced his heart.

At this the survivors took to their heels. Limping and helping each other along, they melted away into the shadows. For a moment she stared after them, and then Neill was beside her on the driver's seat. He caught her by the shoulders. "Are you all right?" he demanded urgently. "You're not hurt?"

"I'm unhurt—" but his hands were red with blood. "You are wounded," she exclaimed.

"One of them nicked me in the wrist. It's nothing." He shoved something into the belt of his trousers—the dead man's pistol—and she began to tremble as he said, "Let's get away from this place. They may have friends nearby."

He whipped the horses on their way, and it wasn't till they were some distance away that she could control her shaking enough to ask, "Why did they attack us? Who were they?"

"Thieves, probably—after easy booty." Neill's voice was grim. "They were clever with their strewn logs and their disabled carriage, but I should have smelled a trap." Then he added even more grimly, "And you were foolish as well. What you did could have gotten you killed."

The memory of the flashing swords, the sight of Neill's blood, the mad careering ride made her shake even more. She tried to control this as she bound his cut with her handkerchief, but what had happened this night seemed to be the climax of all the terrible things that had happened to her since Lampert's men came marching into Laforet. A sob lodged in her throat and she fought it down, but now tears began to stream down her cheeks.

Dimly, she was aware of his calling to the horses and of their stopping. She heard him say her name but it only made her cry harder. She wept for Marthe and her loss, for hotheaded Simon, who might now be dead, cut down in a quarrel with the British, and she thought—I cannot bear it.

"Gabrielle." He had descended from the carriage, come around and was now lifting her down. Held against him, she poured out all her grief, and he stroked the tumbled silk of her hair and murmured words of comfort. "Cry it out," he told her. "It's all right, my brave darling."

The terrible desolation that had filled her eased away in the magic circle of his arms, but now a different tension swept through her like a wind that carried away every other memory and feeling. Darkness and cold vanished, and so did heartbreak and danger, and she raised her face for his kiss.

The touch of his mouth was pure sorcery. Heat, like a flow of hot wine, surged through her blood. As his tongue outlined the periphery of her lips, she parted them to give him entry, gloried in his bold and yet tender invasion. She knew now that all these weeks away from each other, she had wanted him to kiss her, touch her.

And he was touching her, seeking the warm, yielding satin of her body as if reclaiming it. Powerful arms held her to him while his other hand caressed her back and hair and then shifted to cup the fullness of her breast. She was conscious of the almost painful straining of her nipples against the cloth of her dress as his thumb rubbed lightly over the sensitive tips.

Somehow, they had left the side of the carriage and were standing in the sweet-scented meadow that lay beside the road. She drew in the sweet fragrance of crushed grass and flowers together with the scent of him, as his lips left hers and moved hungrily down to her bare throat. She registered his open-mouthed kisses and then he was tugging impatiently at the buttons of her dress, pushing it down to expose shoulders and breasts. For a moment she felt the cool of the night air, and then his mouth brought its own warmth as it caressed her bare skin. Involuntarily, her body arched back against the support of his arm as he kissed the inner curve of her breast and then moved his mouth leisurely, sensuously to skirt but not yet touch her nipples.

"Sweet," he murmured. "My sweet Gabrielle."

She was like honey. Like wine. He heard her moan softly as his mouth closed over the roses of her breasts, and she moved against him in a delicious madness as he held and suckled her. Her fingers twined in his hair, curved about the hard line of his jaw, tickled the nape of his neck. As she pressed still closer, he felt the desire that had always been between them roar into conflagration.

They seemed to move at once, sliding buttons from buttonholes, helping each other. She registered the hard coolness of his chest against her bare breasts, shivered at the erotic rub of his chest fur against her kissed-tender nipples. Now her dress sighed down to her feet, and she stood in her shift. Almost naked beside him, she felt against her softness the hard demand of his still-clothed male body.

He murmured her name as he lifted her toward him, pressing his mouth to the tender valley between her high breasts. She cradled her head against him, and instinctively, she moved so that her softness was pressed against the steel of his passion. Her hips and thighs moved, aping the age-old dance of love, and he held her close to him, savoring her. Again, his mouth claimed her nipples, drawing their honey as she bent over him and covered them both with the curtain of her midnight hair.

Now he went down on one knee and took her with him. She felt cool grass beneath her bare legs, but then all other sensations stilled as he caressed the entire length of her from shoulder to knee and then moved his hand up with a passionate delicacy. Pushing up her shift, stroking her silky thighs, between them.

She felt as if she were shattering under his touch, spasming with an ecstasy that was almost pain. She wrapped her arms about him, kissing his mouth, his throat, the flat male nipples.

In a moment he would lay her back against the grass and the tangle of their clothes. In a moment her shift would be gone, and his breeches, and they would come together. She wanted him. Her entire body was warm and honey-heavy, ready for him. She had always been ready for him. Since that first moment, from that day when he smiled at her.

That thought troubled her, and she put it away. It must not bother her now. She concentrated on the sensual tenderness of his caresses, on the way his mouth sought hers in small, fiery, passionate kisses. But the edge of that concentration was now frayed, and again the unwanted thought came. When Neill had first smiled at her, she was at the church on her bethrothal day.

Before she could close her mind to the

thought, one of the carriage horses snorted and stamped nearby. The noise startled them both, and Neill looked up sharply. And in that moment, all the thoughts she had kept at bay crowded close, repeating one damning fact. Her betrothal day, her betrothed—she was going to Philadelphia to meet her betrothed.

The realization brought with it a sense of loss so terrible that she almost cried out in pain. It was as if somebody had amputated a part of her body. Then shame seared through her, and together with this shame she heard Neill's voice.

"Don't, my love. Don't think. Not now . . ."

But she knew that she must think past the raging fire in her blood. "I am not your love," she whispered. "I belong to Louis Chauvin."

Her voice was low and tremulous, and he read the passionate entreaty in her eyes. Yet he couldn't bear to let her go. The spill of her dark hair cascaded over them both, and her bare shoulders and milk-white breasts were still pressed against him, and his groin ached with want of her. He sensed that if he kissed her again, he could sweep away all thought of this absent Chauvin, realized also that her sweet body would respond to his lovemaking. But at the same time, he knew also that if he did this, she would hate him and herself.

Drawing a deep breath that was almost a sigh, he let go of her. She didn't move at once, as he thought she would, but faced him in the faint moonlight. It caressed the hollows of her temples, shadowed the rich loveliness of her slender body as she said, "This was my fault. You were trying to comfort me, and I forgot—" She broke off, her voice trembling slightly, and he ached to draw her close to him. But at his gesture, she drew back so sharply that he dropped his arms to his sides. She had said it: She belonged to another man.

"It's getting cold, and we'd best be on our way." His voice was flat, controlled. Turning away, he caught up his shirt as he added, "In a few days, God willing, this journey will be over for both of us."

Chapter Eight

"Welcome, sir and Madam—nay, if it isn't Mr. Craddock from Boston town!" Hurrying down the steps of his inn, the jovial, balding innkeeper rubbed his hands together appreciatively. "Glad am I to see you in Philadelphia again, sir."

A ruddy half-moon lit the cobblestoned street and the modest, brick-faced building, which sported a wooden sign ornamented with a scarlet fish. From the inn itself came the sound of conversation and laughter, comfortable, welcoming sounds that made Gabrielle's tired mind yearn for rest.

"Thank you, Mr. Fishe." Leaning down from the carriage, Neill shook the innkeeper's hand. "Can you find rooms for Miss de Montfleuri and myself?"

The innkeeper made an expansive gesture. "Trust me, sir. Have I ever failed ye? But now, come in, come in. There's a rack of lamb roasting on the spit and other good, plain fare. Noah will see to the horses, so rest you. You've come a long way."

A long way indeed, Gabrielle agreed silently. In six days they had covered the long miles between Boston and Philadelphia, riding through the driving rain that had kept them company between New London and New Haven and ignoring the hard stretch of road near Connecticut. It had been a long journey, for they had only stopped to eat or to take their rest at wayside inns.

It had also been a silent journey, and Neill said nothing now as he dismounted from the carriage and came around to assist her down. His hand held hers almost reluctantly and let it go immediately when she had reached the ground. Since that first evening, they had avoided touching and even looking at each other and, by mutual consent spoke only when it was absolutely necessary.

He seemed to think it necessary now. "Fishe is a clever man, as well as discreet. Sam and I are old customers of his, and he'll give us the best rooms in the place. Besides, I'm sure that he'll be able to help us locate Chauvin."

She tried to take heart as she followed him up the steps and into the cheerful common room, dominated by an enormous fireplace, next to which stood a flight of narrow steps leading upstairs. Across from the fireplace and the stairs, long benches had been drawn up to an oaken table that glowed with age and polish, and fresh-faced serving girls were dishing up boiled chickens, half-hams and spit-roasted lamb.

"Are you hungry?" Neill was asking her.

She shook her head. The smells of cooking were suffocating, and she was tired enough to weep. "Only for news," she declared.

"We'll have that as soon as we can talk to Fishe." The innkeeper was urging them up the staircase to more private accommodations, himself escorting them to a dark landing and then to a small sitting room, which adjoined two smaller bedrooms.

Here Gabrielle turned to him. "Mr. Fishe, I have a favor to beg of you . . ."

"Anything, Madam," Fishe smiled, but he looked astonished as she explained the reason for their journey. "I never figured you'd be involved with these Acadian French, Mr. Craddock," he exclaimed.

Neill ignored the comment. "We know that many Acadians settled here. What we need to know is whether Miss de Montfleuri's brother and fiancé were among those given sanctuary. Where would we get this information?"

Frowning, the landlord considered the question. "Benjamin Thurlow's the one to see. He's a Quaker gentleman who does all manner of good works." He paused to add, "Do wash and refresh yourselves, and I'll send someone to find him for you."

As Fishe hurried away, Gabrielle turned to the small sitting room's window and stared outside. It was dark except for the friendly yellow glow that lit the houses around the inn, and as she watched she saw a man walking briskly up to a door. He knows where his home is, she thought enviously.

"You'd better take Fishe's advice and rest and change," Neill now said behind her. When she shook her head, his deep tones took on an edge of impatience. "I'd have thought you'd want to look decent for Chauvin."

Her eyes flew to the image of herself reflected in the glass windowpane and stared at a white-faced shade of herself. Haunted eyes stared from a face taut with fatigue and tension. I look like a *revenant*—a ghost, she thought in horror. Maybe he won't even recognize me.

She didn't realize she had said the words aloud until she felt him move behind her. This time her eyes went to his face. There was an intensity in the mirrored features that echoed her own, and his amber gaze held hers captive. He was close to her, so close that if she stepped backward, she would be in his arms. The memory of those arms and that broad wall of chest seethed unbidden through her senses.

Realizing that she had begun to tremble, she wrapped her arms about herself to try and stop the shaking, then pulled in a sharp breath as she saw him reach out to draw her to him.

But he didn't touch her. Instead, he turned his back to her and began to walk away to one of the bedrooms. "Do as you will," he told her abruptly.

When the door of his room shut behind him, the sitting room grew silent. Without his vital male presence, it seemed suddenly empty and she stood still, until a burst of laughter from downstairs broke the silence and brought her back to reality. She was tired, she told herself, that was why she felt so strangely. And, Neill was right; of course she must look her best for Monsieur Chauvin and Simon.

She spent the better part of an hour in her room, washing away the stains of the road and brushing her black hair till it snapped. Then she dressed in one of the few dresses she had brought with her, a dress Monsieur Chauvin had admired back in Laforet. Compared with the fine clothes she had seen in Boston, it looked simple and countrified, but she could think of nothing else she wanted to wear tonight. She wanted to be close to home, to the fir-scented forests and the lazy golden eagles that soared into the sun. She wanted to pretend that this madness had never happened and that she had never met a man as tawny and as dangerous as one of those great birds.

"Gabrielle." His deep voice, coming at the end of her thoughts, startled her. "Are you ready?" he then asked. "Benjamin Thurlow is here."

She flew to the door and pulled it open, almost running past Neill into the sitting room beyond. Fishe was standing with his back to the closed door of the room, and near him, leaning on a cane, was a stranger. For a moment she thought he was a young man, for though his hair was pure white, his face was unwrinkled. Then he smiled, and she saw the lines of age and experience etched deep about his mouth.

"Friend Gabrielle," he said, and instinct made her curtsey low. "Nay," he said holding out his hand, "do not, my daughter. The Friends do not believe in such posturings."

She crossed the room slowly and took his

hand. It was warm and comforting, and she knew that with this man she needn't pretend. "Neill has told you?"

Sighing, he nodded. "Your brother and your betrothed." Still holding her hand, he led her to a sofa in the room and drew her down to sit beside him. "I wish I had better news for thee."

"They are not here." The words formed in her heart before her lips uttered them. She felt suddenly drained as if all her blood had flowed away from her body.

Unhappily, the old Quaker shook his head. "I have a list of every Acadian lodged with Friends, another of those others who have found employment and other lodging in this city. Both Friend Neill and I have looked over the lists, but neither of us can find the names of thy brother or betrothed nor of the Richauds, thy friends."

She felt dizzy, sick. "Not here," she found herself repeating again, and then in French she whispered brokenly, *"Je suis perdue."* I am lost.

She realized that Neill had now come to stand beside her, and in her desolation his strength was reassuring. She had an almost irresistible impulse to touch him and make contact with his strength, and as the thought filled her mind, she felt his warm clasp on her shoulder. Easy, it seemed to say, don't give up yet. "Can you tell us where the others on *The Royal Princess* went?" She asked.

For the first time, anger disturbed the old man's serenity. "Acadians are being pushed and pulled like baggage from port to port in the hopes that someone will take them in. Nearly two thousand stay here in Philadelphia. Others have been sent on to Virginia and the Carolinas."

There had been a map in Monsieur Chauvin's study and now Gabrielle seemed to see it before her. Virginia—the Carolinas. They were hundreds of miles away. She bit her lower lip to stifle a sob as the old Quaker turned to her.

"Friend Gabrielle, I can see that thee are brave. Are thee brave enough to come among thy countrymen tomorrow and talk to them? Friend Neill here has told me thee met another ship in Boston. Perhaps thee can give some of thy countrymen news of their loved ones."

Neill's hand tightened on her shoulder, and this pressure reminded her of what he had said about never losing hope. She had endured a great deal and could still endure.

Unconsciously, her shoulders straightened and Neill, listening to the new firmness in her voice, knew he had never admired her courage more. "Yes," she said, "yes. Of course I will."

Next morning, while Neill attended to C. and C. business in the city, Benjamin Thurlow took Gabrielle to meet with her fellow deportees. The experience was even worse than meeting *The Galahad*. Though many people from Laforet had remained in Philadelphia, the change in them was so pathetic that she could have wept. These weren't her independent friends but hopeless, helpless creatures who could only cling to her and weep. A few lucky families who had been deported together were trying to make a new life, and some young or single people had work, but most clustered around Benjamin Thurlow like lost sheep. Merciful God, she thought, is this what Simon and Monsieur Chauvin will be like when I see them again?

By evening she was so exhausted in mind and spirit that she could barely drag herself up the stairs to her small sitting room in Fishe's inn. In sharp contrast to her, Neill returned full of energy. There was a spring to his step as he strode into the room, but after one look at her, he stopped. "Good Christ," he exclaimed, "you're ill."

She shook her head in denial, but he was worried. He had never seen her look so beaten. The fine bones stood out against her almost translucent skin, and her lovely eyes had dark crescents under them. He had to check an impulse to go to her and draw her in his arms as she said, "There were just so many homeless ones. And there are more I must meet tomorrow."

"That you won't." Neill spoke sternly, and Gabrielle protested.

"But I have promised Mr. Thurlow."

"Thurlow won't mind your breaking your promise. I've had news of your brother and Chauvin."

With a small, strangled cry, she got to her feet and ran the length of the room to him. She caught his hands in hers crying, "Where are they?"

Hope was sweeping her lovely face like flame, and the warm clutch of her hands evoked responses that he fought down with a stern reminder. This excitement, this hope was because of another man.

"I asked some questions on my own." Control kept his voice even. "One of the C. and C.'s lines is shipbuilding, and some of our finest ships come out of Philadelphia. A ship's carpenter remembers that when some of the Acadians who were to be allowed to remain here were selected, there was a thin man among them—a distinguished-looking man with a large mole on his cheek. This man could have stayed in Philadelphia but chose not to."

"He chose—" Bewilderment caused Gabrielle to hold tighter to Neill's hands. "But why? and Simon—what of him?"

Neill shrugged. "The carpenter I spoke to recalled that a young fellow was with the man with the mark on his cheek. He recalls also that these two sailed for Virginia with the other deportees. At least you know they're well, Gabrielle, and still together."

She realized that she was leaning forward in eagerness, her face inches from his. When she drew in a steadying breath, she inhaled his remembered scent, and that clean and vital fragrance went to her head like wine. Suddenly, she was joyfully, ecstatically happy, and she cried, "But then, it is simple. I will go on to Virginia."

His hands tightened on hers. "You know it's hundreds of miles away. It'd take some time." She nodded and he added, "We'll have no trouble booking passage on one of the company ships and sailing down the Atlantic coastline until we reach the Chesapeake. Luckily at this time of year, there isn't much likelihood of storms."

She laughed up at him, her face alight and

joyous. "I don't care about storms," she sang, and then her eyes went wide. "You said 'we.' You are coming with me?"

He lifted her small hands to his lips. Then, carefully, he disengaged her hold and clasping his hands behind him, stepped away.

"Of course I'm coming with you," he told her, somewhat drily. "Don't forget that the C. and C. has a lot invested in your search for the elusive Monsieur Chauvin."

As Neill had predicted, the journey by sea was long but uneventful. Good weather and calm seas followed the C. and C. schooner *The Consequence* into Delaware Bay and down the long line of the coast. There were no other passengers on this merchant vessel, and since the ship was small, Gabrielle found that there was no avoiding Neill's company.

Not that she needed to avoid him, for Neill seemed constantly occupied with writing notes about C. and C. business dealings in Philadelphia or talking with the ship's Captain. Once she even found him working side by side with the crew.

He explained this later that evening when they met briefly on the deck. It was after the evening hour, and though she generally spent this time in her cabin, she had come up to take some air and found him there. "I'm used to action," he told her when she asked about his unusual activity. "A bad habit from my military days. If there's nothing to do, I must find something to keep me busy."

"Marthe used to say, 'Idle hands are the dev-

132

il's playground,'" Gabrielle smiled and then looked away toward the horizon. "I wonder where she is now."

"Maybe you'll find her—and Guy—in Virginia," he rallied her.

"You are right." She tilted her head to the star-splashed heavens. There was no sound except the slap of waves against the ship's bow, and the whole world seemed to be wrapped in dark velvet. "How lovely it is," she exclaimed.

He agreed silently, but he was looking at her and not the sky. During this long journey, her tension and exhaustion had fallen from her, and she looked as she had when he first saw her in Laforet. "After your last voyage I didn't think you would ever care for the sea again."

To his surprise, she gave her husky, mischievous laugh. "But I love the ocean. When I was a small girl, I scandalized Maman by going out in the fishermen's boats. You didn't see much of Laforet, but it was truly beautiful. In the spring and summer there were flowers and beautiful wild birds, and the autumns were scarlet and gold."

Drawn by the almost dreamy cadence of her voice, he relaxed against the ship's rail. "The winters were harsh, weren't they?"

"Yes, but we didn't mind. In our village, the women spun by the hearth and Simon and I learned our lessons, while the men hunted or mended their farm implements by the fire. That was when there was time for stories, like the one about the Loup Garou, the terrible werewolf, or of Glooscap. He was the Great Spirit of the Micmacs. He was very big and tall and lived in a wigwam on Cape Blomidon, but when the white man came, Glooscap got angry and went away—nobody knows where."

"Sensible fellow," Neill commented drily. His words took her back to what the English had done in Acadia, and she retreated from that ever-present sorrow. Tonight, in this star-washed brightness, she only wanted to remember happy things.

"There was another story that I loved, an Indian legend Marthe told me. Shall I tell it to you?" He nodded and she began to speak about a Micmac maiden called White Lady of the Forest and her lover, Beaver Man. The lovers, she said, were from warring tribes and couldn't marry, but they ran away together one golden autumn day.

"They ran and ran while both tribes pursued them, and finally they came to the edge of a tall cliff." She stopped and in the silence Neill heard her draw a suddenly painful breath.

He asked gently, "Were they captured?"

"I used to think not. You see, to escape their pursuers, the lovers threw themselves over a cliff. And Glooscap changed them into glorious golden eagles so that they could live away from earth. I used to love the story when I was little. I thought then that the lovers lived on forever. Now, I know that they died."

Unable to bear the sadness in her voice, he acted involuntarily, drawing her close to him. She nestled against him for a moment, her cheek against his shoulder, her slender, warm body pressed soft against his hardness. Stroking back her dark hair, he said, "I wouldn't sell old

Glooscap short. And even if they did die, they died together."

She was silent for a moment, and then she nodded. "You're right. That's everything. My father died so far away from us, and that is why Maman grew sick and old before her time. She was so beautiful when we first came to Laforet, but without love a woman ages."

He did not say anything, but instinctively she felt his understanding. She had never seemed so close to him before, and the stars had never seemed so bright or so close. If she reached out, she could perhaps touch their whiteness. If she lifted her head, his lips would find hers. A surge of longing swept through her, a need that was even stronger than passion. It was as if a part of her cried out for the completion that she knew could only be found with this man beside her.

He felt her tremble against him and then grow still, so that her body seemed to merge and meld with his. He looked down into her closed eyes, saw how the dark lashes spread like silk fans against her cheeks, and he forgot why he had kept away from her, kept busy so as not to think of her. Want of her blazed into white heat, and he wanted nothing more than to kiss her until his mouth was drugged with the honey of her lips. He needed to lift her into his arms and carry her below deck to his cabin. There in the darkness, he would relearn the sweet promise of her breasts that would strain like cool satin fruit against his hands. His mouth could draw the honey from her breast's roses and trace the line of her silky belly, her thighs.

The urge to love her was almost irresistible,

and yet at the core of that desire was a warning. She had been hurt and hurt again, his lovely lady of the forest. He must not hurt her again.

She felt his arms grow tense, and unexpectedly, they loosened about her. She looked up at him, first bewildered at his action and then frightened at what had nearly happened. And as the fear grew, she heard him inhale and let it go in a deep breath that was almost a sigh.

"Tomorrow we should catch our first glimpse of the Chesapeake." His voice was carefully emotionless. "Journey's end, Gabrielle."

She nodded. Now she could resume her life with Simon and Monsieur Chauvin. As for this tall Englishman beside her, he would return home to Boston, his business transaction completed. She had looked forward to this time for so long, and she knew that she should feel overjoyed. But instead she could only think of one thing: In a few days' time she would say goodbye to Neill—and she would never see him again.

Chapter Nine

A FEW DAYS LATER THEY SAILED UP THE CHESA-peake and in dazzling early morning sunshine stepped ashore at Yorktown. They were met by Andrew Warrensbody, a soft-spoken merchant in the C. and C. Company's employ. He greeted them cordially and made them welcome in his neatly ordered store, but when they asked him about Acadian refugees, his expression became guarded.

"You'd be talking about the people who were brought over by ship from Canada. I don't know much about them except that they're being held at Williamsburg," he said uneasily.

"Held?" It was an odd word to use, Neill thought.

Andrew Warrensbody hesitated and lowered his voice. "There's been a few incidents involving these people—pilfering and the like—that's set Virginians against them. Also, the poor souls can't speak English and so can't find any work. I hear one young fellow nearly came to blows with Colonel Whitower, commander of the military garrison in Williamsburg."

That could only be Simon. Sensing Gabrielle's anxiety, Neill said, "What happened to this young firebrand?"

But the shopkeeper knew little else except rumors and gossip, brought to him by customers who had traveled to Williamsburg. "The best thing to do is to go and see for yourself," he suggested. "I wish I could help you more, Mr. Craddock. I'll gladly find decent horses for you and the lady. And do you have a pistol or some other weapon? Ah, you do. Then, if there's something else I can do to aid you, call on me."

By midmorning they were spurring toward Williamsburg on a ride that was cheerless in spite of the brilliance of the day and the lush green and gold of the countryside. October was much warmer here than in Boston or Philadelphia, and by late afternoon, when at last they came in sight of Williamsburg, Gabrielle felt as if the dust of the road caked her hot face and arms like a second skin. At the outskirts of the town they were stopped by two English soldiers.

Neill explained that they had come from Boston to seek payment of a business debt. The sentries looked bored at this, and one of them said, "Oh, the Frenchies. They're safe enough. If your man's with them, you'll get your money." He spat in the dust and then added, "Best person to talk to is the Colonel. His house is the big white one on Gloucester Street, not far from Bruton Parish Church."

Gloucester Street was easy to find, and while they rode down the wide street with its neatly pebbled sidewalks and row of two-storied houses, Neill cautioned Gabrielle. "Don't say anything when we get to the Colonel's. Your accent will give your nationality away, and I want to find out exactly what is going on before we tell him the full story."

She gave a small nod of agreement. "You are right, of course, but it is hard to believe that anything terrible could happen in a place like this. Everything looks so busy and pleasant and —ordinary."

She looked about her as she spoke. Nearby, under the large wooden signboard of an inn, some children were playing with a puppy. Some distance away, housewives gossiped in front of a grocery store, which dangled three sugar loaves from its iron trappings. A little farther on they came to a shoulder-high brick wall that encased a gracious church with circular windows and a high-flung steeple. And there at the far corner of the cobbled street was a house larger and more imposing than the rest.

"The Colonel's house." As Neill spoke, they heard hoofbeats behind them, and a carriage conveying a laughing woman and a bewigged, sleepy-eyed man swept past them and drove up to the Colonel's house. "And that must be the man we want to see," Neill exclaimed.

They spurred their horses forward, reaching the Colonel's house just as footmen were assisting the pair in the carriage to descend. Neither the sleepy-eyed man nor his lady spared so much as a glance for the travelers on horseback until

Neill spoke: "Your pardon, sir. Are you Colonel Whitower?"

Very slowly, as if surprised at Neill's presumption, the sleepy-eyed man turned. He blinked several times before saying, "If you wish to speak to me, see my aide and set up an appointment."

He turned back to his companion, who had cocked her head and was studying Neill appreciatively. "You could ask him what he wants," she murmured. "It may be amusing."

If it had not been so serious, Gabrielle would have been amused as Neill turned to the lady and, with a dazzling white smile, swept off his hat so that the late sun burnished his hair to gold. "Madam, your servant. This lady and I have traveled from Massachusetts to seek the Colonel's help. Allow me to introduce myself. Neill Craddock of the C. and C. Company in Boston."

The Colonel frowned, but before he could speak his lady fluttered her eyelashes. "After you have rested and bathed, you must visit us. Perhaps for dinner tonight?" She turned to the Colonel. "It's a long time since we had news of Boston," she purred.

Gabrielle held her breath, but instead of answering his lady, the Colonel was now looking carefully. His eyes narrowed, his sleepiness disappeared and the tip of his thick tongue emerged to run along his upper lip. "Y-yes," he said, slowly. "It has been a long time."

Gabrielle saw the disgust in Neill's eyes mirror her own distaste.

"The White Swan's a decent inn," the Colonel was continuing. "You can get rooms there—if not, mention my name." He glanced at Neill, then stared once again at Gabrielle. "As Mrs. Whitower says, you can give us news of Boston. Come at six."

Neill frowned as the couple went up toward the grand house. "A command appearance, no less," he said, and Gabrielle saw the distaste deepen in his face. "I think it's best that I go alone."

"That is nonsense," she replied briskly. "We are both invited, so now we must go to this inn and bathe and change quickly." He continued to look displeased. "The Colonel is an unpleasant man, but you will be there beside me, and he may have news of Simon and Monsieur Chauvin."

"Maybe you're right." Neill turned his horse back toward the inn.

"Why are you worried?"

"I wish I knew so that I could tell you." He shrugged broad shoulders. "It just seemed too easy."

She chuckled, unexpected mischief bubbling into her dark eyes. "Too easy to charm that lady, you mean? You did it magnificently. The bow, the smile, the manly pose. It is a wonder that she has invited both of us for 'refreshment.'"

"Watch your tongue, ma'am. If anyone was charmed, it was the Colonel, though 'charm' is perhaps too polite a word for it." But he was grinning, too, as they rode to the door of the inn, and when he dismounted and turned to help her down, his hard features had softened. "Let's hope all goes well. We could do with a bit of luck."

She nodded, suddenly breathless as his strong hands clasped her waist and lifted her down. For a moment he held her, and she had the almost irresistible impulse to lean her cheek against his hard chest. And then a thought came to her. "Perhaps," she told him, "it is the end of our quest."

"Yes—perhaps." Was there regret in his voice? She couldn't tell, for he had let go of her and was calling for a stable boy and instructing the innkeeper, who had come to the door, to find them rooms and a bath. "And quickly, too," he added. "We're guests of the Colonel tonight."

The Colonel's name acted like magic. Servants scurried to ready rooms, and baths were supplied for both lady and gentleman. In spite of her haste, Gabrielle found this bath to be the greatest luxury. It was heaven to strip off her dusty, travel-worn clothes and sink deep into the warmth of the water. Here she closed her eyes and leaned back, letting the almost sensuous warmth of the water caress and enfold her like a lover's arms.

His image came to her unbidden and unwanted. One moment she was alone and at peace, the next moment Neill seemed to be there with her, so real in her remembrance that she nearly cried out his name. She could almost feel the crisp curl of his chest fur against her breasts, draw in the clean male scent of him. She could taste his mouth on hers, feel the mind-drugging ecstasy of his lips closing about her suddenly taut nipples.

"Neill." This time she did say it, and the spoken word shattered the magic. She was alone, and the bathwater was cooling about her. But if the water was cold, she was warm, now—hot with a wild honey that was spreading through her veins. Her body felt heavy and waiting, her mouth seemingly bruised with kisses. Sacred name, she thought, what is the matter with me?

Hurriedly, she scrubbed herself with the rough soap the maids had brought, then hastened to dry herself and dress. The undergarments and shift she slipped on were of fine linen fragrant with roses and lavender, but even this soft material was coarse against her sensitive nipples and caused a sensuous hurt. Determinedly ignoring this, she slipped delicate evening shoes on her feet and turned to the dress she was to wear.

It was a green patterned silk that Abigail had given her as a farewell gift, and though travel had worn many wrinkles in the fine fabric, it was a lovely thing and surely would impress the Colonel and his lady as the height of Boston fashion. As she was preparing to slip the dress over her head, the door opened and Neill walked into the room.

He had been so much in her thoughts that at first she thought him only a projection of her mind. Then she realized he was there in truth. He looked elegant in a buff-colored linen coat and breeches with a black ribbon solitaire tied about the white linen stock at his throat, but it was not his finery that drew her eyes. Under the tamed thickness of his fair hair, the tawny eyes were filled with an intensity that reawakened the heat in her veins. If he touched her, she would go to him. If he called her—

"Gabrielle." His voice seemed to come from far away, and she could hardly hear him over the thudding of her heart. Then he said, "I'm sorry. I knocked and thought you bade me enter. Put on your dress and turn around. I'll help with the buttons."

She realized that she was clutching her dress to her breasts. Hastily, she pulled the garment over her head and let it swirl down over her bare white shoulders and arms. As she turned her back to him, she thought she heard him sigh. "I'm sorry I'm late getting dressed," she said formally.

"And I for intruding on you. As I said, I thought you were ready." He felt her tremble as he touched the whiteness of her back, and the silky warmth of her skin made him fight for control as he worked the buttons into their loops. Easy, you fool, he told himself. The eagerness in her eyes, the sweet promise of her body, these were for another man, and if she had turned to look at him with black eyes wide and full of yearning, it was because she dreamed of Chauvin. He finished buttoning her dress and took a step backward. "Are you ready to go and see the Colonel?" he asked abruptly.

The blandness of his voice jerked her back to reality. "At once," she said. Then, reaching for her cloak, she added, "And you?"

He put a hand to the breast pocket of his coat, and she saw the hard outline of a pistol. So he still expected trouble, she thought, but all he said was, "I've hired a carriage so that we'll arrive in style. It's waiting outside."

"Where?" They had reached the inn door, and she looked about her in bewilderment. There was no carriage and no horses. Instead, a number of soldiers stood outside in the courtyard, while an officer spoke with the landlord. As Gabrielle spoke, the man pointed.

"That's them. That's the woman and the man who said he was to see the Colonel," he exclaimed.

The officer with whom he spoke turned his head, and Gabrielle exclaimed in astonishment. There was no mistaking those broad, flat features. "Lieutenant Dray!" she cried.

Instantly, the soldiers trained their muskets on Neill and Gabrielle. "What foul wind brings you here?" Neill demanded sharply.

The flat-faced officer laughed. "That's very simple," he said in the jeering voice they well remembered. "I came with the Acadian rats on *The Royal Princess,* and now these men and I have come to arrest the two of you and take you to prison."

"On what charge?" Neill's hand itched to reach the pistol in his coat, but the muskets leveled at Gabrielle held him back.

"Treason," Dray said, with relish. "We're at war with France, and you've been helping the enemy and consorting with the French." He bowed mockingly to Gabrielle before adding, "That's a hanging offense, my fine friend."

"This isn't Acadia, Dray. This is King George's Virginia, and I am a free Englishman." Neill spoke with cold anger. "I demand to see the Colonel."

Dray nodded to the soldiers, who advanced cautiously, their muskets still pointed at Neill's broad chest. "Save your breath," he advised. "It's by Colonel Whitower's orders that you are being arrested. As for breaking the law—we *are* the law here." Then he paused to add, "Let's see if you like our Williamsburg hospitality, Mr. Craddock."

The warehouse was damp and smelled of mold, and in spite of the warmth outside, it held an unhealthy chill. It was also dark. Thrust unceremoniously through the door, Neill felt the short hairs prickle on his neck, as he stared blindly around and listened to rustles and murmurs about him. As he tensed for possible attack, he heard a voice speak in awed French.

"Heavens, it is Monsieur Neill. Monsieur, it is I, Guy Richaud. Do you remember me?"

His eyes were getting accustomed to the darkness, and he could see a pudgy figure advancing, hand outstretched. Holding out his own hand, he felt sturdy fingers close around his. "Of course I remember. Who else is here? Simon? Chauvin?"

"No, Monsieur, but many here come from Laforet. Others are from Grand Pré and Cobequid," Guy replied.

Neill was now able to discern many shadows in the warehouse. He rubbed a hand against rough planking, looking up at the one window set high on the wall. It let in just enough fresh air, he could see, to make the air breathable. With some effort, a man could reach and get through that window, surprise the guards outside, and make a run for it. "Has anyone tried to get out of here?" he demanded.

Guy sighed deeply. "Yes, but alas, they were caught and brought back." He spread his hands. "Where can we go? We are French. No one will help us here."

"One needs a ship to leave Virginia." Another familiar voice spoke, and Neill recognized Father Mabouef. "But tell us, my son, how is Gabrielle and the others from Laforet who stayed in Boston, and why have you come here to Virginia? Have you come to help us?"

Neill gave a grim laugh. "Don't get your hopes up, Father. Apparently, I'm also a prisoner of the Colonel. Gabrielle, who was with me seeking Simon and Chauvin, is being held elsewhere." He paused. "It's a long story."

He told it as succinctly as he could and they listened, interrupting now and again with comments and exclamations of horror. When he had finished, Guy Richaud sighed. "Ah, my poor Marthe," he said miserably. "My lovely Thérèse. God only knows where they are now. So it was to seek her loved ones the *petite* Gabrielle came?"

"Yes. We know they were with you as far as Philadelphia. Do you have any idea where they are now?"

"Not now, Monsieur," Guy said. "But they were here. With us in this warehouse."

"Monsieur Chauvin is an important man even now," another of the prisoners said. "He was able to buy himself and Simon de Montfleuri out of this place. We have since learned that he and Simon have gone on to the Carolinas."

"Why the Carolinas?" Neill demanded, and Father Maboeuf shrugged.

"Perhaps to raise money with which to help us. He promised to do so before he left, and Simon went with him for that purpose. It's a good thing for Simon that he left, too, for he was put in the English prison for assaulting the colonel. I marvel that Monsieur Chauvin managed to get him free."

Something rustled at the straw near Neill's feet. "Be careful of the rats, Monsieur," Guy advised. "They are big and fearless and, alas, very hungry. They gnaw at one when one is asleep, and the bites carry infection. Two of us have already died from such bites."

Rats and darkness—and Dray who proclaimed himself the law in Williamsburg. "How did you come to be imprisoned in this place?" Neill asked.

Again, it was Father Maboeuf who explained that the Virginians hadn't wanted to take in any deportees but were forced to do so by Colonel Whitower.

"They wouldn't let us work and then they accused us of stealing," the priest said sadly. "The soldiers marched us here from Yorktown, and they made insulting suggestions to the women. One of these was the Colonel, and that is why Simon attacked him. He was imprisoned, and after that, the Colonel ordered us all imprisoned here. Simon, too."

"And the women?" If he could find the answer

to that, maybe he would learn where Gabrielle
had been taken, but the answer did not help
him. The women had also been imprisoned, but
they and the children had been released. Now
some of them worked as servants or begged for
their food. Others were being fed and housed by
kindly people.

"Many would leave Williamsburg, but no Acadian is allowed to leave." Father Maboeuf
sighed. Then he added timidly, "Perhaps you
could speak to the Colonel for us, Monsieur
Neill?"

"How can I when I'm a prisoner also?" but
many voices were raised against this. Neill's
situation was different. He was English, and the
English law would protect him. Besides, he was
a rich man like Monsieur Chauvin, and if necessary he could bribe someone, perhaps their jailer or his assistant, to get him out.

"In the morning," Father Maboeuf said hopefully, "the Colonel might send for you."

His words were interrupted by heavy footsteps
approaching the warehouse door. There was the
rattle of keys, and then a huge, unkempt man
stepped inside, carrying two full buckets. "Here,
you in there, ready for yer grub?" he demanded.

Dinner consisted of a bucket of soup and another of water. A slave who followed the big
fellow carried a lamp and some loaves of coarse
bread. "That's the assistant to the jailer, Phineas Cole," Guy hissed.

The big fellow turned toward the sound of
whispering and stared at Neill with undisguised
hostility. "I heard that a big, Frog-loving Englishman was brought here," he sneered. "Lieu-

tenant Dray took you and your fancy French whore, didn't he?"

Neill's eyes narrowed, but he slid his hand into his pockets, letting the coins there jingle. "I wonder what else you've heard?" he asked. "I'll wager a smart fellow like you could tell me where the Frenchwoman is being held."

After hesitating for a moment, the unkempt man shrugged. "Why not tell yer? Yer visit her, can yer?" He guffawed and then added, slyly, "The slick piece is in Harriet Hook's place off Gloucester Street. Willow House, she calls it." He bent near, tapping a thick finger to his nose. "Held nice and cozy till the Colonel visits her."

Restraining an almost irresistible urge to close his big hands around the assistant jailer's greasy neck, Neill tossed a coin in the air. The gold of it sparkled in the lamplight until Phineas Cole caught it. He examined the coin for a second, then bellowed to the slave and stamped out. Neill thought, at least I know where she is.

But how could he get to her? What the brute had told him gnawed at Neill's guts, for he remembered the way the Colonel had looked Gabrielle over. As the others ate, he considered the window again. Tonight, he thought, and then another thought followed. God send I'll come in time to get her free.

For a moment he toyed with the idea of asking the others if they, too, wished to try again for freedom and then decided against it. One man on his own had a better chance in a situation like this, and Gabrielle's safety outweighed any other consideration. He ate the hard bread and drank the watery soup to give himself strength,

150

and then, as he had learned to do on military campaigns, sat down in a corner to rest until it was dark enough to make a move. Sleep came swiftly, but remembering old and harsh disciplines, he slept lightly, economically, his muscles and senses ready to spring awake at any moment. And when he heard the soft rasp and click of the warehouse door open, he was at once alert.

Neill sat motionless and watched a familiar, large shadow steal into the warehouse and close the door softly behind him. It was late now, and the prisoners in the warehouse slept. Careful not to awaken them, the assistant jailer peered about until he spotted Neill. Then, head down like a dog, he crept toward the Englishman.

Closer the shadowy figure came, until now the faint light from the window glinted off the edge of a knife. Neill waited until the big fellow was nearly upon him, and then moved with deadly swiftness. His knee to the groin, his hand to the back of the neck in a chopping motion that snapped the vertebrae, and Cole fell without so much as a grunt. And as the knife fell from his nerveless fingers, Neill snatched it up.

"Monsieur Neill—" Guy Richaud was beside him. "Take me with you," he implored. "I will go mad if I do not find my family."

Neill hesitated. "You understand that once we're outside and have taken care of the sentries, we separate. You'll be on your own." Guy nodded fervently, and Neill added somewhat reluctantly, "What of the others?"

"Let them sleep." It was a new whisper, which Neill recognized as Father Maboeuf's. "That man came to kill you, my son. Knowing you had money, he came to rob you."

That was the plausible explanation, and yet something nagged at Neill's brain. Why else? he asked himself. I certainly let him know that I had gold in my pocket.

The priest was continuing. "If you will take Guy with you, that will be a good deed. But you can't help everyone, my son. The others will only be hunted down again and treated more harshly than before."

Neill hesitated, looking about him at the sleeping men and at the old priest. It seemed a betrayal, and yet the old man was right. "I must go to Gabrielle," he said, and Father Maboeuf nodded earnestly.

"I understand, my son. Go with God's blessing."

Before he had finished speaking, Neill had already pushed open the door. The chill of the night wind was startling, refreshing after the closed air in the warehouse, and for a moment he breathed it gratefully. Then, he turned to Guy and indicated the two soldiers standing before the warehouse. Guy nodded grimly, and the two men moved stealthily forward. Then Neill's arm went up, arced down, and a man fell, stunned. The other turned, and Guy knocked him flat.

"*Sacré nom*, that felt good." Guy grinned up at Neill as he massaged his fist. "And now what, Monsieur Neill?"

Using the soldiers' belts and handkerchiefs, they bound and gagged the men and carried them to a shadowed corner of the warehouse. Then they went back inside and carted out

Phineas Cole's carcass, dumping him beside the bound guards before carefully locking the warehouse door with keys found on the assistant jailer. "Let them sort this one out," Neill said with grim humor.

Guy said, "We part, then. Where do you go, Monsieur?"

"To find Willow House." Neill reached into his pocket and drew out a full half of the gold he carried. "Don't stay around town, Guy. Get to Yorktown and see a man called Andrew Warrensbody. He works for my company and he'll help you. Tell him I sent you, that he's to smuggle you into the first boat leaving Virginia."

Guy took the money and then shook Neill's hand. With moist eyes he said, "I'll never forget, Monsieur. I pray you find Gabrielle."

"That may take something more than prayer, but I thank you anyway." Neill looked about him. The street was empty, the night silent. "Godspeed," he added tersely.

The Acadian melted away into the darkness, and Neill began to retrace the route by which Dray and the soldiers had brought him to the warehouse. Once back on Gloucester Street, he dusted off his clothes and straightened his solitaire. Then, seemingly a townsman out for a late stroll, he went in search of Gabrielle.

Chapter Ten

HELPLESSLY, GABRIELLE WATCHED NEILL BEING marched away by Lieutenant Dray and all but two of his soldiers. She had no idea where they were taking him, and it seemed as if the tragedy of Acadia was beginning all over again.

"Come along, now," one of the two soldiers left to guard her was saying. "You're going elsewhere, my fine lady."

They marched her past the church and away from Gloucester road. It was turning to dusk, and she could make out only the outline of houses and their surrounding trees. Could she escape? she wondered. Perhaps she could pretend to faint and then push one of these men down and make a run for it.

"I wouldn't try it if I was you," one of the guards mocked her, and the others took up the taunt. "We've orders to take good care of you for the Colonel. Fancies you, he does, see? Likes a bit of French tail."

She felt sickened but did not respond to their baiting, and they fell silent. Their boots made an odd, clopping sound on the hard-packed dirt of the road, and hearing it, several dogs began to bark. A night wind whipped her dress about her, and she shivered from cold, then cried out in pain as a sharp-edged stone dug painfully into the soft sole of her shoe.

One of the soldiers snickered. "Seems like the little lady isn't used to walking." His voice turned vicious as he added, "You Acadians have been nothing but trouble for us since you were brought here. Idle pack of thieves is what you are."

She wanted to throw back at them that it was the fault of the English themselves that they were there at all, but held her tongue. Best not to anger them, better to seek a way of getting away from them. But there seemed little chance of that. They had come to a two-story house with a wide, cobbled yard shaded by willows. There were no lights in the windows, and the house looked deserted until dogs began to bark and snarl viciously. Then a spot of light appeared at the door and a scared voice called a question.

"A visitor for Mrs. Hook," one of the soldiers answered. "By the Colonel's order. She's expecting us."

The door creaked open immediately to silhouette a very tall, gaunt woman on the threshold. The soldiers pushed Gabrielle forward.

"Evening, Harriet," one of them said. "Here's

another of them Acadian Frenchies for you. Colonel wants her treated with kid gloves till he's ready for her."

"I already have my orders." The woman spoke in a cold, rasping voice that had no hint of warmth or even life. "You can take her upstairs."

The soldiers pushed Gabrielle over the front steps and past the Hook woman into the hall. Even with a lamp burning on a table near the doorway, it was almost darker inside than it was out. The silent woman on the threshold appeared to blend with the shadows that gathered about the stairway. Gabrielle started as one of these shadows moved, then realized that a frightened young girl crouched at the foot of the stairs.

"Delcie, light their way upstairs," Harriet Hook commanded, and the girl snatched up the lamp and scurried up the stairs. Urged on by the soldiers, Gabrielle followed, and crossing the landing, was ushered into a large room. As the girl lit the candles in the room, Gabrielle looked about her in surprise.

She had expected a room as stark as a prison, but there was nothing prisonlike about this chamber. It was high-ceilinged and airy with a window that fronted the yard, and it was furnished with fine furniture. A gilt and walnut desk stood near the window, and an ornate and obviously expensive mirror hung next to a large wardrobe. In the center of the room was a feather-bed hung with a canopy of pale lavender satin.

At sight of the bed one soldier dug an elbow in his companion's ribs. "I like our Colonel's taste in love nests," he smirked. "Wonder if his wife knows about Willow House? Not that she'd care —she's got an eye for any well-filled pair of breeches."

"You can go now." She hadn't heard Harriet Hook climb the stairs, but now she stood arms akimbo just inside the door. She gestured to the soldiers, who obediently left the room and began to descend the stairs. "You can tell the Colonel that the girl won't leave here without his order."

She smiled coldly at Gabrielle, who stared back at her, both fearing and disliking the malice in the woman's eyes. "Why have I been brought here?" she demanded as the soldiers rattled and thumped their way down the stairs.

"You'd be no happier in the warehouse with the men." Thin lips twitched sardonically. "There are rats there, I'm told."

So that was where Neill was, in a warehouse. She repressed a shudder at the thought of rats and spoke quietly: "I have asked you why I am imprisoned. Mr. Craddock and I had done nothing wrong."

The Hook woman looked coldly amused. "What's right or wrong got to do with it, my girl? The Colonel wants you, that's all." She paused for a moment and added, "If you're thinking of escape, better forget it. I keep two dogs in the yard, and at night they run loose. I don't feed them too often, and they're hungry and mean. They'll tear you to bloody pieces if you think of letting yourself down from that window and running for it."

The door slammed shut on the last word, and Gabrielle ran to the window. It was not too high from the ground, and a narrow but sturdy ledge ran a yard or so below the window ledge, while one of the great willows that surrounded the house grew close. Below in the brick courtyard prowled twin shadows that snarled and glared upward with almost glowing eyes. She shuddered. The Hook woman hadn't lied about those dogs.

A timid knock announced the young servant girl with the frightened eyes. This time she carried a tray of food. Gabrielle waved it away, but the girl set it down on a table and spoke earnestly. "It's good food, believe me. Orders said as you were to be fed proper."

"I'm not hungry." But Gabrielle noted the way the girl's eyes lingered over the crisp fried chicken, fragrant baked bread, plump, juicy fruit. She said gently, "Do you eat if you want to, Delcie."

Pity filled her as the girl gave a fearful look around before reaching for a piece of chicken. "You won't tell *her*, will you?" she pleaded around a full mouth. Gabrielle shook her head. "She's my mistress for three more years. I'm a bound girl, see. My father died and my Ma had me and four other little 'uns to raise. So she took me to the front of the White Swan Inn one market day, and she bound me over to Miz Hook for six years." She shook her head. "I nearly kilt myself the first year I was here—"

Gabrielle had heard of penniless families "binding" their children into years of servitude for money. Abigail Culpepper had had such a bound girl in her home in Boston, but that girl had been happy with her position and was learning useful skills. Such misery as she saw in Delcie now made her forget her own, and she cried, "Is there no one who can help you?"

"It's the law, lady. I'm bound." The English King's law, Gabrielle thought bitterly as Delcie continued, "One day I'll be free, though, and then she'll need a new slave to see to the people that come here to stay."

Gabrielle caught at a fragment of what the girl had said. "Do many people come here, Delcie?" The girl nodded.

"I don't know as I'm supposed to tell you, but aye, others stay here. Two Frenchies were here just before you. One of them was a good-looking young fellow, maybe seventeen or eighteen. The other was a thinnish, older man. Real dignified-like. He had a mark on his cheek."

Gabrielle's heart had suddenly begun to beat fast. "Was the mark here?" As Delcie nodded, surprised, she caught the bound girl's hands. "Where did they go?"

"I dunno. They didn't stay long." Delcie paused, looking curiously up at Gabrielle. "Did you know them then, lady?"

Before Gabrielle could answer, a harsh voice called from below stairs demanding to know where Delcie was. "I got to go," the bound girl said in real fear. "Do you need anything more, lady? You was nice, giving me that food and all. If there's anything else I can get you—a bath, maybe?"

Realizing that this would give her more time to question the girl, Gabrielle nodded. "That would be kind," she agreed. As the girl scurried away, she tried to collect her thoughts. Simon and Monsieur Chauvin had been here. Perhaps they had stayed in this room. Had the Colonel brought them here, too, or had Monsieur Chauvin managed to escape this warehouse the Hook woman spoke of?

The warehouse where Neill was. She closed her eyes, aching with the knowledge that Neill was being held in some terrible, rat-infested prison. Or was he there at all? "A hanging offense," Dray had sneered as he led Neill away.

There were sounds in the hall, and Delcie now unlocked the door to drag in a large, empty porcelain tub. As she helped the bound girl position it, Gabrielle had a thought. "Do you know the warehouse where the Acadian men are kept?" she asked. The girl nodded warily. "I have to get a message to someone being held prisoner there. Can you do that for me?"

"It'd be dangerous." Delcie peered over her shoulder at the door and then added resolutely, "But you been kind to me, so I'll do my best."

She went away to bring buckets of hot water, and Gabrielle began to search for paper and a pen. There was none in the desk, and she threw open the double doors of the large wardrobe near the bed. Her eyes widened with surprise as she did so, for it was full of woman's clothing. There was a row of shoes and boots for women and above this a row of dresses. Silk and satin dresses for the evening with low-cut bodices and tulle handkerchiefs with which to cover shoulders and neck; velvet and corduroy riding costumes in lovely golds and browns and moss green; afternoon dresses of cotton and linen and sprigged organdy. Could these belong to the

Hook woman? But when she lifted one away from the rest and held it up, it looked more suited for someone her own height.

The little servant reappeared as Gabrielle resumed her hunt for pen and paper. "Don't go writing down your message, lady. Too dangerous if I'm caught. You tell me what to say and who to tell, and I'll give it word for word." Gabrielle began to do so, but again Delcie stopped her. "It's nearly eleven now, and there's no way I can slip away with the dogs running loose. Give me your message tomorrow, and I'll go. It's market day and even Miz Hook has to let me out to shop for food." She indicated the filled tub. "Do you take your bath now, lady. If *she* finds out that you didn't, I'll get beat."

When Delcie had left the room, Gabrielle suddenly felt profoundly weary. She sat on the edge of the big lavender-hung bed, without the energy to get up and shut the open window against the night air that was cooling the hot water. Would Delcie really remember and deliver her message, and even if she did would the message do any good? Dray's mocking remark about hanging haunted her anew. Perhaps right now they were trying Neill on trumped-up charges, marching him out to the gallows, tying a rope around his neck. In purest horror, her imagination took the next and most dismal step, and she could hear the thud of his big body falling into air, the snap of his neck . . .

Snap.

Gabrielle went rigid, listening. Had she imagined that sound? No, for it came again, and close to her—as close as the window. Jumping to her feet, she ran to the window and looked out, then choked back a cry as she saw a dark shadow in the willow tree. As she watched, the shadow leaped catlike to the ledge that ran under her window, and next moment, Neill had swung himself through the open window and she was in his arms.

They clung together wordlessly, thoughtless except for the relief of being together. She heard the steady beat of his heart melding with the leap of her own pulse, pressed herself closer to the welcome hardness of him, while he felt her fragile slenderness and breathed her flower fragrance. Thoughts of escape, danger and death itself faded to some remote and unimportant point in the universe as he heard her whisper his name.

"I was so afraid . . ." Her lips formed the sounds against his throat like small kisses.

He said the only words that would come to mind. "You knew I'd come for you, didn't you?" Then, as she clung even closer to him, he added, "I knew you were being held in a place called Willow House, and when I saw all the trees I hoped this was the place where you were held. Then I saw you in the window, and knew I was right."

"But the dogs—"

He let go of her and placed the wicked blade of a knife on the desk. "I dealt with the dogs," he said and she recalled the incredible quickness with which he had faced four armed men on the road to Philadelphia. "They won't be found until morning."

Suddenly, he stopped talking and tensed, listening. "What is it?" she whispered, And then she heard the still faraway shouting.

Their eyes met. "They've discovered the sentries," he said grimly.

He strode to the window. "Where are you going?" she gasped as he swung a long leg over the window ledge. "They'll see you—catch you . . ."

"Not if I get a head start. I'll be back for you," he said, but she caught his arm and would not let go. His tawny eyes were oddly tender. "I can't be taken, Gabrielle. A man tried to knife me in the warehouse and I killed him. They'll twist that fact around and try to hang me for murder."

"But if you go now they will see you. Listen." Footsteps were pounding down the hard-caked road, and now torches were visible. He twisted free from her grasp, and she cried, "Wait. Your knife . . ."

"Get it for me." At his tense command, she ran back to the desk, then stopped, staring at the tub of water Delcie had brought. Of course, she thought. It's the only way.

Turning back to him, she spoke rapidly. "Into the wardrobe. There is room, behind all the dresses."

"Are you mad? They'll search—name of God, woman, what are you doing?" he demanded, as she began to tear at the buttons of her dress.

"Hurry, help me undress. The buttons in the back—" Gabrielle turned her back to him, twisting her long hair out of the way. "No one will suspect a lady in her bath."

The amber flash in his eyes told her he understood. "No. It's too dangerous—" But she had torn loose the buttons and the leaf-green silk rustled to the ground just as someone pounded on the outer door and a loud voice demanded entrance.

Gabrielle, now in her shift, pushed Neill toward the wardrobe. "If you do not do as I say, we will both be taken, for I will swear that I am your accomplice in everything," she told him fiercely. A reluctant grin curled his lips and she cried in exasperation, "Now what is funny?"

"This is the first time I've left when a lovely woman was taking *off* her clothes." He bent and kissed her, and even at such a time his mouth was leisurely, giving and taking full pleasure. His lips lingered on hers, nibbling gently along the lower lip, sucking it gently before brushing it with his tongue. Her own lips parted under his bold insistence, and for a timeless moment she tasted and felt and breathed only him. Then he drew away.

"If it comes to fighting, duck under the lip of that bath and stay there," he said, and she saw that the laughter had gone from his eyes, leaving them cool and steady. She nodded and he promised, "They won't take us again, my brave lady of the forest."

The door had opened downstairs, and they could hear Harriet Hook remonstrating loudly with the soldiers. Swiftly, Neill slid shut the window, snatched up his knife and opened the wardrobe to step inside. As the wardrobe door closed behind him, Gabrielle removed her shift and undergarments, twisted her hair in a knot on top of her head, and stepped into the now cool bath.

She had barely sunk up to her waist when she heard heavy boots punishing the stairs, and the key rattled in the lock. She tensed as the door swung open, but she made her voice angry and very loud. "What is the meaning of this intrusion?" she demanded.

Three soldiers stopped on the threshold and goggled at her. Behind them, the Hook woman was angrily demanding that the men leave at once. "You can plainly see that she's alone," she was rasping.

Angrily, Gabrielle swished the water and allowed the men a glimpse of white shoulders. She turned to Harriet Hook. "You said that under the Colonel's orders I was to be treated well and allowed any comforts I required. Is this your idea of comfort?"

A young fellow who appeared to be in command cleared his throat. "Madam, our apologies, but there has been an escape at the warehouse. The Englishman who came to Williamsburg with you has taken to his heels. We thought he might come here."

Gabrielle lifted her chin haughtily. "Perhaps you'd like to search my bath?" she demanded sarcastically, and then continued, "you must be mad, sir. Why would that Englishman come here? He merely accompanied me to Williamsburg because he wanted to extract money owed to him by my fiancé." Suddenly, she let her shoulders slump, allowed a tearful note to tremble in her voice. "I have come all this long way only to be imprisoned. And now this . . ."

"Shall we search the room, Sergeant?" one of the soldiers asked, and the young man hesitated.

Gabrielle continued to hold his eyes with her pleading ones, and after a long moment, he looked away, embarrassed.

"It doesn't look as if a man could be hiding here. He must have gone further on."

As the door shut behind them and the key rattled in the lock, Neill thrust the wardrobe door open. "You're all right?" he demanded.

Now that it was over, she found that she was shaking. "I didn't think he'd believe me," she whispered.

"Neither did I." They listened to the sounds of the soldiers moving away, and then he said, "We'll wait a little while until things quieten down and then we must go. They may return to search the house again, and this time no beautiful bather will stop them."

She was suddenly and acutely aware of her nakedness. As if reading her thought, he caught up the thick towel that Delcie had brought and held it up. "Come out, Gabrielle. The water can't be warm any longer," he said.

"Turn your head." She heard him laugh softly as he obeyed, but his hands seemed to have sight of their own. As she stepped out of the bath, he arranged the towel around her, smoothing its softness over her curves.

"You're chilled," he exclaimed.

She knew she must pull away from him, but she could not take the few steps that would remove her from danger. Instead, she let him rub her shoulders and arms. His touch brought warmth that made her tremble even more than mere cold had done, and he said, "You'd better dress, Gabrielle."

166

As she started to step away from him, something made her turn to look at him. The lamp made his eyes burn deep amber, and those golden depths held such desire that she felt the impact physically. And instead of walking away from him, she took a swaying step forward into his arms.

He held her so tightly that she couldn't breathe, but breathing didn't matter. Neither did anything else, except for his mouth finding hers again, except for the joining of breath and the caress of tongues and the fierce fire that swept through her blood. She heard the sound he made in his throat, the deep, growling purr of male satisfaction, and she formed his name like a caress against his mouth.

As if he had heard her, his kiss deepened. One hand rose to loosen the knot of her dark hair, so that the shadowy silk curtained them both. Then that same hand stroked her cheek, outlining the line of her jaw and throat and moving down to trace sensual patterns across her shoulders and back. Under such treatment the towel around her loosened and fell to her waist, and she could feel the cool linen of his coat against her nipples. Then the towel slipped to the floor leaving her completely naked against him. She registered the erotic touch of cloth on her breasts, against her stomach and thighs, for a moment before he lifted her in his arms and carried her to the bed.

She was light in his arms, and he felt her tremble as he lowered her onto the lavender satin. Yet it was a shiver not of fear but of desire, the same desire that swept him like fire. He stroked back her hair, kissing her with swift, passionate kisses and meanwhile discarding coat, waistcoat, stock and shirt. Now he sat on the edge of the bed and drew her up into his arms, while his mouth traced the proud slopes of her cool breasts and their ready flowers. He adored her with open-mouthed kisses that sought the shadow below her breasts, mapped her ribs and belly, and then veered to leave a trail of fire over her silky thighs.

"I've dreamed of this," he told her.

And so had she, thought Gabrielle, as she kissed the muscled broadness of his shoulders, the back of his neck. Her hands roved the musculature of his back, his whipcord-lean waist, and stopped at the line of his breeches before roving over the tenseness of his still-clothed buttocks and thighs.

"Wait, my love." His mouth came back to hers as he drew off his breeches and struggled briefly with boots. She helped him between kisses, listening only to the sound of his endearments and to the wild beating of her heart. Then he gathered her to him again and drew her with him onto the cool sheets.

She had imagined how it must be, and yet the reality of his passion made her tense for a moment in his arms. But for a moment only. He was kissing her, caressing her and changing her blood to seething heat. "My Gabrielle," he called her, "my love," and his mouth was on hers, on her breast, and then he ran his closed lips over and across the yearning nipples until she gasped protest and held his tawny head prisoner against her. "Is this what you want, my lady of the forest?"

Gabrielle shivered with pleasure as his mouth closed over her nipples, suckling her. It was as though she wanted his lips to draw her soul from her. At the same time she was conscious of his hands that roved across her body, the ardent touch that stroked between her thighs.

Now his mouth left her kissed-tender breasts to follow the sensuous pathway of his hands. Here and here and there his lips brought fire, left ecstasy that was like pain until they found the core of her womanhood. Something within her shattered and shattered again, and she could no longer control her body or its movements, and as he knelt between her parted legs she whispered his name, pleading with him to love her. "Neill, my dear one . . ."

Her words drew him back from the edge of his own desire. Though want of her sweet body was a throbbing heat in his groin, a great tenderness for her, a desire to protect her, was for a moment stronger even than passion. He had dreamed of this moment, and yet now he was suddenly afraid of hurting her.

As if she sensed his holding back and its reason, she spoke again. "Dear one, only tonight matters." She touched his cheek in tender caress, ran that hand over his shoulder and arm recalling words he had once said to her. "Don't think of anything but tonight, my Neill."

Her arms went about his neck, drawing him down to her. Her mouth sought his throat and chest and flat male nipples. But even as her light hands caressed him, his thoughts moved from this bed, this moment, to the next hour, the next day, and all the days to come thereafter. Angrily, he willed the thoughts away as having no meaning. Tomorrow might never come if the soldiers caught them.

She moved beneath him, her slender body alive with a need that matched his, her thighs parting trustingly for his pleasure, and it was this trust that made him draw back. He kissed her mouth with regret, and felt an anger directed at himself and at the reason for his presence there. He had come, after all, to help her find Chauvin.

As if she read his thoughts, she herself caught her breath. The full impact of all the dangers that faced them smashed through the golden world they had almost created together, as she heard him speak in a voice hard with control. "It's quiet outside now. If we don't go, we may miss our chance to escape."

In silence he turned from her to draw on his breeches, and suddenly aware of her nakedness, she pulled the satin coverlet above her breasts. I must have been insane, she thought.

At a sudden sound in the hallway outside, they froze to silence, listening, and next moment a knock came on the door.

"Lady," a familiar voice whispered, "something's happened. I've got to speak to you right away."

Chapter Eleven

Moving rapidly, Neill snatched up his knife, but Gabrielle said, "It's Delcie, the little servant girl. She hates the woman who keeps me prisoner and will not betray us."

"She may not be alone."

He strode soundlessly to the door as Gabrielle called, "A moment, Delcie, please."

"Quickly, lady." The bound girl's voice was urgent, and Gabrielle's hands trembled with hurry as she pulled on her clothes. She was still in her shift when Delcie unlocked the door and shut it behind her, "Lady," she hissed, "your friend in the warehouse—he may have escaped and be somewhere near here. I went outside to lock up, and I found both the dogs . . ."

Neill stepped noiselessly up behind her, one big hand covering her mouth to muffle her involuntary cry of alarm. "Who else knows?" he demanded, softly.

"No one." Then as Neill's hand fell free, she whispered, "But there's soldiers posted in the street, and while I was outside, I heard them talking. They said they were going to wait for reinforcements before coming to search the house again."

From the window Neill saw the reality of what Delcie had said. Several soldiers stood guard in the narrow roadway. He could not hope to take them all by surprise, and even though he mastered them in fight, some would escape to give the alarm. "Is there another way out of here?" he asked.

The bound girl's reply was prompt. "The back door. It leads through the yard and away from the house. Nobody is guarding the back, because everyone thinks the dogs are still out there."

"Then we'll go that way." Neill went to the wardrobe and drew out a sturdy travel dress. "Try this. It will be more suitable to wear," he told Gabrielle.

The dress fit almost perfectly and with Delcie's help Gabrielle was soon ready. "Quickly, now," Neill said. "Lead the way, Delcie."

The bound girl slipped from the room like a scared shadow, followed by the others. The dark staircase creaked under their weight, but though Gabrielle held her breath, the Hook woman did not appear. They were led through a narrow kitchen and outside into the yard.

"I daren't come further," Delcie whispered.

Whispering her thanks, Gabrielle kissed the young girl's cheek and Neill pressed a gold piece

172

into her hand. Then he took Gabrielle's arm and they swiftly left the yard.

With surprise she realized that his touch was totally impersonal as they silently hurried through a tangle of willows that led to a narrow, little-used pathway. When they had gone some distance, he finally spoke.

"Our horses are stabled at the White Swan, and we dare not risk being seen. Have you ever stolen a horse?"

"Of course not. I have never in my life taken what belonged to another." She spoke indignantly and saw his sudden, white grin. "Have you?"

His amusement faded abruptly. "Not yet, but there's a first time for everything. Before dawn we need to put distance between ourselves and the Colonel's men."

They were lucky. On the outskirts of the town they found horses standing unwatched, while their soldier owners threw dice. They rode then, setting a bone-bruising speed that found them miles from Williamsburg by dawn. Only then did Neill slacken speed.

"I'm sorry," he told her, "but we don't dare stop to rest. We need to get to the coast."

"And then?" It was hard to speak because she had barely strength left to cling to the reins, but Gabrielle did not protest the lack of rest. She thought of the Colonel's wet-lipped interest, Lieutenant Dray's jeering malice. Better to die in the saddle than be taken prisoner again.

"The Carolinas." She looked at him in bewilderment, and he told her briefly about the events at the warehouse. After she exclaimed over his

meeting with her friends and over Guy Richaud's escape, he added, "I also learned that your
fiancé and your brother have gone on to the
Carolinas."

He spoke as if it mattered little to him, but she
knew how important her answer was. She also
realized that she hadn't thought of either Simon
or Chauvin since the moment Neill had appeared in her room.

Shame made her ask quickly, "How far is it to
the Carolinas?"

"So you want to go after them."

She found herself hesitating before she nodded, for she realized why Neill was asking this.
Her actions last night hadn't been those of a
betrothed woman—or of a decent woman. Forcing steadiness into her voice, she tried to explain. "Simon is my brother—the only family I
have."

An eagerness he couldn't control spilled into
his next question. "And Chauvin?"

"We took an oath in church, before God. It is a
tie that I cannot break, Neill. He is my betrothed."

Wordlessly, he spurred his horse forward. As
her own mount jolted after his, she nearly cried
out with pain that wasn't all physical. She had
seen the flash in those topaz eyes, had read what
could only be contempt in his face. A silence fell
between them, and above the drum of horses'
hooves she heard the drowsy humming of a bee
investigating autumn flowers, the trill of a bird
nearby. These were sounds which should have
recalled Laforet, but instead she thought of a
meadow rich with New England autumn and

the look in a man's tawny eyes. Dear God, she thought in sudden fear, why can't I think of anything but him?

Perhaps he read her thoughts, for he now said, "You mustn't let what happened last night worry you. In times of danger we all do things we're later sorry for." She was shocked to hear how calm, how reasonable he sounded. "Anyway, nothing happened that can't be mended, so it's best forgotten."

Forgotten—the word echoed and re-echoed in her tired mind as she forced herself to keep pace with him. She made no complaint and tried to exhibit no sign of weakness, but soon she felt Neill's eyes on her. "Are you all right?"

"Yes." It cost a great deal for her to square her slender shoulders. "I can ride."

"You certainly can." The real admiration in his voice warmed her, and he added in a different tone, "Chauvin taught you to ride, you said."

"Not he himself, for he was too busy. One of the men who worked for him taught me." She was conscious that her words were slurring a little, and that she was slumping forward in the saddle. It seemed as if she were back in Laforet, being taught to ride, together with Simon. Simon rode like the wind, so reckless and handsome. Simon, her baby brother who looked, everyone said, like the great knight their father . . .

"Gabrielle, wake up." Neill's sharp command snapped open her eyes, and she saw that he'd caught her reins. "You're asleep in the saddle," he accused.

175

"I'll be all right. What are you doing? You said we couldn't stop . . ."

But he had halted the horses and now leaned across to lift her from her saddle, place her in front of him. "It'll be safer if you ride with me."

She had no will left to protest, but even as exhausted as she was, her body registered the warmth of the arms that drew her back against him. "You can sleep now," he told her. "I have you safe."

Secure in the strength of his arm about her waist, she nestled her head against his shoulder. As her thick dark eyelashes swooped down over weary eyes, her last waking thought was that here with him was perfect safety.

She murmured his name as she slid into sleep, and Neill, hearing her, found himself hoping fervently that they would find Chauvin in the Carolinas. It was high time that he and Chauvin's fiancée parted company; otherwise he might not want to let her go.

They spent that day in hiding, while the Colonel's soldiers cantered into Yorktown and spent hours searching Andrew Warrensbody's home and place of business, as well as the waterfront.

Neill was surprised at the Colonel's zeal. Perhaps this was no longer simply a case of unfulfilled lust. Could Whitower be afraid he would use the C. and C.'s influence against him?

Warrensbody agreed. "The Colonel must want you badly, Mr. Craddock, for he's put a reward of a hundred pounds on your head," he said. "Fortunately, no one knows you're here, and that other Acadian fellow is long gone toward Georgia. But we must get you out, too, and soon."

Neill was angry. "I'd give anything to stay and confront the Colonel in a court of law," he told the storekeeper.

"Do you think that would get you anywhere?" Warrensbody dropped his voice to a low rumble. "I'm sorry to say that the King's law has become increasingly hard to bear of late. England sends too many corrupt officials, and unless things change there may be hell to pay."

His words had been gloomy, but they weren't what haunted Gabrielle as they set sail two days later on *The Mary Beth,* a sloop bound for the Carolinas. A new fear filled her. Could it be that so much had happened in a few short months that she had altered beyond her own understanding? It was hard even to remember the kindness in Monsieur Chauvin's shrewd brown eyes, his air of dignified command, the affection in his smile. And yet she was going to marry him.

She avoided Neill during the voyage, staying for the most part in her small cabin and emerging only when she was sure he was not on deck. They came together only when they made landfall several days later, and though Gabrielle wanted to go searching for her men at once, she accompanied Neill to the home of a well-known local merchant who acted as the C. and C. representative in this part of the Carolinas. The man knew little about the Acadian deportees but promised to find out what he could and meanwhile advised Neill to take lodgings at an inn near the waterfront.

News came next day, but it wasn't good. Neill frowned to hear it and wondered how he was going to tell Gabrielle. He thought of several ways in which to broach the subject, as he walked down to the small inn where they had taken rooms, but it didn't make things easier when she opened her door at once, her face eager with hope.

"Did you find them?" she cried.

"No." There was no way around the blunt truth, and yet when he saw the light go out of her eyes, he cursed himself for having to tell her the rest. "They were here, but they've gone on to the island of San Domingo."

Turning from him, she crossed her room to stare blindly out of the small, dusty window. The inn was so near the waterfront that it overlooked the harbor. So many boats were there: shore boats and lighters that hustled between frigates, hulks and bumboats. One proud schooner was on the point of raising anchor, its sails billowing out to catch the wind. It was getting ready to sail away, as Simon and Monsieur Chauvin had sailed away . . .

"I hear Chauvin has property in San Domingo." She hadn't realized that he had crossed the room and now stood directly behind her. "No doubt a great portion of his company funds have been lost because of the deportation, and he needs to raise funds some way."

Her voice was low. "He should know that I would try to find him and Simon. Why doesn't he know?" When Neill was silent, she asked, "How long will it take me to get to San Domingo?"

"It's quite an undertaking to sail there, Gabrielle. It would be better to send him a letter by one of the ships going to the islands. When Chauvin learns you're here, he'll sail back to the Carolinas."

She considered this. "It would cost money to live here for so long a time. I—I must go on."

"Gabrielle."

There was little emotion in his voice, and yet that old, strangely shadowed look filled his eyes as he said, "You know that if you need money the C. and C. will lend you any cash you need. It would be a loan only, to be repaid when we catch up to Chauvin. You could wait here or come back to Boston with me and await him there."

But she was already shaking her head. "I can't. I've already been away from them—from him, too long."

"In that case, I'll try to make arrangements for you to sail on the next ship to San Domingo."

He had said "you" and not "we." He was not coming with her. She felt relief, which struggled with an even stronger sense of loss. "You will return to Boston?" At his nod she added, "I'm sorry that you have to go back without having found Monsieur Chauvin."

"That's certainly no fault of yours." Neill spoke with careful formality as he walked away from her toward the door, and she turned back to stare at the harbor. While they talked the sun had gone behind the clouds, and now the waterfront seemed lackluster. She realized that she herself felt dull and without life, and she found herself wondering whether the ache that had developed within her was to be her companion forever. It was the same bone-deep pain she had felt when her mother died, when she had seen Laforet in flames.

Somewhere deep within her, she knew that fissures of loss were cracking open because she and Neill were parting, and yet she was grateful. At last she had to face the truth that if Neill had decided to come with her to San Domingo, she would not have stayed true to her betrothal vows.

She forced herself to concentrate on those vows during the next few days. Though she would have liked to leave immediately, there were no vessels bound for French-controlled San Domingo from this English port, and it took both persistence and hard cash on Neill's part to finally discover a Dutch merchantman that was sailing there after a detour at the French port of New Orleans. Then there were negotiations, for Captain Van Haemstra was superstitious and at first roundly refused to let a woman on his ship, *The Cameroon*. Women, Van Haemstra swore, could bring bad luck on a sea voyage.

It took a great deal of gold to allay his fears, but at last he agreed, and on a bright gold and blue November morning, Neill escorted Gabrielle to *The Cameroon* and cautioned her to be careful.

"The Captain seems to be an honest man, but there's no telling about his crew. Merchantmen attract all types of sailors," he told her. "Best to hold onto your goods and keep to your cabin as much as you can."

"You must not worry." She offered him her

hand, and he smiled and lifted it to his lips, as he had done so long ago in Laforet.

"Godspeed, Gabrielle."

His deep voice seemed to caress her name, and she carried it and the memory of his touch away with her as she went up the gangway. When I turn around he'll be gone, she warned herself, and yet when she did turn and could no longer see him, she felt an almost physical ache. Ignoring it, she walked to the lee side of the ship and from there stared steadfastly into the horizon, where Simon and her betrothed were waiting. She strained her ears to listen for the orders to weigh anchor, but other noises now filled the air.

A group of painted women had come out to bid the sailors on board *The Cameroon* farewell, and Gabrielle listened to their laughing sallies about eternal remembrance, eternal fidelity.

"I'll never forget you, darling," one of the women called, and the words brushed like an open-mouthed kiss against her memory. She clenched her small hands on the ship's rail and thought: I must forget him. He's already gone.

But Neill had not yet left the dock. His long strides had taken him into the shadow of the warehouses at the edge of the dock and there he stopped and waited for the ship to sail. As he stood there a rowdy group of sailors and drunken, painted women brushed past him. The women were laughing and crooning obscene endearments, while the men, almost as drunk as their companions, hurried to board the vessel before it sailed.

Apparently, they were colonials recruited here

181

in the Carolinas, for they spoke English. "Captain'll have us keelhauled for being late," Neill heard one of them grunt.

One of his comrades made tipsy reply. "You be grateful if that's all the Dutchman does to you this voyage. You know we got a damned woman on board, don't you? Women on board ship are unlucky. Jonahs. If I had my way, I'd throw her overboard . . ."

Neill stared after the men as they stumbled toward the ship. The man was drunk, of course, but Neill thought of how far Gabrielle had come and how far she must still go, and he remembered her outburst of a few days ago. Dammit, she was right. Chauvin should have waited for her or, better, searched for her, instead of drifting from place to place.

He did not realize he had begun to walk back toward the ship. The order had just been given to raise the gangway when he reached it, and he had to summon the surprised Van Hamestra and explain his change of plan. Negotiations this time were brief, and by the time the order to weigh anchor had been given, Neill was searching the deck for Gabrielle.

He found her staring out to sea. Her shoulders were held erect, but the dark hair that she had sternly repressed in a knot at the back of her head had come free, and she looked very young and somehow fragile. His anger at the absent Chauvin rose to a boiling point as he crossed the deck and came to stand beside her.

It took a moment before she became aware that she wasn't alone. Then she stared up at him, and her eyes went wide. "What are you doing here?" she gasped.

He'd been asking himself that same question and he'd found no answers. This, plus the need to control his conflicting emotions, made his voice colder than he had intended it to be. "I changed my mind about coming. I've chased Chauvin too long not to be at the end of the trail. God grant that we find him this time."

At his words the joy and eagerness that had blazed briefly in her face died away, and her small hands curled tightly around the rail of the ship. With a control as great as his own, she turned away from him to stare again at the distant horizon.

"We *must* find him," Gabrielle said.

Chapter Twelve

GABRIELLE LEANED AGAINST THE SHIP'S RAIL AND watched the seabirds skim and wheel in *The Cameroon*'s wake, while the sun beat down out of a blue sky. All she could see was an expanse of blue sea and sky without a trace of land.

"Sail, ho," came from the bow of the boat, "sail on the weather beam."

In the distance she could make out a feather of white against the perfect blue. "A barque, perhaps, or a merchantman like *The Cameroon*," Neill's deep voice said behind her.

She knew why he was reassuring her; this was the arena of privateers who would seize and take cargo for their profit.

"How far do you think we are from New Orleans?" she asked.

He didn't answer for a moment but watched the shadows and the sunlight trace their patterns across her upturned face. When she was out of sight, he often wondered why he'd come with her. When he was near her, he knew he hadn't had any choice.

"Not long," he finally said. "Two, three days' sail at most."

The guarded note in his voice troubled her. When she had seen him standing next to her on the day of *The Cameroon*'s departure, she had felt such inexpressible joy that she had wanted to run into his arms. His cold words had stopped her, and yet she knew that the impulse expressed her deepest feelings. She hadn't just been grateful for his continued protection; she had come alive because he was there.

But he obviously didn't share these feelings, and the next days on *The Cameroon* had proven it. Though he didn't try to avoid her, he treated her with the cool courtesy of a stranger. And yet not quite a stranger. She could sense that below the calm surface seethed a restless tension.

She could feel that tension, but when she looked up at him, he was watching the fast-approaching ship. Now they could both see that it was a nervous-looking, high-bowed vessel with a taut rig. "That's no merchantman," he declared. "A warship. A British brig by her colors."

She could see the Union Jack whip smartly from the ship's mizzen. "It's moving very fast."

Neill nodded agreement and then exclaimed, "She carries human cargo."

On the deck of the warship was a longboat, and in this longboat a group of men appeared to be huddled. It was still much too far to make out their faces or expressions, but she could see from the way they cowered together in that cramped space that they were terrified.

She watched them pityingly as the warship came within hailing distance of *The Cameroon*, and though Gabrielle could not catch the quick signals, Neill managed to decipher a few words. "It seems that the warship makes for England with a cargo of 'recruits' to fight against the French."

Now she could see how muddied and filthy the prisoners were, how they blinked and stared at the sun. "They look as if they haven't seen sunlight for days."

Neill said, "They've probably been confined to the hold of the ship."

"But," she cried indignantly, "if they're going to fight for England why are they being treated so badly?"

"I doubt that they're going willingly. Have you not heard of youths being 'impressed'? That's a polite way of saying that they were kidnapped into the King's service."

"Another demonstration of English justice," she began scornfully, and then added contritely, "I am sorry, Neill. I know that France, too, does such things, for governments and kings are all alike. My father served Louis XV all his life, but when he died the King forgot all about us."

"So I heard. Marthe Richaud told me that Chauvin was the one who kept you from starving."

To his surprise, she shook her head. "He did more. Marthe did not know this, but Monsieur Chauvin used his own money to hire lawyers in

France to see if anything could be salvaged from the de Montfleuri estate there."

"And?"

"Unfortunately, some legal clause in the documents that made our father a rich man stipulated that the estate, together with all his wealth, was to revert back to the crown when he died." Gabrielle paused and added slowly, "It was hard for Maman to accept this at first, but even she agreed that it was better to know how things stood. And Monsieur Chauvin's lawyers fought hard for us, managed to get a small allowance for Maman as long as she lived. Monsieur Chauvin also was going to send Simon to France when he turned seventeen—" She broke off and turned to him, her dark eyes full of a plea for understanding.

"So you're marrying him out of gratitude." She didn't know whether it was her imagination or whether his voice had hardened.

"You once told me that there were many reasons to marry. Perhaps gratitude is one of them," she replied in a low voice.

She saw the tawny eyes narrow, registered the intensity of feeling in their depths, and it was as if some part of her was waiting for him to protest, to sweep aside her words and take her into his arms. She was suddenly filled by memories so powerful that beside them, mere gratitude paled to nothing.

Hastily, she looked out to sea, and after a few moments he spoke again. "Seems as though that man-of-war brought us ill weather." He nodded into the distance, and when she followed his eyes she saw a line of cloud lying on what had been the unmarred blue of the horizon. "We may get rain by nightfall."

The rain caught up with them that evening, and with it came heavy winds and seas. Captain Van Haemstra gave orders that his two passengers were to go below during the storm so as to take no hurt. Gabrielle did as he suggested, but as the storm worsened, the pitch and roll of the ship and her hot, airless cabin made her feel ill. So did the sight of the whale oil lamp jerking on its chain to the back-and-forth wallowing of the ship. She fought her seasickness stubbornly, but by midnight *The Cameroon* was bobbing about like a cork, and she was struggling to control her nausea when Neill pounded on her door and asked how she was.

Even with all his strength he could hardly keep her cabin door open against the violent pitch and yaw of *The Cameroon*. How could a ship take such punishment and stay afloat? Gabrielle wondered sickly, but Neill told her not to worry. "We've seen the worst of the storm now," he reassured her. "Stay in your cabin, and you'll be safe."

"And you, too," she told him, but he said that he was going on deck.

"One of the officers has been injured and the Captain sent word that he needs my help. I only came to see how you were faring." Then he was gone, and she returned to her lonely battle against seasickness.

She had not been ill on the way from Laforet to Boston, but as the storm's ferocity continued unchecked she felt sick enough to die. She was starved for clean air, and her nausea-strained stomach roiled again as the ship yawed into the trough of a wave. She needed fresh air desperately. Surely it could be no worse on deck than it was here . . .

Her thoughts came thickly, almost incoherently, and she envied Neill. He was fortunate to be up on deck with the clean wind blowing through his hair, the cool rain on his face. Suddenly, she knew that if she didn't get on deck herself, she would go mad. She tugged and clawed at her cabin door, until at last it opened, but as she pushed outside, she was inundated by a deluge of water that poured down like a waterfall from the deck. Next moment the pitching of the ship tore the cabin door out of Gabrielle's hands, and it slammed tight shut.

The shock of the cold water cleared her head, and she realized the danger of what she had wanted to do. It was crazy to even think of climbing the deck now, and she caught hold of her cabin door and tried to pull it open. It wouldn't budge. Then the ship rolled again, and she was swept away from the door and thrown against the ladder that led up to the deck. As she clung to it, more water poured down on her, and a loud voice behind her shouted, "You—get up that ladder right this minute, or I skin you!"

Automatically, she obeyed, and as she climbed the first step she heard a roaring. It was as if some huge animal was loose, prowling the sea and bellowing for its prey. She halted on the ladder and heard swearing behind her.

"Damn your eyes, move. Call yerself a seaman?"

She tried to explain but the storm tore her words away, and in the darkness she knew the man couldn't see her. Nor could she stand there blocking his way. She'd have to go up and then come down again and try to get her cabin door open. If she could only find Neill, he would help her. Neill . . .

She didn't realize she was repeating his name to herself as she climbed onto the deck. It had been dark below deck, but here she couldn't see at all. Upwind, everything was blinding grayness, and as the wind shifted a little, the grayness became mountainous seas that towered high above the ship. As *The Cameroon* slid into a trough between the waves, one of the wave crests broke off and smashed down onto the deck, foaming over them all. A flash of lightning lit the sky, and she saw the shocked, bearded face of the seaman who had climbed the ladder behind her.

"So it's you. I should've broken your neck on the ladder—would have, if I'd known. Goddamned woman Jonah. You brought the storm . . ."

His voice was so full of fear and menace that she recoiled involuntarily and threw up both hands to ward him off. At the same time the ship rolled again, and the water on the deck sluiced toward her and knocked her legs from under her. She tried to find something to cling to, but couldn't, as the momentum of the water swept her across the deck. She had no time to think or try to save herself—time only for one scream.

Then she was plunging backward over the rail into the sea. The shock of hitting water knocked the breath out of her, and for a moment she went limp. But when the waves closed over her head she began to fight instinctively for the surface.

The surface she reached was a nightmare world. Bobbing like a cork between huge swells, she tried desperately to tread water and to locate the ship. Where was it? She could barely see the hulk of it in the wind-driven rain.

Nobody could have seen her go over the rail—nobody but that fright-crazed sailor, and he, blaming her for the storm, would be only too glad to see her go. She was going to drown, she thought, she was going to die. Oddly, she did not feel fear but rather a passionate regret. Not to see a sunset again or to walk in the forest, or to hear Neill's voice beside her in the starlit evenings—and one more 'never' that tore her heart. Neill, she thought, I have never even told him that I love him—and that was when she heard him call her name.

She'd heard that people who drowned became lightheaded in their last minutes. Even so, she looked desperately around, trying to pierce the raging darkness about her. Then she saw him. He was swimming as quickly as he could against the wind, and she heard him call to her again.

At the sound of his voice she found new strength and began to swim desperately toward him, but she couldn't make headway against the wind and the giant waves. It was all she could do to stay afloat until he was near enough to reach her and wrapped one strong arm around her.

"I have you," she heard him say. "Now hold on. We're in for the swim of our lives."

Spent, she lay across his big body and felt the unfamiliar roughness of a rope he had around his waist. Turning, he began to pull his way back to the ship. Once, she was nearly swept away from him, and another time the rope went slack so that she feared that they had been cut adrift. He did not seem to have such fears. Inch by hard inch, he pulled them toward safety until they were flung against the side of the ship.

Even then there was danger. As seamen hauled them up, the ship yawed sharply so that the rope tightened suddenly and Neill was smashed against the ship's side. The impact tore her arms loose from him, yet he somehow managed to keep his hold on her. He heard her gasp his name as they were being dragged over the side of the ship, and in spite of everything managed reassurance. "It's all right, I have you."

Her answer was a ragged gasp of sound. "I thought—I was dying. Neill, I could not die without telling you—hold me close. Please hold me."

As they fell onto the deck, he kissed her sea-wet hair and her eyes and her cold lips. He wanted to tell her that she was a part of him, a part of his heart and flesh, but no words formed in his exhausted mind. All he could do was to repeat, "I have you, Gabrielle." And he thought, I'm not going to let you go.

Two days later the weary and wounded *Cameroon* limped into the port of New Orleans for repairs as well as trade. Much of the cargo she carried had been damaged by the storm, and Captain Van Haemstra emphatically told Neill and Gabrielle that their stay in port would be a long one. "That is," he added, "if Madam wants to attempt another sea voyage."

Gabrielle only replied that she was grateful to be on land again. As Neill helped her climb the levees or mounds of earth that edged New Orleans and held back river water, she repeated: "I had forgotten how good it is to stand on ground that doesn't move."

Neill agreed. "I think we've both had enough of ships for a while."

There was no doubt in her mind that he was talking about their postponed voyage to San Domingo. They hadn't discussed it yet, but on the night of the storm they had clung together, their emotions so raw and honest that there could be no turning back. What had happened then had changed everything, and yet there had been no time to talk. Because of his military background, Neill had been requested to continue to take the hurt officer's place and help bring *The Cameroon* into port. For the last two days Gabrielle had only seen him in the company of others.

Now she was suddenly afraid of what he might say. She had an almost irresistible need to tell him how much she loved him, and yet something held her back. Even though he'd risked his life for her, even though it was clear he desired her, he had never told her that he loved her. And even if he did love her, was this enough for her to throw duty and honor away?

"There's something we need to decide," he

was saying now, and she went suddenly rigid, waiting. But he only added, "We'll need a place to stay for a few days. It'll take some time for the ship to be repaired, and I've had my fill of noisy waterfront inns."

Grateful that he wasn't talking at once of personal matters, she looked about her at the bustling river port. It was very warm, and all the colors seemed intense, from the bright blue of the sky and the thick, muddy gold of the great river to the colorful headscarves of slaves and the cheerful clothing worn by workers and peddlers on the dock. Some distance away, a ship was unloading, a small cluster of slaves was being readied for auction and vendors shouted loudly as they hawked their goods. As Neill said, the noise here was deafening.

"What do you suggest?" she asked.

"The C. and C. man in the Carolinas does business with some of the Spaniards who live here in New Orleans. Learning that you were bound this way, he suggested a place where you might wish to stay while in port. It seems that the widow of one of his late business associates makes a practice of letting rooms at her house near Chartres."

He spoke with careful detachment, and she replied in kind. "After all this traveling, one place is like another, but if you wish I'll go and look over this widow's rooms. Are you coming with me?"

"I have an official call to make first at Government House." She looked at him, surprised, and he explained. "As an Englishman in a French port, a visit to the local authorities is in order.

It'd be a cursed shame to spend my first visit to this part of the world in prison."

"Let me come with you," she begged, but he would not have this. Instead, he hailed the driver of a nearby carriage and instructed him to take the lady to the Señora Alejandro's on Chartres Street.

"If you like the rooms, engage them," he then told her. "I'll meet you there in an hour or two."

"Supposing I don't like them?" but he was already striding away.

The grinning driver descended to help her into the carriage. "Of course, you will like the house of Madame Alejandro," he told her in French. "Who could not like paradise?"

He was a talkative little man, gray-haired and stooped with laboring, he told her, on farms before he had become too old to do more than drive a hack. His talk of farms made her think of Laforet, and she began to ask him questions as he proudly showed her his city.

"Ah, it is not yet a full hundred years since the great Sieur de Bienville came here with six carpenters and thirty laborers to cut the city out of mud and canebrakes," he told her. "You who come from Acadia should know the great man, for he was born in Canada. He fought off Indians, established us for what we are—the pearl of the St. Louis River—or, as the Indians say, the Mississippi."

She could see that the city was very new, but what she saw of it was impressive. The driver swept her past the Governor's residence with its imposing galleries and courtyard and pointed out the brick of the Place D'Armes across the way. "Several hundred brave men can live there at a time and fight off any foe that an enemy can throw at us," he boasted.

Just listening to French being spoken again was marvelous, Gabrielle thought. She found herself relaxing, enjoying the view as the carriage swept around the river to Chartres and the widow Alejandro's home.

Even at first glance, she was pleased with the house. It was built of graceful pink stone and was surrounded by a high wall that enclosed a large garden, and later when a smiling Indian manservant showed her into this garden, she exclaimed with pleasure. Jasmine, roses, orderly bushes of honeysuckle were only some of the flowers that bordered a well-swept path that led to a pond full of waterlilies. The house itself was shaded by a tall oak, and songbirds twittered and warbled in its branches. As she looked about her, she thought she caught the flash of an egret's wings.

The Señora Alejandro herself did not live in the house but arrived soon after Gabrielle. She was a plump, dark-haired woman, French by birth, enthusiastic about Gabrielle as a tenant. "But it is the entire house I wish to rent, not mere rooms," she explained. "Since my husband died, I live with my daughter, and so only my servants stay here. They will continue to stay and serve you, if you permit. But will you take the place alone?" Gabrielle hesitated, then shook her head. "Good," she said with Gallic tolerance. "It's time the house knew laughter and love again."

Gabrielle started to explain, but then held her

peace. It did not matter what this woman thought, and she wasn't even sure she wanted to take the place. But a closer inspection proved that she would be foolish not to do so. Besides its beauty and privacy, it was sturdily built, with two separate wings each equipped with a large bedroom. There would be more than enough room for two people to live here and still maintain privacy, and she had no doubt that Neill would approve of the place.

The widow expressed her delight at Gabrielle's decision. "You will enjoy the city, Mademoiselle," she exclaimed. "You are only staying for a short time? But that does not signify. You must meet the Baron de Sandoville. He is an aristocrat and the leader of New Orleans society. And he gives such parties, such balls." She kissed her fingers. "My husband and I often attended such affairs, and even though I do not go out anymore, I am still invited."

Events moved swiftly. Her luggage was brought in, and the two servants, a smiling Houma Indian called Jeanot and his wife Maria, were placed at her disposal. After the Señora left, she was kept busy discussing suggestions for the evening meal and supervising the changing of linen, and it was only when she realized how late it was getting to be that she realized Neill had not yet come.

Remembering his errand, she began to worry about him. She held off real anxiety for a while, unpacking her trunk in the airy bedroom she had chosen for herself, and later bathing and changing into a simple dress that she had worn on summer days in Laforet. But when sunset was near and the long shadows had begun to sweep across the garden, anxiety became a tight knot in her breast.

She was on the point of telling Jeanot to find a carriage to take her into town, when she looked outside and saw that the sun was setting. Even in the midst of her worries, the sight of the great crimson ball sliding below the tall oak was so beautiful that she went out into the garden to see. The songbirds were settling in the trees for the night, trilling and squawking as they did so, and so she didn't hear the footsteps on the garden path behind her, until she heard him say her name.

She turned so swiftly that she was nearly unbalanced. He stood just behind her, the sunset burnishing his hair to near bronze. "Is everything all right?" she cried.

"Never better. Governor de Kerlerac was at first inclined to be suspicious of an Englishman traveling in these parts, but apparently they know about the C. and C. here in New Orleans, and of course they'd heard about the Acadian deportation." He was smiling as if well satisfied, as he added, "A gentleman called the Baron de Sandoville was visiting His Excellency, and he extended his personal welcome to me. There's much more hospitality here than in Williamsburg."

She exclaimed in relief. "I was getting worried," she confessed.

"No need to be concerned." He looked around him to add, "I see you've rented the house."

She had had a moment to catch her breath, and now she could smile as though very much at her ease. "Is it not lovely? It seems we have the entire house. We'll have a great deal of room."

A small, flower-fragrant breeze rustled the vines of the bougainvillea nearby, tossing the flowers like jewels. Then, he said, "A pity that neither of us may be staying here."

"But I thought . . ."

She stopped as his eyes came back to hold hers. "While I was with the Baron, word came that a ship in port now will be sailing for San Domingo tomorrow. It could take a letter. Or . . ."

He fell silent and she whispered the rest. "Or I could go myself."

He didn't answer, and she turned her back to him and looked blindly at the glorious sunset. The moment she feared had come, and now there was no escape. She knew the full weight of honor, the heaviness of the vow she had taken. But as she tried to form her decision, he spoke again.

"When I saw you go over the side of the ship, I knew that nothing mattered to me in the world but you. I swore then that I would do everything in my power to prevent you from going to Chauvin. I knew about this house and I planned to be alone with you and make you see the truth about my love for you."

She turned to face him, and her lips formed the words almost soundlessly. "And now?"

She saw the muscle leap in his lean jaw, the way he fisted his hands and thrust them behind his back, but he spoke quietly. "I know I can't do that to you. I love you." He repeated the words again with a wonder that was almost pain.

"Whatever you want, I'll do, even if it means you want to go—to him."

"But I don't want to go." This time her words broke on a sob. She took a blind step forward and found herself in his arms. She clung to him, drawing in the beloved scent of him, rejoicing in his almost painful embrace. The cool linen of his shirt was crisp against her bare arms, her cheek felt the tender-tough rasp of his. Then her mouth was opening to his, surrendering as their lips came together.

"Christ, but I love you," she heard him repeat against her lips, and she tilted her head back, breaking the long, passionate kiss and touching his cheek, his chin, his lips and throat with swift butterfly kisses.

"And yet you would have let me go?" she whispered and caught her breath as his mouth lowered to her still-clothed breast.

"Never again. You belong to me."

Their lips met again, their kiss wilder now, fierce with remembered desire as their tongues touched and caressed. He was right, she thought. She had never belonged to Louis Chauvin. She was Neill's.

When he drew her toward the house, she went with him eagerly, guiding him up the stairs toward her room. He shut the door behind them and drew her to him, and it was she who kissed him first and then again and still again, until she was dizzy with the wine of his lips. There was no slow arousal today as they helped each other with buttons and laces. She arched her back with almost unbearable desire as he bared her shoulders and neck and breast and bent to take the upthrust nipples into his mouth, and she moaned her pleasure as his lips closed lightly over each aching peak. The heavy wine of her need spread through her entire body until she could no longer wait.

But when their clothing had fallen to the floor, their hurry seemed to ease. He lifted her into his arms and held her against him, rubbing his cheek between the slopes of her breasts, kissing her throat and her mouth and murmuring her name. She stroked his tawny hair and the line of his jaw, kissed his eyes and his hands.

She told him softly. "I have loved you for so long."

He lowered her onto the wide bed and eased himself beside her. He had envisioned this moment so often, remembered the feel of her silk hair against his fingers and lips, the taste and feel of her breasts and thighs. He had imagined what it would be to sink into the depths of her, to slake his passion for her at last. Yet now he felt a tenderness greater than his own urgency, a need to spin out her pleasure and his delight in loving her. His lips traced the delicate line of her stomach, her thighs and knees, then moved upward between her thighs to worship the sweet honey of her.

And meanwhile she stroked his shoulders, streaked her nails lightly across his back and down his buttocks and thighs, then touched, wonderingly, the cool hardness of his passion.

"But you are beautiful," she exclaimed. "I didn't know a man could be beautiful."

Registering the soft curl of her hand about him, he could wait no longer. He knelt between her parted thighs and looked down into her upraised face so that she could see herself reflected in tawny gold. Once she had thought a woman could drown in such eyes. Now, as she saw the passion and the tenderness, she was sure.

She whispered his name as he came to her, poising himself on his elbows, his hips hard against hers. Slowly, he told himself, gently—

But she would have none of this slowness. As she felt the power of his desire, she opened herself heart and soul and body to his loving. At his first thrust she tensed a little and he grew rigid in turn, holding himself back for fear of hurting her. But she held him closer, kissing his mouth and his hands and whispering his name with a tender joy that held no shadow of regret. And when he moved again, she lifted her hips to meet him, took him deep within the yielding warmth and satin of her love.

Then they were together. Moving slowly, then faster, then faster still, until no longer earthbound, they soared higher than the golden eagles could ever fly.

"I love you," she heard him tell her, "I love . . ."

And with the hot, heavy honey of his seed within her, she soared with him into the heart of the sun.

Chapter Thirteen

SHE AWOKE TO VELVET DARKNESS AND THE
sound of wind. It rustled through the open windows of her room bringing with it the cool fragrance of flowers, and she nestled closer into
Neill's arms.

"*Je t'aime*—I love you." Loving his body, too,
she rubbed her lips against the muscle of his
shoulder, his broad chest. Ripples of pleasure
still thrilled through her, and when his arms
tightened about her, they coalesced in a honeyed
fire. "Neill, *je t'adore*."

Without words he began to stroke her hair and
then ran his hand lightly across her arms, the
curve of her breast and hips. The shadow touch
was sensuous and loving, and she shivered deli-
ciously against him.

"There aren't any right words—at least, I
never learned them," he said, then. "'I love you'

doesn't seem enough to tell you how I feel. There should be something more."

But there is, she thought, and her lips curved happily as she rested her cheek against his chest and remembered the magic of their coming together. As if reading her thought, he turned in the big bed, drawing her on her side to face him, easing her body against his own. Like two parts of a whole, they seemed to fit together, and her lips nestled in the hollow of his throat as he began to claim her again with deliberate, erotic skill.

No need to lie to him or to herself any longer. "I've wanted you to love me like this for so long," she told him. "Ever since that first night in the forest when you carried me away."

"It was even sooner for me than that, my love. When I saw you in church, I knew you were mine." He felt the tension in her as he spoke, and he held her closer. "Gabrielle, marry me," he said.

Registering his words in the deepest core of her heart, she still had to say it. "You know I cannot marry you while I am betrothed to Monsieur Chauvin."

She tried to draw away from him, but he would not let her. "I know the vows you took that day. I was there. But a bethrothal can be dissolved." She didn't answer, and he added forcefully, "You love me, not Chauvin."

Now she pulled away from him and sat up. Limned against the faint moonlight he could see her proud breasts rise and fall with emotion. "I love you more than life," she was saying, "but I am a knight's daughter, dear one. I—I can't break a pledge."

He propped himself up on his elbow and took her hand, turning it over and kissing the palm. "Then we'll make Chauvin let you go."

"If he would only release me—" Her breath came in a low sigh, and he pulled her down to him again. She came eagerly, and he kissed her eyes and her soft mouth. "Do you think he would permit me to break the betrothal and marry you?"

"I've no doubt that he will."

There was a determined note in his voice that made her frown. "Promise me that you will remain his friend," she begged. "He has been so good to me and to Simon . . ."

"So you've told me often. Now forget him."

His lips were taking away all other thought, and yet she persisted. "Neill, I truly mean this. I don't want Monsieur Chauvin hurt. I—I fear he loves me and that he still wishes to marry me."

He kissed her. "I can sympathize with the man, since I feel the same way. Don't worry, dear love, Chauvin is a man of the world. When he realizes how you feel, he'll have the grace to let you go." The determined note in his voice intensified as he added, "That ship bound for San Domingo will carry a letter to him from me. I'll write it at once."

But she protested this. "In the morning," she whispered.

His lips sought hers again. As his mouth drank her honey, his hands began their loving journey over her body. He curved his fingers to cup the sweet fullness of her high breasts, then lightly rubbed his thumb around her nipples. When she protested his avoidance of the taut peaks, his mouth left hers to draw a circle of kisses about the now aching buds.

"Neill, you are not being fair," she half-laughed, half-moaned and heard in turn his deep-throated male laughter.

"But you are fair, my lovely lady of the forest, fairer than the morning sun." His deep voice vibrated with longing, and she shivered with answering desire. "You're made for loving."

His tongue lightly flicked the base of her nipples, touched them, then grazed her smooth young stomach and the joining of her thighs. She felt as if gems of fire had been scattered over her, and her body moved involuntarily under the teasing of his tongue and lips. She tried to clasp her arms around him and draw him to her, but he would not do her bidding. Instead, he brought delicious torment to all the small, secret places of her body. The bend of her knees, the sensitive inner thighs, her ribs, and now at last back to her breasts again.

She gave a little cry as his mouth closed over the roses of her breasts, and she held him close to her as he suckled her. Waves of ecstasy, undulating through her as he took his pleasure, grew stronger and more fierce as he lowered his mouth to retrace his earlier kisses. But this time those kisses were not light, they did not tease. He sought out the curve of her belly, the warmth of her thighs with deliberate, open-mouthed kisses.

She whispered an entreaty as he knelt be-

tween her parted thighs and worshiped the honeyed secrets of her womanhood, but he did not
heed her. With exquisite slowness he pleasured
her until her hips were thrusting against him,
mimicking the age-old dance of love. Then, still
slowly, still deliberately controlled, his mouth
returned to her breasts, to her lips.

Her body moved to a primal rhythm, and her
mouth seemed to have a will of its own as it
traced his now-familiar line of shoulder and
sought the flat male nipples. Meanwhile, her
hands caressed the hard line of his back and the
tense thighs, curled about the demand of his
manhood. Lovingly, her fingertips stroked his
power, her delicate touch an invitation.

It was an invitation he could not long resist,
and yet he spun out the golden moments for as
long as possible. When at last he came to her,
her eyes were wide with love and desire. As
his hardness sought the warmth of her, he
heard her whisper, "Neill, *je t'adore*. Always.
Always . . ."

As he loved her, Neill found himself still
capable of rational thought. Here and now there
was no shadow of Chauvin between them.

And he intended to keep it that way.

Next morning they woke to a dazzling sunshine that set the course for the days that followed. Neill wrote to Chauvin and dispatched
the letter to San Domingo and then a few days
later wrote to Sam Culpepper, explaining that
he would be detained some time in New Orleans.

He had a good reason for this prolonged stay.

His initial talk with the Baron de Sandoville, the aristocrat he'd met at the Governor's, had been interesting. "Louisiana is a vast area," Neill wrote. "At the moment there is only one major French company, John Law's Company of the East Indies, which is seeking to monopolize trade. Louisiana is in French hands, of course, but de Sandoville hinted that there are several prominent people here who don't care for Law's monopoly. They may be interested in what the C. and C. can offer. Besides, the war with France can't last forever."

Gabrielle, who read the letter, was thoughtful. "Then you are going to try and do business with New Orleans?"

He put his arm about her. "I've always wanted to lock horns with the Company of the East Indies, but you know it's not the main reason for my stay."

She turned swiftly to clasp her arms about his neck. "How soon will we have a reply, do you think, from San Domingo?"

"Perhaps as soon as a few weeks. It depends on how the ships run." He kissed her then, adding, "What does time matter as long as we wait together?"

Neill was right. Time did not seem to matter, except that it passed too quickly for their liking. New Orleans was an ideal place for lovers. It was as if the warm climate made the people here affectionate and tolerant, for even the slaves were well treated, protected by the so-called black code. The Baron de Sandoville introduced Neill to several prominent figures in the financial world of the riverport city, and while he attended to C. and C. business, Señora Alejandro insisted on showing Gabrielle the sights.

Filled with the joy of loving Neill and enchanted with the city, Gabrielle found herself forgetting the harshness of the past few months. Though the horror of Laforet was still with her, and though she worried constantly over Simon's whereabouts and welfare, she felt more content than she had ever been. Sometimes she would find herself humming a song learned in faraway Laforet, but she knew that she was happier now than she had been even in Acadia. With Neill, the restless longing and loneliness she had always felt had vanished, and as they walked in the gardens or toured the bustling city or lay in each other's arms through the long flower-scented nights, she knew a joy that was almost painful in its intensity.

Señora Alejandro commented on the change in her during one visit several weeks after their arrival in the city by the river. "You are blooming like a rose," she exclaimed. "New Orleans agrees with you, Mademoiselle Gabrielle."

"It does indeed, Señora," Gabrielle said, and the plump widow smiled.

"Did I not say that this house was in need of lovers? If I were but twenty years younger, I would envy you *le tigre d'or*, your golden tiger." She chuckled throatily at Gabrielle's heightened color and added, "But, *ma petite*, what is there really for a woman but the love of a good man? I have seen how he looks at you, how you seem to glow with happiness when he is near. There is an unbreakable bond between you, yes?"

There was something in the shrewd, kind eyes that made her think of Marthe Richaud. "Yes," Gabrielle agreed, "it is that way."

"You are very lucky. I, too, felt this way for my husband." Señora Alejandro sighed a little and added, "It was as if we were one soul in two bodies from the moment we met until the day he died."

Gabrielle could not help saying, "How could you stand it when he died?"

The widow shrugged with Gallic common sense. "One must live. But, *alors,* I didn't come to dwell on sad things. I met one of the servants of the Baron de Sandoville, on the way here and assured him I would deliver this to you in person."

She handed Gabrielle a large white envelope that contained an invitation to a ball given within the week. The Baron, the invitation explained, would be enchanted if Monsieur Craddock and Mademoiselle de Montfleuri could attend.

Señora Alejandro was enchanted by this, exclaiming that this ball was the highlight of the New Orleans social season and that to be invited was a very great honor. Neill also was pleased. "I've been pursuing business talk with the baron, but this is the first opportunity I'll have of meeting him on a social footing." Gabrielle nodded somewhat hesitantly, and he said, "What is it, my love?"

"I was thinking that perhaps some of the people there would have known my father in France. I—I am not trained in etiquette, Neill. I don't want to do anything to shame my father's memory."

"Like having an Englishman for a lover?" he asked her and then cursed his bluntness when he saw the trouble in her eyes. Drawing her to him, he caressed the dark silk of her hair. "My darling, we needn't go if you don't want to. I'd much rather be in your company than in that of all the crowned heads of Europe."

Under her cheek she could hear the strong beat of his heart. It steadied her, and she shook her head. "We will not stay away," she told him firmly. "I don't care what anyone thinks. You are my love, my man, my life."

"And you are my lady. Do you think that anyone will dare to do you less than honor?" He was smiling, but she sensed the hint of savagery just below the surface. He was truly her golden tiger, she thought with a sudden ache of love. If only she were his wife. If only Monsieur Chauvin would write and release her from her betrothal vows.

"No one will dare to greet me at all if you look so fierce." She forced her voice to lightness and stood on tiptoe to kiss the lean line of his jaw as she added, "But now I must not disgrace you. Remember what happened to me when I went to court for the first and last time!" He began to laugh, and her eyes danced for a moment before she gave a soft shriek. "Neill, what will I wear? I have nothing grand enough. Do you think that the Señora will help me find a decent dressmaker in the city?"

The delighted Señora Alejandro insisted on

taking Gabrielle in hand. Like a stout fairy godmother, she bustled her tenant around the city, taking her shopping first for silks that were the color of a summer sky, then on a search for the finest laces from Holland. Next, she unearthed an ancient dressmaker who had once sewn for the court of Louis XV and who produced, with his trembling hands, the most beautiful creation that Gabrielle had ever seen. The Señora's eyes gleamed when she saw Gabrielle in the dress.

"What man at the ball will be able to keep his eyes off you?" she cried. "Your golden tiger will growl with pleasure when he sees you thus."

Goodnaturedly, Neill endured the feminine excitement that hummed through the house on Chartres Street on the day of the ball. He cared little for fashion and thought it foolish that men and women overdressed for social gatherings, but he was glad to see Gabrielle enjoying herself. To please her, he had ordered a coat of heavy honey-colored satin that fit the broad wedge of his shoulders and followed closely the line of his chest, before sloping away from the fastening buttoned over on embroidered single-breasted waistcoat. He was fastening the four small buttons and buckles on his breeches when Maria entered to announce that Madame was ready for the evening.

He had always known that Gabrielle was beautiful, but he still wasn't prepared for the woman who now swept into the room. She wore a sky-blue dress with a square décolletage edged with fine lace ruching. A bow, placed in the center of her bosom, called attention to the proud rise of her breasts and emphasized her slender waist before the dress swirled out over oval hoops reaching to the ground. As she curtseyed deep before him, he saw that bows, like the one at her breast, cascaded down both sides of the flaring overskirt.

The effect of her dress was breathtaking—but after an initial glance, his eyes went to her face. There was a new look in the dark eyes under the upsweep of unpowdered dark hair, a confidence in her always graceful carriage. She was no longer afraid and alone, he thought with pride. She was a woman beloved and protected, who was giving back that love with all her heart.

"Don't you like the dress?" she was asking, a little anxiously. "Perhaps it is too much, all these bows and laces."

He walked quickly over to her and bent low over her hand. "I expected Gabrielle, and I'm visited by the Queen of France," he told her. "Turn around and let me look at Your Majesty."

Her eyes showed delight in his approval and she stood on the tips of small silver and blue shoes and turned slowly. "Does the golden tiger like me?" she asked demurely.

"I've seldom liked you more. *What* did you call me?" he asked, and when she had explained he did not laugh as she had expected, but took her by the bare shoulders and drew her toward him. "The Señora is right about one thing. Tigers are possessive about their own. Remember, when you are surrounded by all the nobility of New Orleans, that you are queen of my heart."

The vibrancy of his voice brought tears to her

eyes. "This I could never forget," she whispered. "But, my dear one, you mustn't look at me like that. Otherwise I don't think we will ever get to the Baron's ball."

"Hang the Baron's ball." She laughed softly as he drew her closer, bent to kiss her eager lips. Then, sighing regretfully, he drew away. "It would be a pity not to show off that pretty dress, but the ball won't last forever. And the night belongs to us."

Jeanot, the Houma manservant, was waiting to drive the carriage that Neill had engaged while they resided in New Orleans. He knew the way to the Baron's estate, and so his passengers could lean back and enjoy the warm star-spangled night and the cool breeze that blew in from the river. January, Gabrielle reflected, would be cold almost everywhere else, but here it was comfortably warm. As they clattered down Chartres and then past the new school and hospital built and run by the Ursuline nuns, she drank in the flower-scented air. But when they drove past St. Anne Street and the Governor's residence, she looked up at Neill in surprise.

"Isn't the Baron's house on St. Anne Street?" she asked.

"I heard that he built it on the city's out-skirts." The truth of this became clear when Jeanot guided the horses away from the main streets and down a mile or so of what looked to be uninhabited countryside before coming to an avenue of oaks. This pathway was lighted by hundreds of lamps, and in this light the branches of the trees seemed to drip with silvery clouds.

"How lovely," she exclaimed and then saw the wry look in Neill's eyes. "What are those silvery things?"

"Spiderwebs, I'd say."

"Spiderwebs!" She gave a little shriek and shrank against him. "You mean there are such big spiders in New Orleans?"

He laughed and held her close. "Not the kind to fear, dear love. But I heard that the Baron does everything in a big way. To prepare for this ball he had thousands of spiders imported from China. He freed them around here so that they could spin their spectacular webs."

The webs were beautiful but also eerie, and Gabrielle was grateful when they were out of the shadow of the spiderwebs and driving down a well-cleared pathway toward a gracious, two-story house, which was surrounded by formal French gardens lit by torches and lanterns. The gardens were exquisite, and Gabrielle was enchanted by the time Jeanot had driven them to the door of the baron's fine house and bowing footmen were helping her to descend.

She had expected to find a residence such as Governor Shirley enjoyed in Boston, but de Sandoville's home bore little resemblance to anything she had seen. Although it was clear that everyone of consequence in the city was there, the house still retained a sense of space. Someone had planned the Baron's residence with an eye to proportion, and though candles flared in crystal and bronze chandeliers, their light fell on the uncluttered elegance of the hallway. This hall led away to a staircase garlanded with roses, and then to a large room from which came the sound of music and dancing.

As Neill and Gabrielle were announced, a slender, slight man appeared in the doorway to greet them. He was elegantly attired in silver brocade and satin, and the aristocratic features beneath the powdered and queued wig proclaimed him to be the Baron even before he introduced himself. He bowed over Gabrielle's hand and shook Neill's as if they were his most important guests.

"I am grateful you have come," he told them. "My friend Monsieur Craddock and I have talked business often enough, but until now I have not had the honor of meeting a daughter of the Chevalier de Montfleuri."

"You knew my father, sir?" she asked, eagerly.

"I had the honor to serve at his side when we were both younger and fighting for Louis XV." He seemed about to say more, then checked himself. "He would have been proud and delighted to see the woman his daughter has become. Now you must both come and meet my wife and our friends."

The Baroness was taller than her husband, a gentle, gracious lady who performed the introductions to bewigged and bejeweled men and women. Though Neill seemed to know many of them, she did not, and as she tried to remember everyone's title and name, Gabrielle saw that many of the young men were eyeing her with frank admiration. Wait until I tell the Señora that she was right, she thought, amused.

One of the peers to whom they were introduced had also known Gabrielle's father and spoke of him in glowing terms. "It was a tragic day for France when the Chevalier died. He was a good soldier, a gallant officer and a fine man. I often wondered why your mother did not bring his family back to France."

Seeing that Gabrielle hesitated to speak of the family's poverty, Neill intervened. "Circumstances prevented this return," he explained. "It is a long story, sir."

"As long as it does not have to do with politics, we must hear it someday." The Baroness de Sandoville now interrupted. "I am exhausted with talk of politics, which my husband indulges in each day. The British did this, the British did that—we are never free of talk of this miserable war with Britain." She checked herself and added with concern, "But then, forgive me. I forget that you are English yourself, Monsieur Craddock."

"Alas, Madame." Neill's smile was somewhat dry. "The courtesy my countrymen have offered Mademoiselle de Montfleuri and myself lately hasn't endeared them to me."

The Baron pursed his lips. "Since you have said so much, my friend, let me add that many here abhor English policy in Acadia. Some wretched deportees have come here, and I for one have done my best to welcome them and help them rebuild their lives. I wonder what would happen in the English colonies—say, in Boston—if your King suddenly tried to impose his will on his people and deported them from their homes?"

The Baron's words caused several people to

crane their necks to hear Neill's terse reply. "We wouldn't stand for it, sir. The King would have to rescind his decision. But I could hardly credit King George with such idiocy, unless he were badly advised by his ministers."

"He is right—*sacré Dieu,* he's right," yelped one of the old men who was standing nearby. "What do kings know, *hein?* Our own King's court is riddled with intrigue and he appoints fools and rascals to high positions. Look at de Rochemore, who has more than once attempted to blacken the name of our good Governor. De Rochemore was appointed by addle-pated ministers at court . . ."

Other voices now joined in. Noblemen, men of business and young officers argued or agreed passionately. Catching Neill's eye, the Baron smiled.

"We are fortunate that we are able to speak our minds here. But free speech may not always be wise here in Louisiana or in your own colonies, Monsieur Craddock."

Before Neill could answer, the Governor and Mademoiselle de Kerlerac were announced, and soon afterward dancing began. As the Governor and his lady led the first set, Neill offered Gabrielle his arm. "Do you want to dance and show off that lovely dress?"

She shook her head. "The floor is so crowded now, and the Governor and his lady are leading a set. Perhaps later."

"In that case let's walk a little and see the gardens." Pleased, she nodded, and Neill sidestepped a pair of young officers who had been eyeing Gabrielle and twirling their mustaches, obviously trying to work up the courage to seek an introduction. "There are too many people here. I find I want to be alone for a moment with my lady of the forest."

"That's what I want, too." They left the great room and stepped through a side door into the cool fragrance of a formal French garden. Here chairs had been set for the guests' comfort, and lamps glowed softly over the carefully trimmed rosebushes. Ignoring the chairs, Neill drew Gabrielle into the darkness beyond the perimeter of lamplight.

"What are you thinking about? Your father?" he prompted.

She raised her face to him, her dark eyes a little troubled. "How did you know? I was thinking that our host the Baron might know something that he did not tell me about my father. It's a feeling I have."

He bent and brushed the soft mouth with his own. "We'll find a moment to talk with the Baron later. Meanwhile . . ."

Her mouth was eager for his kiss, and as they took their pleasure with a deliberate passion that left them both shaken, Neill knew that he could never have enough of the taste and feel of her mouth or of the cool, flower-scented fragrance of her skin. Not though they lived forever would he tire of the way she trembled when he pleased her, when she wanted his loving . . .

"Oh, Monsieur, Madame, please. Don't step on the roses!"

The agitated voice brought them back to reality. Guiltily, they looked about them and saw that they had strayed from the carefully laid-out path and stood among the flowers. A man, obviously a gardener, was on his knees in the dirt, carefully scooping earth over exposed roots.

"Pardon, please," he was saying apologetically, "but these little roses, they were planted only this morning."

His voice was somehow familiar. "But I know you, Monsieur," Gabrielle exclaimed.

At the sound of her voice, the gardener lifted his head. "Oh, *sacré Dieu*," he exclaimed. "Gabrielle! Monsieur Neill!"

Clumsy with astonishment, he got to his feet and the lamplight fell on his face.

It was Guy Richaud.

Chapter Fourteen

ALMOST BESIDE HERSELF WITH ASTONISHMENT
and joy, Gabrielle embraced the stocky gardener. "I can't believe you're here! Are Marthe and
Thérèse with you?"

Weeping, Guy nodded. "Yes, by the grace of *le
bon Dieu* and Monsieur Neill." Then, turning to
Neill, he shook both the big Englishman's
hands. "If it had not been for your help and the
money you lent me, I would never have left
Virginia."

"How did you find your family?" Neill asked,
and Guy launched into his story. Andrew
Warrensbody had found passage for him on a
ship that had taken him to Georgia, where
Marthe and Thérèse had been let off *The
Lovely Lady*. After the initial joy of reunion,
however, the Richauds had decided to move on.

"We were not welcomed there," Guy explained
sadly. "We were outcasts, regarded always with

221

suspicion. We heard rumors that farther south, in New Orleans, French people would welcome us, and as I had your gold, Monsieur, it was possible to come here." He shook Neill's hand again, this time with reverence. "It took us many weeks to come here, but then the good God smiled on us again, for Monsieur *le* Baron engaged me as a gardener and my Marthe and Thérèse have been employed as maids. We have been given a little house behind the baronial residence."

"Please take me to Marthe and Thérèse," Gabrielle begged, but Guy was shocked.

"You are guests of the Baron," he protested. "You can come and see us anytime."

That was not good enough for Gabrielle. "I have worried about you and prayed for you so long that I won't wait another moment," she declared.

Neill agreed. "I, too, would like to see your family again, Guy."

Beaming, Guy led them away from the gardens and down a well-swept path that led to the servants' quarters. A good-sized building housed the Baron's unmarried employees, and many smaller cottages had been built for married servants. Guy pointed to one. "Home," he said proudly.

Gabrielle's eyes filled with tears and her throat contracted. Limned against the starlight, Guy's wooden house was no more than a shack. There was no resemblance between this place and the neat, well-to-do farmhouse he had had back in Laforet. But her sorrow only lasted for a moment. At Guy's shout, Thérèse and Marthe came running out of the small house, and Gabrielle nearly tumbled into her old friends' arms.

"*Petite*—my dear little one, I am so glad to see you again, I don't know whether I am standing on my feet or on my head," Marthe wept. She then turned to Neill and embraced him also. "When Guy told me what you had done for us, I swore that when you came to my house, I would seat you in the best chair in my house and cook you the best meal you had ever had in your life. I can't say much for the chair, but the meal you shall have immediately."

"Marthe, they must return to the ball," Guy protested.

"At least, come back to the house with us. I will make some *chocolat* and we can talk—ah, we have so much to tell each other." Laughing and crying, Marthe drew them into the hut, and once inside, Gabrielle blinked back tears again, for in spite of its smallness the place was home. The dirt floor had been swept neatly, and a bouquet of wildflowers stood in a large clay vase by the door. Guy had fashioned some chairs, a table and two bedsteads out of wood and palmetto leaves, and in a special corner of the room was Marthe's spinning wheel. Gabrielle went to the wheel and touched it gently, running her fingers over the fine old wood.

"You managed to keep this during all your journey," she murmured.

Marthe nodded. "It was a heavy weight to carry around, but I knew it wouldn't be home without my spinning wheel."

Neill, watching Gabrielle's face, knew that she was thinking of the terrible day when Dray had smashed her spinning wheel. He came to her and put an arm around her waist, and she leaned back against him. "It doesn't matter, you mustn't worry," she told him, but he heard the sadness in her voice and damned Dray and Lampert and all the other stupid, callous officials sent by King George.

"This way, Monsieur Neill." Marthe was dusting off one of the chairs. "Sit you down and be comfortable with Guy, while Thérèse and I make the *chocolat*." Gabrielle offered her help, but Marthe was scandalized. "In that beautiful dress? *Petite*, you must not even come near the cooking. Still, I want to hear everything that happened to you."

The cooking fires were outside. Standing under the white stars, Gabrielle recounted the story of her journey to Philadelphia, their adventures in Virginia and the Carolinas. When she came to the story of the storm and her rescue, Marthe stared at her young friend.

"Monsieur Neill is strong," she exclaimed. "It's not everyone who can fight seas like that and win." She paused and then asked, "Is he your lover?" Gabrielle met the older woman's eyes and nodded. "What about Monsieur Chauvin?" Marthe persisted.

"I looked for him and Simon. God knows I tried—" She made a little, helpless gesture. "I love Neill," she said, simply. "I think I always have."

Marthe sighed. "I understand. Maybe if we were back in Laforet, I would have been horrified at your breaking the betrothal vows, but everything that has happened since we left our home has taught me that love is the most precious thing in the world." She kissed Gabrielle's cheek. "Be happy with Monsieur Neill, *petite*."

Gabrielle felt as if a heavy weight had rolled away from her heart. Heedless of her dress and Marthe's shocked protests, she hugged her old friend joyfully. "I didn't care what anyone would think or say except you," she confessed. "And, Marthe, I am happy with him. I sometimes feel as if I could soar with the eagles."

Marthe grinned. "Obviously, *le bon Dieu* meant you for each other."

The steaming chocolate was served in crude mugs fashioned of clay, but Gabrielle thought she had never tasted anything as delicious. She was happier than she had ever been, as she sat close to Neill and listened to her old friends talking. If only Simon were here, she thought, her joy would have been complete.

She carried that happiness back to the Baron's ball when at last they returned, and she was radiant as she danced throughout the glittering night. Whether she danced with Neill or graced the arm of de Sandoville and later the Governor, Neill saw how all the men at the ball followed her with their eyes. The ladies, too, seemed captivated by Gabrielle and her story. Many invited her to their homes before the long night had at last grayed into dawn, and the Baron's servants began to offer cups of coffee and gumbo to refresh homegoing guests.

All during the ball Gabrielle had not seemed at all tired, but going home in the carriage, she nestled into the familiar circle of Neill's arm. She sighed her contentment as he bent to brush her lips with his. "You must be happy," he commented. "You're purring like a kitten."

"It was a wonderful ball. And to see our friends again after so long—it's like a miracle. Marthe and Thérèse and Guy look wonderfully happy."

"I hope it will last." There was a sober note in his voice, and she looked up at him surprised. "There was a lot of talking going on while you were capturing everyone's heart, my love. New Orleans isn't a perfect paradise. There's trouble with nearby Indian tribes, problems between religious factions in the city, political bickering between the Governor and his aides. There's also some fear that there may be an English invasion."

All thought of sleep gone, she broke in. "I hope you are wrong. Haven't we had enough wars and pain to last us twenty lifetimes?"

He didn't answer her directly. "Do you remember what Paul Revere said in Boston? The people of New Orleans feel the same way—that many of their problems arise because France is too far away to govern its colonies properly." He added thoughtfully, "I've just had a strange notion. It's not impossible that someday the colonies of France and England might become allies."

Her laughter stopped him. "Now I know you are joking."

He laughed, too, shaking off his serious mood. "You're right. I should never discuss politics. They have a strange effect on me."

He began to kiss her in the dark carriage, his mouth turning her bones to warm honey so that she hardly realized when they returned home to

226

Chartres Street, and once in their room, they kissed again, their tongues touching, their breaths mingling as they sought more and even more closeness.

One hand rose up to let loose the upswept masses of her hair so that they fell loose about her bare shoulders in fragrant profusion, and he kissed her again before turning his attention to the hooks and clasps of her dress. "This is a beautiful creation, my love," he told her, "but it has too many damned buttons."

"That's because you're so impatient." She pretended to scold him, but her own fingers trembled with hurry as she helped him undo the laces and buttons and the beautiful dress sighed to the ground, followed by her hoops, the lace and silk of her shift. He would have stopped now to kiss her shoulders and breasts, but she would have none of it. "I'm in a hurry, too," she admitted.

His coat, the vest, the immaculate linen and lace of his shirt—and then a pause to hold each other close, breast to chest. Now it was she who undid his breeches and drew them down, making an erotic ceremony of running the palms of her small hands down his tense thighs and legs. And when, free of clothing, he turned to take her in his arms, she stopped him once more. "Let me," she murmured.

Standing close together, swaying a little, they kissed, and he let her have her way as she kissed his shoulders and the thick fur of his chest and caressed the flat male nipples with her tongue. Then she knelt to follow the line of the tawny fur to his belly, caressing and teasing with her lips while her hands stroked downward, over the front and back of his thighs, feeling the spring of iron muscle under her fingers.

"In this way and this, the golden tiger must be pleasured." He heard the soft huskiness of her purr and held himself under control as her hands and lips brought indescribable excitement. Her hair touched him like silken fingers, her upright nipples thrust against his thighs as she began to retrace the sensual path her lips had made on his body, straying nearer and nearer yet to his hardness, but not yet touching him.

"Gabrielle," he protested, but when he would have drawn her up into his arms, she only laughed softly and shook her head.

"You've had your way too often, dear love. Tonight, it's my turn."

Her hands roved willfully over his back and buttocks, holding him prisoner while her lips grazed the periphery of his passion, touched, drew back. But when he felt the warmth of her tongue and lips on him, he could wait no longer. Lifting her in his arms, he drew her softness against him, felt the leap of her heart against his.

"The tiger is thoroughly tamed," he told her between swift, passionate kisses.

Glorying in the tremor of his strong arms, she let him draw her to the bed and onto it, and sinking deep into the welcome of cool sheets and pillows, she wrapped her arms about his neck and held him to her. "Show me how tame you have become," she commanded.

His first, deep thrusts brought a gasp of pleasure. Enveloped in the wine-sweet richness of her, he now paused to kiss and stroke her hair, suckle first one and then the other nipple. Then they moved again, together. Deeper. Faster. His hipbones grated against hers, and her soft cry of pleasure formed against his mouth.

"Neill, let this be forever. I want to be together like this—for always."

"For always," he agreed.

And when they were swept up beyond the earth, when they shattered again and yet again and slowly spiraled back to reality, they were still together. Still one.

Throughout the warm winter months, their happiness grew unchecked, and it seemed to Gabrielle that they did little besides grow closer, did nothing except enjoy each other's company and find new pleasure and tenderness in each other's arms.

Actually, it wasn't so. The Baroness de Sandoville had taken a fancy to Gabrielle and often sought her company. So did the Señora Alejandro and many other ladies. Neill's days were also full, for he was becoming more involved in plans to challenge the trade and development monopoly of the Company of the East Indies. And, Neill wrote Sam, future expansion of the C. and C. into this new and fertile area seemed indeed possible.

Sam's enthusiastic agreement, together with a supply of gold, arrived via a Dutch schooner at the end of February, and there was also a warm and friendly letter from Abigail to Gabrielle. Glad as she was to get this letter, Gabrielle knew it wasn't the one she had been waiting and hoping for. There was still no news from San Domingo, and because she worried that Neill's first letter had not reached Louis Chauvin, he wrote another. This, too, remained unanswered.

"Do you think he has received the letters and is too angry to reply?" Gabrielle asked Marthe, who frowned as she shook her head.

"If it were any other man, I'd say perhaps you were right, but Monsieur Chauvin has always been so kind to you," she said. "I'm sure there's another reason for his silence, so don't worry."

Gabrielle tried to follow Marthe's advice, but it was not easy. Even if she could put Louis Chauvin out of her mind, there was Simon to think about, and she constantly worried over him. She tried not to let these anxieties cloud her happiness with Neill, but he couldn't help knowing how she felt and damning Chauvin for his silence.

One afternoon he found her sitting on a bench in the garden staring unseeingly at a blaze of bougainvillea and hibiscus that grew near the pond. An unread book was in her lap, and a line of worry puckered her forehead. She hardly heard his steps until he was beside her, and even then the anxious look didn't leave her eyes.

"They're worrying you again, Simon and Chauvin," he said abruptly.

"Jeanot told me that a ship from the islands put into port today. I sent him down at once to see if there was word, but . . ."

"I, too, heard of that ship." He sat down beside her and took both hands in his. They were cold in spite of the warmth of the day, and he rubbed them gently and wished there was something he could say to explain this continued lack of news from Chauvin.

Before he found the words, she spoke again in a low, fearful tone. "Supposing he doesn't agree to dissolve the betrothal pledge?"

"There's no reason why he wouldn't." And, Neill thought grimly, he would make sure of that. "There's no need to worry, Gabrielle. I'll sail to San Domingo and speak to the man personally."

He was unprepared for the force of her reaction. "No," she cried and turned to throw her arms around his neck. She pressed her cheek against his as she whispered, "You must not. I cannot let you go. It has taken us so long to find each other, and I never want to be away from you again."

Holding her tightly, he stroked her dark hair to soothe her. "Darling, listen to me. It's high time we were married, and I'm willing to seek Mr. Chauvin out, even though I care little for his blessing."

She drew in a deep breath of his beloved scent and listened to his deep voice. "There's no need for you to go to San Domingo," she said then. "We have done all we could. Rather than have you hazard another journey for me, I will marry you without Monsieur Chauvin's consent."

"Are you sure?" He had waited for this moment a long time, but now he was uncertain. He wanted nothing to mar their life together. But now that her decision had been made, her voice had an unmistakable lilt of joy in it.

"You are my man, my life. Wherever you are will be my home."

He knew that this was a hard decision for her, and that for love of him she was giving up the code and beliefs of her people. His voice was rough with feeling when he spoke. "Strange that you should mention home. That's why I came out here to find you." She asked what he meant, and he took the book away from her and got up to draw her to her feet. "Come with me and you'll see."

She followed wonderingly, but he would not answer her questions and, when she persisted, told her such outrageous fibs that she was laughing her lovely, husky laugh as they came into the main room of the house. Then the laughter died away and her eyes grew wide.

In the middle of the room stood a spinning wheel like the one she had wanted to bring with her from Laforet. It had been painstakingly crafted, and the wood gleamed with hours of polish.

"Do you like it? I had it made specially, with Marthe's advice," Neill said, but she couldn't answer him. Wordless, she took a few steps forward and touched the wheel. It turned against her hand, the wood warm and welcoming. Memories filled her mind and heart: the quiet voice of her mother as she talked of France and the brave chevalier who had been her husband; Simon, dark eyes snapping with pleasure as he praised a shirt that she had made for him; the bright fire snapping logs in the fireplace and the winter howling outside, while Guy Richaud told her and Simon the story of the Indian lovers . . .

"You always know what I feel, what I think." She whispered and turned her head away so that he wouldn't see the tears. He saw them anyway and lifted her chin to kiss them away. "Only you could have understood how much I have missed this." She turned the wheel again and gave a small, shaky laugh. "I fear I'm no knight's daughter after all, but only a simple village woman at heart. I'll be happiest when I am spinning for you and for our children."

His voice was husky as he said, "And I'll share your happiness. But you are wrong about being a great lady. Don't you remember that you're the queen of my heart?"

Before she could reply, Maria entered the room with a letter for Neill. He opened and read it, then handed it to Gabrielle. It was an unexpected invitation from the Baron, bidding him to an early supper. "But you must hurry," Gabrielle exclaimed, "or you will be late."

He rubbed a thumb along the wooden wheel in front of him. "I can think of better things to do with my evening."

She kissed him and then reproved him gently. "But this is what you have wanted and waited for. Of course you must go. There will be much business talk, and I know how hard you have been working to get these important men together so that you can convince them to trade with the C. and C."

"You sound as if you're a wife already." She chuckled and he kissed her, adding, "I'll make sure it's an early evening."

"Don't worry on my account." She gave the

spinning wheel a turn. "Do you know that I have with me some fine, carded wool from Laforet? I never threw it away, even though I knew it would be useless without a spinning wheel. Tonight I will begin to spin thread so that I can make my golden tiger a shirt for our wedding day."

Arms around each other they went upstairs, and while he dressed for his evening with the Baron, she hunted and found the wool. Later, she accompanied him to the door of the house and kissed him a loving goodbye before he mounted the horse Jeanot held for him and rode away. For a long moment she stood watching him, and then she returned to the spinning wheel.

The first spin of the wheel brought memories back again, but as soon as she had begun her work, her mind slid away into a warm and happy contemplation of the future. She thought of how the thread she wove would become a warm shirt for Neill, how someday she would get the finest wool to create the finest of clothing for their first child. A child with Neill's hair and eyes, a golden, beautiful babe.

She heard the sound of carriage wheels in the courtyard outside, but she was reluctant to stop her spinning. Perhaps Señora Alejandro had come to visit, or Marthe wanted to see how she did with her new spinning wheel . . .

She heard Maria opening the front door and the sound of a man's voice, and reluctantly, she stopped her spinning. No doubt some business acquaintance of Neill's had stopped to call. She got to her feet as footsteps approached down the hall and the door opened.

"I regret that Monsieur Craddock is not at home—" she began, then stopped. Her eyes went wide, her hand to her mouth.

"*Sacré nom,*" she whispered. "It's you!"

Chapter Fifteen

"THIS WAY, MONSIEUR, IF YOU PLEASE. MONsieur *le* Baron is expecting you."

Dusk had fallen while Neill rode to the Baron's residence, and the candles in the hallway had been lit. No musicians or exquisitely gowned women graced the house today, but half a dozen carriages, including one that carried the Governor's coat-of-arms, stood outside in the courtyard. The Baron himself came forward, hand outstretched, to greet his guest at the door of his study.

"My friend—you are welcome." Bowing in response to the Baron's greeting, Neill glanced around the room. It was evidently de Sandoville's study, for the walls were lined with books and a finely carved desk stood in a corner. Ensconced in a comfortable-looking chair by this desk was the Governor. A dozen other men of wealth and prestige also graced the room, and

Neill felt both surprise and pleasurable excitement. The fact that he had been invited to such a gathering boded well for his efforts in behalf of the C. and C.

"We've been awaiting your arrival impatiently." The Baron linked his arm in Neill's and drew him to the center of the room. "His Excellency, especially, has been anxious to hear your ideas concerning trade."

Neill greeted the Governor with respectful interest. After his initial brief meeting with de Kerlerac, he had hoped for a longer interview with him. "Your Excellency does me honor," he said. "However, my ideas are not original. Monsieur *le* Baron and many others here in New Orleans share my opinion that monopolies stifle healthy competition." As everyone in the room seemed to be listening he added, "John Law's Company of the East Indies may not be in the best interests of New Orleans. This is a large and rich area, and trade and development should be undertaken by more than one business concern."

The Governor's rather severe face was thoughtful. "As you know, your country and mine are at war."

"True, Your Excellency, but wars don't last forever, and today's enemies may be tomorrow's allies."

De Kerlerac shifted uneasily in his chair. "De Sandoville tells me that you were a military man. So was I. For years I have been afraid of an English naval invasion of New Orleans, but I can tell you that I am even more afraid of backbiting bureaucrats and powerful monopolies." He paused. "How does your C. and C. differ from the many other trading companies anxious to challenge the Company of the East Indies?"

Neill had his answer ready. "The point I would make is that we are a company of the New World," he said. "While John Law's company has its roots in Europe, ours are here. The C. and C. isn't as large as its rivals, but we're a young and aggressive concern that does business with almost all of the English colonies."

"You also conducted this business in Canada, did you not?" the Baron prompted as Neill paused.

"British Canada," one of the other men in the room pointed out somewhat disdainfully.

"Not exclusively. We hoped to open trade negotiations in furs with Chauvin Company in Acadia. Unfortunately, Lawrence's order to deport the Acadians ruined that hope." Neill turned back to the Governor and added earnestly, "A company bred and based in the Americas can understand and deal with colonists in this country. A company based in Europe thinks differently."

Before he could continue, one of the guests rose excitedly to his feet. "He speaks the truth," he exclaimed. "It's the same with governments. Why else would our King be considering the idiocy of handing Louisiana over to Spain?"

Neill was astonished. "I've not heard of this."

"It's merely a rumor," the Baron protested, but the heated words had set off a chain reaction. Amid the arguments that followed, Neill found himself listening thoughtfully. The loud, often passionate voices were French, but otherwise they reminded him of Sam Culpepper's friends, speaking at the Red Dragon Inn. He couldn't shunt aside what he was hearing as mere rhetoric, either, for these men were talking about freedom and opportunity, of colonies that governed themselves.

"A heady concept, though probably unworkable." The Baron had made his way to Neill's side. "Colonies, alas, are meant to be governed, and my loyalty is still to His Majesty King Louis. And you, Monsieur Craddock?"

Neill hesitated. "I find that what has happened to me and those dear to me in the past few months has made me question those loyalties."

"You are, of course, talking of the lovely Mademoiselle de Montfleuri." The Baron shook his head and smiled a little. "Not that you are to blame. My wife has become enchanted with the lovely lady, and so have I. Our only regret is that the daughter of a French aristocrat was subjected to such unhappiness. She and her brother should have been raised on their father's estates."

"It wasn't possible. After the Chevalier's death, his family was left penniless in Acadia. There was no money to return to France."

"So she told my wife, but I don't believe a word of it."

Neill frowned. "Meaning what, sir?"

Servants were offering refreshments: goblets of chilled wine and fine pastries, thick gumbo and coffee served in eggshell-thin porcelain. The Baron chose two goblets of wine and offered one to Neill.

"I don't mean to say that I doubt Mademoiselle de Montfleuri's word—not at all. But it's not true that there was no estate for her and her brother. There's an inheritance in France awaiting your lovely lady, an inheritance that will make her very wealthy indeed."

"But that's impossible." Neill set down his glass of wine and spoke earnestly. "Forgive me, sir, but how do you know this?"

"I have made inquiries, Monsieur Craddock." The Baron put a hand on Neill's arm, adding, "Perhaps it was meddling, but what my Baroness learned from Mademoiselle Gabrielle disturbed me. I had been a friend of the Chevalier, after all. I wrote letters to men of integrity at court, inquiring about the de Montfleuri inheritance."

"And?"

The Baron leaned closer. "My friend, the replies I received were almost identical. The Montfleuri children are heirs to an enormous sum of money. The lawyers in charge of the estate wrote of this to Acadia when the Chevalier died, but it appears that his widow put her whole trust in the hands of one, Louis Chauvin."

"Chauvin." Neill's voice suddenly cracked with understanding. "That's why he was so kind to her. Christ, sir, why didn't you tell me this before?"

"I only received replies to the letters today." Apologetically, the Baron cleared his throat. "That is the real reason I asked you to come today, my friend." There was a small pause and then he added, "My wife has told me that your lady needs Chauvin's consent before she breaks her betrothal vows and marries you. He'll never give his consent, of course."

Neill would have liked to question his host further, but there was no more chance for private discussion. The talk had turned from politics back to trade, and Neill was asked many questions about the C. and C. He tried to answer them as best he could, but he couldn't concentrate. Instead, he thought of Gabrielle as he had first seen her on her betrothal day, her arm linked with Chauvin's. His blood seethed when he realized how Chauvin had lied to her family all these years and had trapped her into marriage. What would she think of Chauvin now, and more important, how would this new knowledge affect the future?

He considered this question sometime later when he was riding down the Baron's long tree-shaded carriageway. The evening's disclosure brought problems. Gabrielle, and Simon, too, wherever he was, were heirs to a great fortune in France . . .

The incomplete thought trailed away from Neill's mind as he heard a sound in the trees ahead of him. His senses alert, he slowed his horse imperceptibly, and the sound came again: the soft, swiftly hushed stamp of a concealed horse. Then, as if to offer further proof, he heard the unseen animal snort and whicker. He had no idea how many were there or why, but he was being stalked.

And he had come unarmed to the Baron's house. Neill spurred his horse forward but as he did so saw mounted shadows spilling into the path ahead of him. With a sudden, loud shout to startle them, he made straight for them and saw them scatter to avoid a collision, then group together to ride in pursuit. Let the bastards try to catch up to me, he thought grimly.

Thundering hooves tore at the ground as he careened through the dark canopy of trees. He was almost at the end of the roadway and could see the open sky beyond when he realized that the way was blocked. At the end of the row of trees waited another half-dozen mounted men. Neill turned to look over his shoulder and saw that more pursued him.

He swerved his horse toward the trees and saw men waiting there, too. Perhaps he could crash through them—but as the thought formed, one of the men spoke jeeringly in gutter French. "Don't try it. I've got a pistol trained on you. Move, and you're a dead man."

"If you fire that thing, they'll hear the report at the house and come after you." He spoke with cold deliberation, but his mind was working furiously, looking for a weak link in the circle that surrounded him. Meanwhile, the one who had spoken ordered him to dismount.

"We want to talk to you, Englishman."

"Think I'd waste my breath on scum like you? From what gutter did you ignorant bastards crawl?" Neill's voice dripped with contempt, while his powerful body tensed to move as soon as they took the bait. "You're filthy swine, fit only for the dungheap where you were conceived . . ."

With a yell of fury, one of the shadows sprang forward, and faint light flared off the blade of an ugly curved sword. At that moment, Neill spurred his horse forward and rode full tilt toward his attacker. At the last moment he veered a hair's-breadth away, and, catching the fellow by the shoulder, dragged him out of the saddle. As the man shouted and fell, Neill broke through the ring about him and galloped free.

He heard the shouts and threats that followed him and then the crack of a pistol and the burning rush of a ball passing close to his head. There was another crack and a ball passed closer. A third crack and his horse stumbled and went down.

For a moment the heavy weight of the struggling animal pinned him down, then Neill managed to pull loose and get to his feet. The horse, uninjured, struggled up also, but before he could remount, his attackers closed in on him.

There was not much hope against such numbers, but he fought grimly, charging the first of the ruffians and knocking the wind out of the man. Then he tore the knife from the man's nerveless fingers and with it parried a vicious cut aimed at him by a saber-wielding shadow, then lunged forward to find that shadow's heart. As this adversary fell, he heard the leader's bellow.

"Don't waste any more time. Sacred devil, do you want to fail like the others did? Get out of the way so I can shoot the bastard."

How many of them were there? Ten—no, nine, for one man lay dead. Neill slashed up with his knife and sent another of his attackers to hell. Desperately, he kept them between him and the wavering pistol, and as he did so, his mind flashed back to what their leader had said. What others?

There wasn't time to think of it now. Neill parried a blow with his knife, and then, as he sidestepped another attacker, slipped on spilled blood. It was what they had been waiting for, and they closed in. As he tried to get to his feet, he saw the man with the pistol aiming it for his chest.

"Goodbye, Craddock," the man jeered.

The pistol cracked and Neill's body, expecting its death blow, jerked with tension. Nothing happened. Then Neill saw that the man with the pistol was slowly crumpling forward and that more riders were cantering toward them through the trees.

"Au secours, to the rescue," it was the voice of the Baron de Sandoville, and taking advantage of their momentary confusion, Neill regained his feet and hurled himself at the ruffians. He knocked one down and wrested away his sword, and the man took to his heels followed by his companions. Neill's mounted rescuers swept after them.

"Ah, I feel young again tonight. That's how we all acted when we were in our youth and hunting game in France." Looking up, Neill saw that Baron de Sandoville had reined in beside him. "Are you hurt? You're covered with blood."

"It's not mine. Thanks to you, I'm still alive," he said gratefully.

The Baron shrugged off such thanks. "We were standing outside my house saying our goodbyes when we heard you shout, and we sensed you needed help. You fought heroically. If you hadn't, you'd have perished." He looked contemptuously at the dead on the ground. "Have you any idea who these swine are?"

Neill shook his head, for a new and greater anxiety had formed in his mind. "No, but they knew me. I must get home. Gabrielle is alone."

He whistled for his horse and remounted, but as he pulled on the reins, the Baron caught his arm.

"I, too, am concerned. I will ride with you. Wait until I have called the others."

But Neill did not wait to see who followed as he galloped back toward the city. Again, the ruffian leader's words returned, and now he understood them. The attack on the road to Philadelphia, the reception he had received in Williamsburg, Phineas Cole who had tried to murder him in the warehouse—all these formed a pattern. Everything that had happened to them since leaving Boston had all been part of a plan—and the plan could only be Chauvin's.

He turned the corner of the street and swore aloud as he saw the gate of his rented house swinging agape. The front door was open, too, and in the hallway lay Jeanot, moaning and covered with blood.

Stepping over him and shouting Gabrielle's name, Neill ran into the room where he had left her. The room gave mute evidence of a struggle. The spinning wheel lay upended on the ground, the wool she had been using was scattered all over. Chairs and a small table had been overturned. "Gabrielle!" he cried again.

A low moan came from nearby, and the sound

froze his blood. As he followed the moans to the next room, he found Maria lying tied and gagged on the ground.

Neill fell on his knees to free her. "Maria, where is she?" he cried.

Her first words confirmed every fear he had had. "They took her, the men," Maria groaned. "Jeanot and I—tried to stop them. No use . . ."

Killing rage filled Neill and he struggled with it. That wouldn't help Gabrielle now. With an effort he pulled his thoughts together into a single purpose. "What did they look like, these men who took her?"

The Houma servant struggled to a sitting position. "There were many of them, but their leader was a thin man with a big black spot here." She indicated her cheek. "Madame knew him, that one. She argued with him, pleaded . . ."

"Chauvin."

Neill didn't know he had snarled the one word aloud until Maria nodded. "That was his name, yes. He ordered his men to bind and gag Madame. He said he was going to take her away on a ship."

"Where, Maria?" Neill's voice was urgent, but it was the Baron, striding now into the room, who furnished this vital piece of information.

"Your manservant remembers the swine mentioning a word as they carried your lady away," he told Neill. "It was an unfamiliar name and they hit him soon after, but he remembers that it sounded like 'William.'"

"Williamsburg." Neill got to his feet. "Chauvin's taking her to Virginia. He'll have taken her to the dock—perhaps I can still stop them."

But at the docks, Neill was greeted with more bad news. There had been a sloop sailing for Virginia, yes, but it had sailed with the tide three hours ago. As Neill demanded the next available transport, the Baron interposed.

"My friend, I feel responsible for this. Had I told you earlier what I suspected about your lady's inheritance, this might not have occurred. I keep a vessel for my own personal use. Permit me to put it at your disposal. You'll need weapons, too, and I would like to send as many of my servants as you may need to help you recover your lady from this beast Chauvin."

Neill shook his head. "Frenchmen in an English colony would be a liability. I'm going alone, but I gratefully accept your offer of a ship and of weapons, sir." His voice was tautly, furiously controlled as he added, "As for Chauvin, he's going to answer to me."

Chapter Sixteen

IN AN AGONY OF IMPATIENCE AND ANXIETY, GAB-
rielle paced the floor of her luxurious cabin and
listened to the shouting as Chauvin's ship prepared to drop anchor off the coast of Virginia.
During this long journey from the mouth of the
Mississippi, she had been treated like captive
royalty. Nothing had been too good for her comfort except her freedom. After all, this was
Chauvin's ship and she was his prisoner.

Chauvin—the name stuck in her throat like a
bone she couldn't dislodge. Ever since she'd
looked up from her spinning wheel and seen his
face, she had been living a nightmare. She had
tried to explain in New Orleans, but he hadn't
listened. Nor had she seen him since the evening he and his henchmen had subdued her,
gagged and bound her and carried her to this
ship. She knew that he was on board also, but he
never came on deck when she was permitted

fresh air, and he did not visit her cabin. He had ignored all her requests that they meet, and when she pleaded for news of Simon, he had sent word through the ship's steward that Simon was in Virginia and that she would see him when they made landfall.

Through her cabin's round window she could see the familiar sweep of coastline and the wharf and dock. She knew she should be glad about the prospect of seeing her brother again, and yet she could only think that even though it was now February, Yorktown in winter hadn't changed since she had come here with Neill.

She spoke his name in her heart, wishing desperately that he could hear her and knowing that this hope was futile. She had seen poor Jeanot lying in his blood and feared he and Maria were dead. Neill would have found them so. There was no way he could know who had kidnapped her or where she was. And though her yearning for him was a physical ache, though she had never loved him more, she also had never felt so far away from him.

It was this that had made the journey such a hell, for she wasn't really afraid for herself. She knew that Monsieur Chauvin had acted out of anger at her, but she couldn't believe that he would hurt her. If she could only talk to him, as she had talked to him in the old days in Laforet, she knew that she would be able to explain. Perhaps then Monsieur Chauvin would send her back to New Orleans and the man she loved.

There was a knock on the cabin door, but instead of the ship's steward it was Chauvin who opened the door. "Time to go ashore, Gabrielle."

"Please," she began, "we must talk . . ."

"Later. We'll have time on the way to Williamsburg to do all the talking you wish." He was smiling as he added, "A great deal has happened since we were separated."

Following him on deck and into the waiting longboat, she studied him. Dressed in the height of fashion with a warm, fur-collared cloak over natty corduroy breeches and coat, he looked prosperous and confident, not like a man whose fortunes had been wiped out by Governor Lawrence's deportation order. But then he'd probably been able to raise money in San Domingo. Memory of how she had honestly tried to follow him gave her the courage to try again to explain.

"Monsieur Chauvin, I tried to find you."

He smiled as he cut her short. "Of course you did, Gabrielle. After all, I had Simon with me, and you were concerned about him."

"He's well?" she asked anxiously. "You never told me anything about him, except that I would see him here in Virginia." He didn't answer and she begged, "Please, Monsieur, tell me."

"He's well." There seemed to be a smug note in his voice, but he looked serious as he continued, "Simon is worried about you, of course. Neither of us imagined that you would so forget yourself and your vows as to come under the influence of that scoundrel Neill Craddock."

"Monsieur, I love him." When Chauvin didn't react, she added, "I know it seems like a betrayal. I know how angry you were and why you brought me here. But, Monsieur Chauvin, I'm going to marry Neill."

Chauvin's face hardened suddenly and she

thought she was looking at a stranger. When he spoke, his voice was cold, too. "You forget that I haven't released you from the betrothal vows," he said, sternly.

"Neill wrote to you so many times, Monsieur, but you never answered him." Desperation crept into her voice as she added, "Surely, you can't want to marry a woman who loves and—and has given herself to another man?"

The longboat touched the dock, and without answering he got out and helped her ashore. His grip was painful, but all he said was, "This way, Gabrielle. A carriage is waiting to take us to Williamsburg."

She asked him if Simon was in Williamsburg, but he didn't answer and there was nothing to do but follow him. As she set her foot on the step of the carriage, however, her heart leaped into her throat with sudden hope. Not too far away stood Andrew Warrensbody, talking to a group of men.

"Mr. Warrensbody." She had spoken without thought, and now felt the hard pressure of Chauvin's hand. She looked up to see the hard glitter in his eyes.

"Get in the carriage, Gabrielle," he was saying, but as he urged her into the conveyance, Gabrielle saw Warrensbody turn and look at her. Then Chauvin was pushing her into the carriage and following her. "Drive on," he called to the driver.

Had Warrensbody recognized her? Gabrielle's heart beat wildly. If he had, then he would write to Neill, surely. She felt her hopes soar, and then she heard Chauvin's chuckle. "You think you've been clever, don't you?" he said. She didn't reply and he added, "You really think that your Englishman will learn your whereabouts from his business agent and follow you?"

"How did you . . ."

His chuckle had become a laugh. "Poor innocent. I know a great deal about what goes on, believe me. However, even I didn't think you would so forget yourself as to take an English lover."

The distaste in his tone was shaded by mockery, and she looked at him sharply. Before she could question him, however, the carriage jolted forward, throwing her against him. Instantly, his arm clamped around her, drawing her close. "Let's see if I can't dislodge Craddock from your memory."

As moist lips sought hers, Gabrielle felt disjointed panic first and then disgust and anger. Wildly, she struggled against the kiss and heard him swearing. His arms became steel bands that clamped her against his chest, while one hand clawed at her breast. Sickened, hardly able to breathe, she still fought until finally he let her go.

"So," he said in an ugly voice, "the little dove has grown wild." He sucked at his wrist, and she saw that her nails had drawn blood. "It'll be a pleasure to tame you, Mademoiselle, but you'll knuckle under," he continued. "Our wedding night will show you who's master."

"I'm not going to marry you." She hadn't meant to spit it out at him, had meant to reason gently with him, make him see how deeply she loved Neill. Now she added, "Neill Craddock is the only man I want to marry. I won't let you touch me."

To her surprise, he began to laugh. "Bravo," he said, "I like a woman with spirit; they're more fun in bed." Then he added, "And you'll beg me to bed you, Gabrielle. You'll beg on your knees if you care anything about your brother."

She felt a new and terrible fear, but her voice held a quiet dignity. "Explain, Monsieur," she said.

He was silent for a moment, and when he spoke again his voice held reluctant respect. "Simon, my constant traveling companion, is about to go on another voyage, this time without me." He paused and then added softly, "I regret to say that he's going to England."

"To Eng—" she couldn't even finish the word but stared at him. "Why, in the name of God?" she gasped.

He explained that the Acadian men had been kept in the warehouse for most of the winter, but that eventually they had been freed. "Most of them cannot get decent work, of course, and King George in his infinite mercy is allowing Acadian volunteers to join his army so as to fight in the French-English wars. Simon was one of those who volunteered to fight for England."

"Volunteered—" into her mind swam a memory of Simon's unfaltering hatred for the English and also a picture of the English man-of-war she had seen en route to New Orleans. Its prisoners had likely been "volunteers" too.

"Not Simon," she whispered.

"I'm afraid that in my absence he got into

trouble, and Colonel Whitower decided that it was wisest to rid Williamsburg of the young firebrand." Chauvin paused and then reached out to take her hand. "But I could help—perhaps. Should I try?"

Wincing at his touch, she forced herself not to jerk her hand away. "Monsieur, you know how much Simon means to me," she said earnestly. "Anything you could do would make me forever grateful to you. But what could you do?"

"Perhaps nothing, perhaps a great deal." He let go of her hand to rub his thumb down her jawline and under her lower lip. "It would cost a great deal of money, Gabrielle, and I would have to humble myself before Colonel Whitower. But I would do it—for you. You see, I still want you to be my wife."

The thought of Simon conscripted into an army he loathed tore at her heart, and yet the idea of belonging to any man except Neill—she felt nauseated, and her breasts heaved with the effort it took not to pull away from his touch. "But I don't love you," she cried in desperation.

"That doesn't matter. You're young and have been through a terrible time." His voice had shed its mockery, become again the reasonable, kind voice she remembered from her childhood. "Poor Gabrielle, I don't reproach you for anything," he soothed. "After we are married, we'll leave these colonies and return to France, where you will live as the great lady you should be. And Simon can come with us."

He took her hand again and kissed it gently. Totally bewildered at this change in him, she couldn't even answer him. She shrank back into her corner of the carriage and watched him apprehensively as they rattled and banged along the uneven road toward Williamsburg. She dreaded what he might say next, but for a while everything was quiet. Then, suddenly, the driver of the carriage uttered a sharp exclamation and drew rein.

"Now what's the matter?" Chauvin opened the door of the carriage and looked out. Then, in an impatient tone, he snapped, "Start the horses again, you fool. Go ahead around them."

"There's no room on the road," the driver remonstrated. "See for yourself. We can't move until these carts pass."

With an oath, Chauvin got out of the carriage and stared down the road, and as he did so Gabrielle heard the sound of heavy wheels approaching. She leaned across the carriage seat to look outside and saw what seemed at first glance to be a thick cloud of dust rolling toward them. Then she realized that four or five horse-drawn carts were lumbering down the road. By the side of each cart rode uniformed English soldiers.

The driver of Chauvin's carriage shook his head. "Poor miserable buggers," he said. "Off to drown at sea or fight and die in the war with them Frenchies."

Gabrielle's breath caught in her throat as she realized that these were the "volunteers" that Chauvin had told her about. And if he didn't or couldn't do anything, Simon would be riding in one of those carts soon. She craned her head farther out of the carriage. It was so easy to picture Simon in one of those lumbering, dusty carts. She could almost see him . . .

Then she realized that she *was* seeing him. "Oh, dear God," she gasped, "Simon—"

She tumbled from the carriage into the dust of the road and, evading Chauvin's attempt to stop her, ran for the carts. As she called Simon's name, a lean, dark-haired youth sitting in the forefront of the first cart raised his head and looked about him in bewilderment. Her heart contracted in agony as she saw how thin he'd become, how pale and sickly he looked. In spite of the February cold, he wore no coat or cloak, and his face wore a dull, hopeless expression, but when he saw her his eyes came alive.

"Gabrielle!" he gasped. "Holy Mother, it's Gabrielle . . ."

Before any of the mounted soldiers could stop her, she had reached the side of the cart. Simon leaned down to embrace her, and she clung to him, the tears streaming down her cheeks as she whispered endearments from their childhood. "I've found you at last," she whispered.

"Oh, Gabrielle." Against her cheek she could feel his icy skin and the rasp of his beginning beard, and his thin shoulders heaved with sobs. "I worried about you all the time. I was afraid something horrible had happened to you. You don't know how much I wanted to find you, but naturally he couldn't permit us to meet . . ."

"What are you talking about?" she asked in bewilderment, but before he could answer, rough arms were forcing them apart.

"None of this, now," a familiar voice snarled,

and she turned to look into the familiar face of Lieutenant Dray. "It seems that you're always interfering with His Majesty's business, Mademoiselle."

Gabrielle clung to Simon. "You don't understand. This is my brother . . ." She saw Chauvin coming toward them and turned to him. "Monsieur Chauvin, please help us."

"That's rich." Lieutenant Dray began to laugh and Simon turned black, hating eyes toward Chauvin.

"Gabrielle, this man is the reason why we're here."

Her bewilderment was now complete. "What do you mean, the reason?" she demanded.

"I mean that he's sold me into slavery under George of England just as he sold us all in Laforet. He was the traitor, he brought the English into our village . . ."

With a brutal shove, Dray tore Simon loose from Gabrielle and hurled him back into the cart. "Be quiet, scum, or you'll feel the bite of my whip," he snarled, then turned to the driver of the cart. "Drive on."

"Simon!" Gabrielle began to run after the cart, but this time Chauvin caught and held her back. The dust of the road filled her eyes and mouth , as half-choking on the gritty sand, she screamed her brother's name again and again.

Turning in the cart to look back at her, the boy shouted, "Don't listen to him, Gabrielle. He's the devil. Blood is on his hands. He and Lawrence planned it together for blood money."

Lieutenant Dray snatched a whip from his saddle and brought it down across Simon's shoulder. Gabrielle screamed in horror as the whip rose and fell again and yet again. In her ear she heard Chauvin say, "Remember, Gabrielle, I can save him from that."

She twisted in his grasp to face him. Her tears were cold on her cheeks, but her eyes blazed. "Simon accused you of selling him to King George, of betraying us all."

Still holding her in an iron grip, he forced her back to the carriage. "When we get to Williamsburg, I'll see what can be done for him."

Ignoring this, she demanded again, "What did he mean when he said that you and Governor Lawrence had a plan together?"

Forcing her into the carriage, he got in behind her. "Ravings," he said. "Prison and the prospect of fighting for England has unhinged his mind."

The black eyes that had stared into hers had been tormented but sane. "No, he wasn't crazy, but I can't believe that you brought the British to Laforet. Why would you do such a terrible thing?"

For a moment he was silent, and she could see the hesitation in his eyes, then he shrugged. "Why are most things done in this world?" he asked her. "Money."

"Money!" she repeated, aghast.

"Or profit, if you will. Governor Lawrence had already decided to take over Acadia and bring in English settlers to replace the French. My cooperation with him didn't change anything; it just expedited matters."

She couldn't believe he was saying these terrible things. This couldn't be Monsieur Chauvin, the kind, good friend of her childhood, the suitor who had wooed her so respectfully, the man to whom all Laforet had looked for guidance. But he was smiling, and in that smile she saw again that terrible September day—the women wailing for their men, lost children crying for their mothers, Dray smashing her spinning wheel and Neill lifting her from the dust of the road.

"Be reasonable," he was saying. "What good would it have done anyone if I had opposed Lawrence? He summoned me to Halifax to talk to me because I had influence in Laforet. After we had spoken, he agreed to give me a percentage of the land value after the Acadians had been driven out and the English settlers had moved in. In return I agreed with him that there should be an organized, orderly evacuation. No bloodshed."

"What about Gaspard?" she cried. "What about Marthe Richaud, who lost her husband for months, and poor Céline who lost her child—what about all of us who lost our homes, Monsieur? Simon is right. You've got blood on your hands."

There was a silence in the carriage. All she could hear was her own tortured breathing. The beat of her own heart sounded loud in her ears, and when he moved, the rustle of his coat against the leather of the carriage was like a scream. She pressed herself flat to the side of the carriage. "If you touch me," she told him, "I'll throw myself out of this carriage. I swear it. I'd rather die than have you touch me."

"We'll see." But he left her alone as they rattled on, and she tried to draw her tangled thoughts together into some logical order. It didn't work. She had prayed so hard to see Simon again—and now that she had seen him, knowledge of his fate left her beyond horror. Worse, no one could help except this man here in the carriage, and his price was monstrous. To marry him, to feel his mouth on hers and his body claim hers—nausea racked her, and she thought, I would rather die. Simon would rather see me dead. Neill . . .

Suddenly, her fraught mind was filled with images of Neill, so real and strong that for a moment she forgot who sat beside her in the carriage. She felt Neill's arms about her, holding her close. She felt his strength and his support and his love, and somewhere within herself courage flared defiance against Chauvin and any of his hellish tricks. She had been Neill Craddock's woman. She was the queen of his heart. Nothing could touch that part of her or take it away . . .

"Gabrielle, we're nearing Williamsburg."

The fragile bubble of bravery disintegrated at the sound of Chauvin's voice, and yet she clung to a remnant of her hope. Neill would come for her. Surely, he would find her and Simon, too.

As the thought took hold in her mind, he laughed as if at a good joke. "Let's see how you feel a little later, Mademoiselle Wildcat."

She did not respond to his jibe. Now or later, she thought, she could not despise him more. In silence she heard the driver of the carriage call to stop his horses, and in the same frozen silence descended to find herself standing in front of

Willow House. Chauvin climbed the front steps to knock on the door, which was opened by Delcie.

The little bound girl's eyes opened wide when she saw Gabrielle, but she ran to fetch her mistress. Chauvin spoke with Harriet Hook for a moment, then motioned to Gabrielle. "Come, Mademoiselle. You remember Mistress Hook and this comfortable abode of hers. If you had remained here as you ought to have done, everything would have been much simpler."

So Chauvin had been behind her imprisonment in Willow House. As she followed Delcie up to the remembered chamber, Gabrielle felt pieces of the jumbled puzzle slide into place. Of course the dresses in the wardrobe had fit—they'd been made with her in mind. He'd intended for her to be kept prisoner here until he returned from San Domingo to claim her. But then Neill had come . . .

A small, workworn hand slid into hers and Delcie whispered hoarse comfort. "Don't you fret, Lady. Your golden man'll rescue you again."

Gabrielle squeezed the young girl's hand. Delcie continued, "*She* was in a state when she found you gone—and I would've caught it if they hadn't found the dogs and figured it was all your man's fault. The Colonel himself came. He was hopping mad. He kept saying, 'Do you know how much money this is going to cost me? The Frenchman was going to pay, and now he won't. Who'd pay for a bird that's flown?'"

"That means that Colonel Whitower, too, is in

Chauvin's pay." Gabrielle sank down on one of the chairs by the bed. She felt so exhausted that she was almost numb.

Harriet Hook began now to shout for Delcie. The girl hurried away, and Gabrielle sat where she was for a long time. Finally, she forced herself to her feet and went to the window. It was turning to twilight, and she could see the February wind whipping at the bare willow branches. She shivered suddenly, and wrapped her arms around herself. Neill, she thought, where are you?

"No doubt your foolish lover is nearer than you think." She didn't realize she had spoken the thought aloud until Chauvin answered. She hadn't heard him come into the room, and as she whipped around in surprise, he laughed and withdrawing a key, held it up for her inspection before returning it to his pocket. "Why wouldn't he come? I have bait he can't resist."

She repeated his words silently. Chauvin wanted Neill to come. For a moment she grappled with that thought, and then she realized what she had been too upset to see before. In Williamsburg, Neill was still a fugitive from justice. Accused of treason, suspected of murder, he would be arrested and brought before Colonel Whitower—who was in Chauvin's pay.

"I see that you've puzzled it out," Chauvin was saying. He had changed from his travel clothes into a coat and breeches of fine embroidered satin and in spite of his civilian status sported a sword on a sash at his waist. "He only has himself to blame. Neill Craddock is a hard man to kill. However, he will follow you and the clues I scattered along the trail. I purposely left your servants alive so that they could tell him where we were going, and of course your Mr. Warrensbody saw you and recognized you in Yorktown."

"Because he loves me you want him killed." Her knees felt rubbery under her. "You are a monster," she cried.

He looked a little surprised. "I'm just a businessman who wants everything orderly. I could hardly enjoy you and the fortune you'd bring with you were Craddock alive. He would not let you go, my dear Gabrielle, and so he must be eliminated." He saw the bewilderment struggling with horror in her eyes and he added, "I mean, of course, the de Montfleuri fortune, which will be yours when we return to France to claim it together."

"You're insane. There is no fortune. You yourself said . . ."

"I lied."

She could only listen in horror as he told her how he had lied to her mother, told the grieving widow that there was no money when indeed there had been an enormous fortune waiting in France.

"The terms of the will, I discovered, were that any heirs to the de Montfleuri fortune would have to return to France and live there," he told her. "Naturally, I couldn't let any of you return to France before I was ready. To prevent your return, I made sure you were taken care of and educated in Laforet. And, you must admit, you wanted for nothing." He took a step forward, smiling at her. "I always intended to make sure that my bride-to-be was intelligent as well as beautiful."

As if delighted by his own cleverness, he told her how he had decided to claim her fortune by marrying her. "You were grateful for my kindness, and I knew you would gladly agree to marry me," he explained. "As for Simon, I encouraged his hotheadedness. I knew that this would give me an excuse to remove him from the picture and make it possible for you to inherit everything."

Though her mind was reeling with shock at what he said, that much was clear. Chauvin held not only her fortune in his hand but Simon's and Neill's lives. He had told her that she would beg him to marry her on her knees, and now she understood why. She clasped her hands and bowed her head, truly beaten at least. "Monsieur, if I agree to marry you, if I do whatever you say without question and without argument, will you help Simon and leave Neill alone?"

He seemed to hesitate before shaking his head. "There's no need for me to buy your cooperation. Whether you will or no, our marriage will take place. Don't forget that we are betrothed." He paused. "I am sorry to grieve you, but you will learn that in life there are those who win by seizing the opportunities that come their way, without foolish sentiment or remorse." He came toward her, took her limp hand from her lap and kissed it lightly.

She snatched her hand away. "You cannot be sure of that," she told him, and now her voice was as cold as ice, her eyes burned cold fire. "I swear to you on the honor of my father and my mother that I will kill myself before you have a chance to marry me. See if you can inherit money from a dead bride."

The room was suddenly very quiet, so silent that a sudden shouting in the street outside sounded unnaturally loud. Chauvin frowned. "Don't be dramatic, Mademoiselle. There's no weapon, no way of hurting yourself in the room. Even the window locks from outside, so that you can't open it and thus accidentally injure yourself." His smile was cool, a little pitying. "As for our marriage, it takes place in an hour. Arrangements are being made as we talk, so give it up. Your brother will sail for England tomorrow, and your lover is as good as dead. You're all alone."

There was the rustle of a curtain, the creak of the window swinging inward. She saw Chauvin's eyes widen, heard him suck in his breath, and her heart leaped as she heard the deep voice behind her. "I wouldn't put it quite that way," Neill said.

Chapter Seventeen

HE WAS STANDING, SWORD IN HAND, JUST INSIDE the window. He had discarded his cloak, and in spite of the February cold, dust and sweat streaked his face. His eyes were coldly murderous as they held Chauvin's.

"About time we met, you treacherous cur," he said, and then to Gabrielle he added, "I came as quickly as I could. Are you all right?"

The words were almost harsh, but she could read the riptide of feeling in his voice. Wanting to run into his arms, she checked herself. She must do nothing to ruin his concentration. "I'm unharmed," she said, and then, as joy gave way to fear, "but he has been expecting you. He's set a trap for you . . ."

"I'd have been disappointed else." Grim humor flickered in his deep tones as he addressed Chauvin. "You may have heard a shouting down the street a while ago? What we used to call a 'diversionary tactic' in my military days. A small brushfire that will do no harm but will keep every soldier you had posted around this house occupied for the next few minutes." He stepped forward, the sword blade twitching. "A few minutes are all I need."

Chauvin spoke for the first time. "You add arson to treason and murder. You'll hang, Craddock." He started to ease backward toward the door, and Gabrielle cried warning. But before the warning had even left her lips, Neill strode forward to catch the Acadian by his shoulder and spin him away from the door.

"I see you wear a sword, too, Chauvin. Draw it."

At the grim command, Chauvin's face grew paler. His eyes narrowed, his mouth set. "You intend to murder me," he protested.

"You're an expert at murder, aren't you? There was the attack on the road to Philadelphia, and then the legal murder you tried to carry out here in Williamsburg with the help of the Colonel. Was that brute of a fellow who tried to slit my throat in the warehouse your idea, too?" He heard Gabrielle's gasp of horror and his rage at Chauvin grew even greater. Without looking at her he knew how she had fared since being kidnapped. Though she seemed unharmed, he had seen the dark smudges under her lovely eyes, the haunted thinness of her face.

"I was only trying to protect what was mine." Chauvin's voice had a whine in it.

Neill gestured with his sword. "Draw. If I

think of the other things you've done to Simon and my lady, I may run you through and be done."

"Your lady." Chauvin's sneer, Neill knew, was calculated insult. He wanted his opponent to lose his temper and be thrown off balance.

His voice was tense but controlled as he said, "Your fine plan won't work. Gabrielle is coming with me tonight, and Simon isn't going to oblige you by dying on the battlefield. He's free and on his way out of Virginia by now."

"Free!" Gabrielle couldn't control that glad cry, and involuntarily Neill's eyes turned to her. In that second, Chauvin leaped forward, sword in hand.

"You meddling fool!" he cried.

Gabrielle choked back a scream as Chauvin's sword rang against Neill's parry. Then the slighter Acadian was being pushed back against the far wall of the room. As he righted himself, Neill said, "I came upon the Acadians who had 'volunteered' for King George's army and also on Lieutenant Dray, who led them. He and I had a few words to say to each other, and he tried to take me prisoner. During the scuffle, Simon and many others managed to escape from the carts into the forests nearby." He parried Chauvin's weak sword blow and added, "I'm not concerned about those escapees. They have gold, and Simon has my pistol. That's the reason I don't shoot you now, Monsieur Dog, though I must confess killing you this way is more pleasurable."

Chauvin again went staggering backward.

Clumsily, he parried Neill's wickedly thrusting blade. "Murderer," he hissed.

"I'm sorry to say that even Dray isn't dead, though I gave him the beating of his life and left him with a good-sized hole in his shoulder. With you, I hope to be luckier." His sword point stabbed forward again and caught the Acadian in the right arm.

Chauvin dropped his sword and made as if to clutch at his arm, but Gabrielle saw what he was really after. "He's got a pistol under his coat!"

Even while she was crying out her warning, she knew that it came too late. Neill was too far from Chauvin to stop him from firing. As Chauvin whipped the pistol from his jacket she acted instinctively, throwing herself between Neill and the Acadian.

"If you shoot, you'll say goodbye to a fortune," she cried.

Chauvin hesitated. As he did so, they all heard the rush of footsteps outside in the street and then the Hook woman's voice. "I tell you, they're fighting upstairs. The man you want is here in this house."

Neill surged past Gabrielle and, holding his sword point to Chauvin's neck, spoke tersely. "Monsieur Dog, we're leaving this house together. Gabrielle, take his pistol, and get behind me. Our friend here is going to make sure we leave Williamsburg safely."

Chauvin made a choking sound. His eyes were almost starting out of his head, but he obeyed when Neill ordered him to open the door. Out-

side on the landing stood several soldiers who
fell back at sight of Chauvin.

"It pays to know a man who has friends in
high places." Holding Chauvin in place with his
sword tip, Neill walked him toward the stairs,
while Gabrielle kept her pistol trained on the
soldiers behind them. "Down the stairs and out
of the door, and give the order for three horses,"
he ordered Chauvin.

The outer door stood open and a blast of
cold night air swept through the hallway as
they made their way toward the street. Gabrielle had a glimpse of Delcie's white face, and
the enraged Harriet Hook, who stood helpless behind the soldiers at the foot of the stairs.
A few more steps, she thought, and we'll be
free.

"Hold. Don't take another step—or this man
will suffer for it."

The new, hard voice came from outside, and
now an English Captain came through the open
door, dragging a struggling, ragged figure with
him. "Simon," Gabrielle cried, but her voice was
drowned by the boy's despairing cry.

"It doesn't matter about me, Monsieur Neill.
Take Gabrielle and get away."

For a moment, Neill was tempted. Then he
heard Gabrielle's cry of protest and saw the
boy's eyes, so frightened in spite of their effort to
be brave. In despair, he lowered his sword.

At the Captain's order, one of the soldiers took
Gabrielle's weapon from her. Chauvin hurriedly
moved out of Neill's reach as the Captain said,
"Sentries found the boy on the outskirts of
Williamsburg. He's an Acadian deserter, armed

and dangerous. He says he's the brother of Gabrielle de Montfleuri."

Simon spoke in English, his eyes on Neill. "I am sorry," he muttered. "I didn't go on to Yorktown, as you told me to, but followed you here. I only wanted to help you free my sister from this animal, Chauvin."

With a wordless cry, Gabrielle ran forward and into her brother's arms. As soldiers moved to separate them, Neill spoke bitterly. "They've not seen each other since this bastard sold their entire village out from under them. Does it violate some new law of the Colonel's if you let them be?"

The Captain motioned back his men. "I'm Captain Harroway, and in Colonel Whitower's absence I command the Williamsburg garrison. I arrest you, sir, on a charge of treason, murder and attempted murder."

"And arson. He was responsible for that fire some time ago," Chauvin interjected. His color had returned and he was smiling. "There's nothing like a long night in prison to make a man appreciate hanging, Craddock."

Noting the faint distaste that flickered across the Captain's face, Neill turned to him. "Am I to have a trial, Captain, or has British justice been changed to suit traitors?"

Captain Harroway stiffened. "You'll have your trial, Mr. Craddock, as soon as the Colonel returns. He's away visiting the Governor today, but we expect him back tomorrow."

"I'm willing to wait." As Neill spoke, Gabrielle turned from Simon to him, her lips forming his name. She did not reach out to him or touch

271

him, but he felt the depths of her love, and again he was filled with killing rage at Chauvin. And also at himself. Why hadn't he spitted the Acadian when he had the chance? Then, at least, Gabrielle would be safe.

Captain Harroway had stepped aside to speak to the Hook woman, who seemed unhappy at what he had said. Now he returned to his prisoners. "As ranking officer here, I've decided not to take you to jail," he said formally. "I've heard of the events that took place when you were, er, incarcerated last time, and I don't want a recurrence." He cleared his throat and became even more formal. "Until you stand trial, Mr. Craddock, will you give me your word that you won't try to escape from this house?"

Obviously, Chauvin couldn't believe his ears. "This house—his word. Captain, you are mad. You'd take the word of a criminal?"

Ignoring the Acadian, the English Captain kept his eyes on Neill. No, Gabrielle wanted to cry, don't promise. Bide your time and escape. You know what "justice" awaits you.

He could read her thoughts, and as he turned to her, his eyes softened. He would have given anything to do as she wished, but this time there was escape. There was an outside chance that he could fight himself clear and take Gabrielle with him, but it would be impossible to rescue Simon. Harroway, he knew instinctively, was a man of honor. If the Captain learned the true story behind Chauvin and the Montfleuris, he might help Gabrielle and her brother.

"It's all right, dear love," he told Gabrielle. Then bowing to the Captain, he added, "You have my word—if you will give me yours, as an officer of the King and a gentleman, that no harm will come to this lady while I am unable to protect her. I also need certain letters delivered."

Chauvin began to laugh incredulously, but a cold look from Harroway silenced him. The Captain ordered half a dozen of the soldiers present to fall out and stand guard on the house, while others were to convey Simon to prison. Then he said, "As for the lady, she remains here. As an important witness, she must be kept safe. There's room for two in the house."

"And what of me?" Chauvin demanded wrathfully. "You have turned this house—a house which I have engaged for my own use—into a jail for a well-known criminal. The Colonel will hear of this, I assure you. Meanwhile, if you insist on this madness, I demand that I be given suitable accommodations. And this lady must come with me."

The contempt that had flickered in Captain Harroway's eyes now flared openly. "I've just placed this house under military jurisdiction," he snapped. "Where you go has nothing to do with me." He turned to the soldiers and issued another order. "Until a court of law sits in judgment on Mr. Craddock, no one is to disturb him or try to communicate with him or with this woman. No one."

"Damnation."

Pacing the room by the light of a solitary flickering lamp, Neill swore softly under his breath and tried to think past tonight to tomorrow. He had done all he could as a prisoner who had given his word not to attempt escape. He had written three letters, one to Sam Culpepper, amending his will in favor of Gabrielle, a second to Baron de Sandoville requesting that nobleman's aid for the de Montfleuris and a third to the Governor of Virginia. In this last letter he had set down the details of Colonel Whitower's involvement with Chauvin.

Now, the letters handed personally to Captain Harroway, there was one other letter that he knew he must write. It did not come easily, but he knew that it was essential that he write it, for he might never again have the chance to communicate with Gabrielle. If he knew Chauvin and Whitower, his "trial" would be a swift, trumped-up affair, and by tomorrow night he could be swinging from a hastily erected gibbet. And if he did not tell her, Gabrielle would not know all he was trying to do to protect her.

He turned back to the table on which stood the lamp. A sheet of paper rested there, with ink and a quill, but he hadn't progressed beyond, "My dear love." And, Neill wondered, sinking down onto a large chair between the table and the bed that had been provided for him, what else was there really to say? They had spoken of that love so often, in words and through the language of their bodies. And yet there was so much he wanted to tell her: that he would carry—to the grave and beyond—the flower scent of her skin, the warm honey of her lips and breasts, the sound of her laughter, the memory of her humor and tenderness and her brave loyalty.

Outside in the hall, he could hear the shuffle

of the two soldiers who acted as token guardians. Ignoring the noise, he tried to think of words to give her comfort and offer his love. As he did so, he heard one of the guards clear his throat. "Where are you going with that tray, girl?" the man was demanding.

Delcie's low voice answered, "The Captain said as the prisoner was to have food."

Neill put down his pen. He'd forgotten about Delcie, but now he realized that the young girl could be his link with Gabrielle. As the door was unlocked, he addressed the soldier who stood behind the hunched form that carried the tray. "I'm going to write another letter to send by this girl. It'll take me some time."

"Take all the time you need." The door was closed and locked behind Delcie, and Neill noted that tonight she looked even more terrified than she usually did and that she kept her head, already half-concealed by a white cap, bent low as she placed the tray before him on the table. Her action unsettled his barely begun letter to Gabrielle, and he frowned up at her in irritation.

"Be careful, girl, and take the food away," he began, and then stopped, staring. "Christ," he breathed.

"After all my efforts, such gratitude." Gabrielle's eyes were shining, and when he caught her in his arms, the white cap fell off. "Ah, be careful. It is the only one that Delcie owns," she whispered.

She pressed her cheek against his shoulder, and closing her eyes, drew deep breaths of him. Her hands roved his shoulders and back, reaffirming his reality. "How did you get here?"

Her words made kisses against his shoulder. "Delcie helped me. She is in my room now, and the soldiers who guard me think I haven't left my room. We changed clothes and I stooped very low and acted very humble and they didn't suspect. But—but we don't have much time, my dear one."

She lifted her face to him and her dark lashes swooped down over her eyes as he kissed them, then the corner of her lips, finally claimed her mouth with fiery-sweet kisses. She clasped her arms about his neck, willing herself to become a part of him, meld with his hardness. But after a long moment he pulled away.

"Gabrielle, we've got to talk." Still holding her, he drew her to the armchair near the bed and sank down into it with her. "I've written to de Sandoville and Sam. Both will help you. After the trial tomorrow, you'll be set free. Captain Harroway will help you to get to Yorktown, where the Baron's ship is awaiting me. Sail immediately for New Orleans." He spoke carefully, because it was important she understood all of this. "Before I came here, I took the precaution of giving Andrew Warrensbody most of the gold I had on me. He'll give that gold to you. I've instructed Sam to send you more gold by way of de Sandoville, and the Baron will also help you get to France." He gave her a little shake. "Are you listening?"

She listened to the urgency of his words, but they did not register in her mind. Now she placed her fingers against his lips. "You know I won't go anywhere unless you come, too."

He drew her hand away. "My sweet love, be

realistic. Colonel Whitower isn't likely to let me get away a second time."

"A man like that could be bribed," she cried, but again he shook his head.

"He's Chauvin's man, remember? He'll realize what a formidable adversary I could be to him. If he lets me go, I'll make sure that he's exposed as the scoundrel he is, and he can't afford that." She started to protest, but he kissed her silent. "Gabrielle, promise me you'll do as I say."

She drew a little away from him and in the sputtering lamplight her eyes were like bruised velvet. "If Simon is freed, I will go for his sake."

"Whether Simon is freed or not, I want your promise, Gabrielle." He spoke sternly now, the gold of his eyes turned to bronze. "You mustn't fall into Chauvin's clutches again."

He would have said more, but now she began to kiss him, her lips urgent and passionate. "I swear that Chauvin won't have his will with me. Now I beg you, no more talk of tomorrow. We have been too long away from each other."

He knew that he should insist on her promise, but his body had its own insistence, and he could no longer resist the passionate entreaty of the slender, cool-fired body pressed against his. One hand went up to smooth the remembered silk of her hair, the other stroked the line of her chin, her throat, traced the proud rise of her breast. As his fingers rediscovered the remembered grace of her body, she whispered love words against his lips.

"When I was taken away from you, I thought I'd die of loneliness. My darling, my golden tiger, my heart. Love me now, let me be with you again."

Their hands trembled with hurry as they tugged clothing loose from buttons and laces, removed boots and sashes. Then they stood pressed together, all barriers removed, their bodies savoring the feel of each other for a full moment before he lifted her into his arms and carried her to the bed.

She kept her arms around his neck as he lowered her onto the cool sheets, and he kissed her mouth and the fragile lobes of her ears and her shoulders. She murmured with pleasure as he sucked first one, then the other of the roses of her breasts, then drew a path of fire with his mouth across her belly and smooth, velvet thighs. When his mouth came back to hers, she met his probing tongue with hers, arching her back so that her breasts with the taut, yearning nipples were pressed against his hard chest.

"My queen," he named her. "My lovely lady of the forest."

Again his mouth moved downward, conquering the eager breasts, the silken concavity of her navel, the soft rise that guarded the secrets of her womanhood. As his mouth and tongue stroked and adored her with the most intimate of kisses, she shivered with a pleasure that seemed to radiate to the innermost core of her being.

"No more. Not now," she begged. "I love you. Want you."

He returned to her, his weight poised above her, and she kissed his lean, hard jawline and his throat and shoulders and the hands that stroked her hair. Let it last, her eyes implored him, let this last forever. Drowning in the golden fire of his gaze, she raised her hips to take him deep within her.

Never before in all their loving had it been like this. Her body met and melded with his so perfectly that there seemed no separation between them. There was only a flawless joining, in which his urgent hardness, her soft warmth, mingled together in heart-stopping ecstasy. The strong, sure strokes of his loving filled her completely and her warm flesh took him deep and still deeper, until neither could bear the pleasure that was almost pain. Then, waiting, stilling, they shivered on the brink together, holding back so as to cling to the moment a little longer. She kissed his eyes, he bent to her breasts, and they spoke to each other with words they knew only they had ever used. *My love. My dear one. My heart.*

She sobbed with pleasure as he started to move inside her her again and now there was no holding back. Each convulsive movement of their bodies brought them closer to the ultimate ecstasy. As she took the hot, thick honey of his seed deep within her, as she herself shattered against him, Gabrielle heard him call her name.

And she knew that no matter what happened to them tomorrow, they could never be truly apart again.

Chapter Eighteen

"MR. CRADDOCK, YOU'RE REQUESTED TO COME with me before the commanding officer of the military garrison in Williamsburg. He requests a preliminary meeting before a civil court is called in judgment upon you."

Captain Harroway stood at attention, his eyes staring straight forward as he delivered his message. A bad sign, Neill decided.

He kept his own reply light. "I see the Colonel's losing no time in seeing that justice is done."

Harroway made no answer but bowed and stood aside from the door. Neill picked up the hat and cloak with which the Captain had provided him, and stepped into the hall. There Gabrielle was waiting. She looked pale and frightened, and he smiled at her in reassurance as he offered her his arm. "A good day for a walk," he said bracingly.

Remembering last night and the joy they'd had in spite of everything, she tried to smile bravely into the loving depths of his eyes. Then she shivered. The memory of those stolen moments was a cruel reminder that after today there might never be time again for them. As the thought touched her mind, Neill pressed her arm closer to his hard side. "Remember," he said quietly, "there's one great rule in life."

"Never despair—I know it." She forced herself to smile again at him, and squared her slender shoulders as they stepped together into the bright sunshine. The crystal clearness and cold of the winter morning hurt her lungs when she drew a deep, steadying breath. She would never despair, she promised herself, as long as he remained alive.

Again, he seemed to hear her thought. "Whatever happens today, I love you and honor you," he told her.

Tears filled her eyes and she looked hastily away lest he see them. But he did see them, and his heart contracted sharply with pain for her. His lovely lady of the forest had suffered too much already, and today she'd have to sit through this mockery of a trial before having to grapple with her own problems. He turned to Captain Harroway, who was walking with his soldiers a few yards away.

"When this is over, Captain, I remind you of your promise to help this lady and her brother," he said.

Instead of replying, the Captain pointed. "There's the military garrison, sir, where the meeting will take place."

Now Neill could see that a group of people waited in front of the garrison. One of them was Simon. Even though he was still guarded by soldiers, he had been given a warm suit of clean clothes and with his dark hair brushed back into a queue at the back of his head, he looked like a young aristocrat. Next to Simon and obviously in a bad temper was Chauvin.

"Why have you given orders that I not be permitted to see the Colonel the moment he returned?" he demanded. He glared at the Captain and then at Gabrielle on Neill's arm. "You'll answer for this disrespect to me, Captain."

"Everything's been done at the commanding officer's order, Mr. Chauvin." As usual when addressing Chauvin, Captain Harroway's face expressed a profound distaste, but he spoke courteously. "Now that we've assembled, we can all go in." He nodded to one of the soldiers, who went ahead to push the doors of the military garrison. "The commander's waiting for us."

After the brightness of the day outside, the interior of the garrison seemed very dark, and for a moment Gabrielle could see little. She mechanically followed the soldier who led through a much-worn anteroom to swing open the door of a larger chamber. Then, standing at attention in the doorway, he announced, "The Acadians and Neill Craddock to see you, sir."

"Send them in." She heard the command through the frightened pounding of her heart and forced herself to step forward. Though her hands were clammy with perspiration, she did not allow herself to show fear as she walked into the Colonel's presence. She couldn't bear to look at him or appeal to him, so she merely bowed her head to him in cold silence and stepped to one side to make room for the others. As she did so, she hear Chauvin's gasp.

"But—sacred name—where is Colonel Whitower?"

Neill was staring, too, and Gabrielle at last looked fully at the man behind the desk. This was no sleepy-eyed Colonel but a dark-haired, youngish man with a scar across his forehead. He was smiling a little at Chauvin's exclamation, but the eyes under the scar were unamused.

"Colonel Whitower is no longer in command of this garrison. He was relieved as commanding officer by His Excellency the Governor yesterday. I'm Major Kittery."

Gabrielle saw Neill frown as if in thought, as Chauvin exploded into speech. "But—*sacré nom*—that isn't possible. Why wasn't I told? When was the Colonel relieved of his command?"

"It is indeed possible. Colonel Whitower's performance of his duties has been highly unsatisfactory. And, sir, you weren't told because it was none of your concern." He turned to Neill, and his smile became genuine. "Are you still struggling to remember me, Major Craddock?"

Neill shook his head. "I'm not sure. Did we serve together?"

Nearly numb with disbelief, Gabrielle saw the new commanding officer nod eagerly. "Yes, in France. I was the Lieutenant, newly assigned to your command when you were ordered to burn the village of Layons. You refused, and I honored you for that." He rose from the desk to reach out a hand to Neill. "When I heard you'd left the military, I was sorry, sir, for we lost a fine officer and a brave gentleman."

Clearly, Chauvin could no longer hold himself back. "Do you know that this so-called gentleman is a murderer who has committed treasonous acts?" he demanded. "I demand justice, Major Kittery."

No longer smiling, the dark-haired officer resumed his seat. "Mr. Chauvin, as an Acadian you have few rights. However, you'll have your chance to speak. Meanwhile, please be silent as Captain Harroway reads the facts we've assembled so far."

Captain Harroway stepped forward and began to read from a sheaf of papers in his hands. At first he merely stated facts. Neill had been accused by Lieutenant Dray and Colonel Whitower of aiding the French. He had further been accused of murdering Phineas Cole, an assistant jailer, in the warehouse where the Acadians had been kept. Simon was accused of desertion. Gabrielle appeared merely as a witness, Chauvin as a plaintiff.

Chauvin tried to speak but was silenced as the Captain read on. Now he read written depositions given under oath. One deposition came from Father Maboeuf, who swore that Neill had acted in self-defense against Phineas Cole, and another was from Andrew Warrensbody, who gave the true story of Neill's dealing with Colonel Whitower. Further, there was a letter from the Governor of Virginia, who wrote of the colony's friendly and excellent business dealings with the C. and C. Company.

"Your version of what happened, Mr. Craddock?" the Major asked. Neill told it, including the story of Chauvin's fraud against the de Montfleuris. Simon corroborated this.

"I learned of Chauvin's treachery when we were both aboard *The Royal Princess*," he said. "Lieutenant Dray was very friendly with Chauvin, and it was immediately clear that Chauvin had been the traitor who helped Governor Lawrence deport our people. Later, he boasted to me that he'd get money from Lawrence for his betrayal and also that he'd marry my sister and get more money. Naturally, after I learned all this, he didn't dare let us meet."

"He lies!" Chauvin sputtered, but again the English Major ordered that he be silent.

"You'll please continue, Mr. de Montfleuri," he said.

Words spilled out of Simon. He explained that while they were in Philadelphia, he had heard Chauvin order ruffians to find and kill Neill. "He was afraid that my sister would be influenced by Neill Craddock. He feared she might even fall in love with him, even though he was an Englishman," he added with contempt, "but he wasn't man enough to meet Monsieur Neill face to face, so he tried several times to arrange to have him killed."

Gabrielle's testimony came next. She spoke of trying to find Simon and Chauvin, of the dangers she and Neill had faced, the storm at sea when Neill had saved her life. The English officer listened intently, but when she described how Chauvin had kidnapped her and brought her to Virginia, he stopped her.

"Madam, I know that the telling of these events must be painful to you. I think I've heard enough. We must now listen to Mr. Chauvin's testimony." Chauvin stood up at once but was checked by the Major, who added, "A moment. Louis Chauvin, you stand accused of attempted murder and fraud and kidnapping."

Chauvin's teeth were bared in a smile that was almost a sneer. "You have only the word of these people. There is no proof anywhere."

"On the contrary, sir. There's a witness against you."

This time, the sneer was completely obvious. "Who? The de Montfleuri whelp? An old, addle-brained Acadian priest?"

"Our witness is an English officer. Since he stands accused of corruption and misuse of authority, Lieutenant Dray has been persuaded to tell us all he knows about you."

Gabrielle thought she had been beyond surprise, but she was shocked at Dray's appearance. The man's flat face was ghost-pale and wore a look of total misery and humiliation. One arm was bandaged high against his chest, and he could hardly walk. "Seems to be having a hard time of it, the bastard," Neill murmured in her ear. "I did better work than I thought."

Dray spoke shortly and to the point. It was Chauvin, he said, who had bribed Colonel Whitower to imprison Neill so that the assistant jailer could kill him. He added that Chauvin had also boasted to him that he had defrauded the de Montfleuris and was going to marry a rich heiress. "Once he married the woman, he was going to dispose of her brother. That's why he 'volunteered' the boy to serve in the army. He was sure that Simon de Montfleuri would be killed while fighting."

He would have said more, but before he could do so, Chauvin's hand went to his coat. Next moment, he had reached across to catch Gabrielle by the shoulder. "Make a movement toward me and I kill the woman," he snarled.

Gabrielle felt the cold, hard muzzle of the pistol against her spine. She saw the horror in the English officers' faces, Simon's incredulity and the look in Neill's eyes. She knew that cool, murderous look well and she realized how every muscle and sinew in that great body was tensed for action. A sense of *déjà vu* swept her mind as she held his eyes with hers. Neill, her gaze told him, now . . .

"I can't bear this, it's too much . . ." As she gave her theatrical gasp and sagged forward in a pretended faint, Chauvin's attention was momentarily diverted. In that split second, Neill surged forward. One big hand caught Chauvin's pistol arm, the other closed around the Acadian's throat.

Releasing Gabrielle, Chauvin struggled to free himself of the iron grip around his larynx. "Now, you bastard," Neill said quietly, "will you confess to everything you've done, or do I choke the life out of you?"

Chauvin's mouth opened soundlessly on a plea for help, but nobody moved. The Major sat where he was, and Captain Harroway seemed interested in something that was happening out in the street. The bandaged Lieutenant Dray didn't dare move. Simon hissed, "Break his neck, Monsieur Neill. Steel is too good for a swine like that."

But now Chauvin was making small nodding motions. "Wait," he gasped. "I—confess." With some reluctance Neill let him go, and he sank onto the floor gagging and massaging his throat. As Gabrielle ran to Neill and flung her arms about him, Major Kittery stirred to life and cleared his throat.

"Mr. Chauvin is obviously ready to confess." He turned to Simon to add, "Under the circumstances, Mr. de Montfleuri, you are cleared of all charges of desertion. A man cannot desert what he never joined to start with."

A wild, sweet triumph filled Gabrielle. It was over at last! They were together, the three of them, and they were safe. Nothing could hurt them now. And as that thought touched her mind, Chauvin spoke again.

"Before I make my statement, I want to talk to Craddock."

"What would you say to Mr. Craddock that you can't say to all of us?" the Major demanded suspiciously, and some instinct made Gabrielle catch at Neill's arm.

"Don't listen to him," she begged.

"He can't do anything to us, love. Let him have his few minutes." He stepped away from Gabrielle and walked over to a far corner of the room, and Chauvin rose from the floor and closely watched by the others, limped over to where Neill stood.

"Well?" Neill demanded.

Chauvin leaned forward and spoke rapidly. "You think you've won. You think you've got it all, don't you?"

Neill didn't care for the Acadian's tone. "Spit out what you have to and be done," he said curtly.

"By the terms of the will, Craddock, Gabrielle and Simon de Montfleuri can only claim their inheritance by going to live in France. How will you fit into that scheme of things when France and England are at war?"

Neill turned to look at Gabrielle. She was standing beside Simon, and as he drank in the sight of her radiant beauty, Chauvin spoke again.

"You're an honorable man, Craddock. You know that Gabrielle deserves to be an heiress and the revered daughter of the Chevalier de Montfleuri. You can't keep her from her fortune and you can't go with her. I wonder what you'll do?"

"Damn you, be quiet," Neill snarled. His fingers itched to strangle the man before him, but he couldn't take his eyes away from Gabrielle. He knew that Chauvin was speaking the truth, and every word filled him with despair.

"Even if she wants no part of the money, and she may not, Simon won't be able to wait to claim his inheritance. And do you think she'll let her little brother go to France alone?" Chauvin's voice was gloating now. "Face it, Craddock. If I've lost, so have you."

Chapter Nineteen

"I CAN'T BELIEVE IT—I'M FREE." SIMON LOOKED about him at the gardens that surrounded Major Kittery's house, then turned dramatically to his sister. "After all these months of being dragged around by Chauvin, half-starved, threatened at every turn. Sacred name, but it's good to be alive."

Seated on a garden bench under a drifting branch of early-budding dogwood, Gabrielle smiled, but her smile did not quite reach her eyes. If everything could be so simple, she thought. Everything that she had hoped and longed for had come true, and yet she wasn't completely satisfied. There was the de Montfleuri inheritance for one thing—and Simon wanted to leave for France as soon as possible. She hated to think of his going without her, and yet she knew there was no way that Neill could accompany them to France.

Neill was another problem. Something had gnawed at the corners of what should have been perfect happiness, ever since Chauvin had begged a few moments alone with him. She hadn't been able to hear what had passed between them, but ever since then . . .

"Everything's changed," Simon was saying exuberantly. "A few months ago I was a penniless Acadian deportee. Now I find that I am a very rich man and I have even grown to appreciate that there are *some* good Englishmen. This Major Kittery, who invites us to stay with him as his guests, isn't too bad, and of course, there's Neill Craddock." His smile slipped and he looked askance at his sister. "I haven't seen him today."

"Perhaps he is with the Major, talking about their military days." She spoke calmly, but she felt anything but complacent. Though she had seen a great deal of Neill in public since Chauvin's confession, it seemed as if he was avoiding being alone with her.

"I need to talk to you about Craddock, Sister." Pretending to flick dust from the sleeve of his elaborate satin coat, Simon added slowly, "I know he loves you, and we both owe him a great deal, so perhaps this sounds ungracious, but— well, he's English, and we're at war with England. There can be no future in a relationship with him, as you know."

His words had given her the opening she needed. "It's true that we must talk," she said. "Also, we need to discuss the money Father left us."

"What's there to discuss?" The young man

turned to stare at his sister. "Are you all right, Gabrielle?" he asked anxiously. "You sound strange."

How to tell him of her own love for Neill? How to break the news that she couldn't go to France with him? Trying to find the right words, she hesitated, and he came to sit beside her on the garden seat. He tried to sit in a dignified way, but his long legs made him awkward and she realized how young he still was. She finally began, "Of course, you must go to France to claim the inheritance."

With a burst of renewed eagerness, he caught her hands in his. "It'll be wonderful," he told her. "All these months, I've thought about you—how hard you worked in Laforet. I'm afraid I took you too much for granted," he added with embarrassment, "but now that we have money, it's going to be different. I'm going to attend the University and learn, Gabrielle. Governments and politics fascinate me, and I'm going to find out more about them. And naturally, we'll be presented at court and all the French aristocrats will fall in love with you. How wonderful it will be to live in our own country, among our own people. And we can be together."

His innocent words made her feel even more unhappy than she already was. "Supposing I can't go with you?"

He stared at her, disbelieving. "You're joking, aren't you?" When she didn't reply, Simon added, "I couldn't do it without you, Sister. You've always been my guiding light. I didn't realize it until that swine Chauvin separated us. I went crazy worrying about you, and at the same time, it was the thought that we would be together someday that kept me sane."

Before she could speak again, she heard a footstep behind her, and turning, saw Neill standing there. There was a determined look in his eyes, but he was smiling as he came forward to shake Simon's hand.

"Ha, Simon. Your fine new feathers suit you very well," he exclaimed.

The boy attempted dignity. "It's time I started dressing to fit my new station in life. I was just telling Gabrielle what we'd do when we got to France to claim our father's inheritance."

Why didn't Neill look at her? Gabrielle wondered. She rose from the garden seat as Neill said, "I'd like a word alone with your sister, Simon, if you permit."

The haughty aristocrat-to-be collapsed at once into a still-awkward youth. "Of course," he said. "I know you've got a lot to talk about before— well, you don't need me around." Swinging around on long legs, he marched away, and Neill grinned.

"These months have been hard on him, but they've helped him grow up."

"You said you wanted to talk to me." He nodded but still didn't look at her, so she whispered, "Neill, I have missed you so much."

She held out her hands to him, but he didn't seem to see them and clasped his own behind his back. "Chauvin stands accused of bribery, attempted murder and kidnapping, and his trial date has been set. At your request a lawyer has been appointed to represent him. He doesn't deserve this, but it's been done."

"I know that he's done terrible things, and yet I can't forget that once I thought him the kindest of men." Why were they talking as drily as lawyers themselves, when she wanted only to be in his arms? But now he was telling her that, also at her request, he'd seen to it that Delcie's indentured time had been paid for and that the girl had been reunited with her family. "I'm afraid that there's not much that can be done to Harriet Hook herself. She insists that anything she did for Chauvin was by direct order of Colonel Whitower." Neill paused. "As for the C. and C., it's being reimbursed the money owed to it by Chauvin."

"Neill." She sounded so unhappy, that reluctant as he was to do so, he had to turn and look at her. She was dressed, like Simon, in the height of fashion, but the fine lace ruching at her throat was no paler than she. "What is wrong between us?" She asked him.

When she looked at him like that, when her voice grew low and so sweet that he felt a loosening in his heart, he could hardly bear what he had come to do. He struggled with the urgent need to take her into his arms, as he said, "Nothing is wrong, Gabrielle, but we have to realize that circumstances have changed for both of us."

"You mean the de Montfleuri fortune. But I don't want it." She closed the distance between them with a few, eager steps and put her hands on his broad shoulders. "My dear one, do you really think that I'd go away to France? No amount of money could make me want to leave you."

"Is that what Simon feels also?" A shadow fell across her face as he continued, "I heard you talking. I know he wants to leave for France immediately, and I don't blame him. There's nothing to keep you here now."

"There is everything to keep me here." She moved closer to him, and the movement brought the faint, remembered flower scent to his nostrils. "I told you once that my life was where you were. Nothing has changed." He didn't respond and she added, "Simon will understand. He will see that I must stay here with you."

It was bravely said, and yet he knew it wasn't so simple. If she chose to stay in the colonies with him, she would worry desperately over the boy—and with some justification. Simon, though goodhearted, was still young and foolhardy. Introduced to the corrupt court of King Louis XV, he might fall in with bad companions and grow corrupt himself. "I can't do it without you," he had heard Simon say, and Gabrielle would always remember those words with guilt.

He held himself stiff as he said the words that would give her a solution to her terrible problem. "Gabrielle, my love was for a lovely Acadian deportee and not for a great heiress."

"But I am unchanged," she cried.

He took the hands from his shoulders and returned them to her sides. "Not so. You've a fortune and a future before you, and frankly, I don't see how I can fit into that future." She began to speak, to deny this, but he cut her short. "You are a French aristocrat, Gabrielle. By the terms of your inheritance, you would have to live for several years in France before you could claim the bulk of your father's fortune, and that's as it should be. As for me, I'm a sometime English soldier, partner in an English firm. Even if there were no war between our countries, I would not join you to live in France." He paused. "You see? We belong to different worlds."

Her eyes were enormous in her paper-white face as she whispered, "When have differences mattered between us?"

If he stayed, he would forget his good intentions, sweep her into his arms and tell her that he wanted to marry her now, this minute, and that his heart and soul and body were hers forever. He turned away from her and spoke as coolly as he could. "The differences are greater than either of us can overcome. Even supposing you were foolish enough to stay here and waive your right to your inheritance, you would always be French-Acadian. Our loyalties would be to our countries, no matter what we did. And—I regret to tell you this, but it's true—having a French-Acadian wife could be a liability to me. Just as having an English husband would be to you."

He started to walk away, but before he could do so she stepped in front of him. Her head was high, her eyes snapping with indignation. "What lawyer's talk is this of 'liability'? I do not believe one word you say. Have you risked your life for me—have I been willing to give up honor and family and home for you—so that we can talk of 'liabilities'?" Then the indignation crumbled, and her dark eyes filled with pleading. "I will not go to France. I cannot go. This is where I want to be, only here. Simon is a man now, and he must live his own life. Neill, my dear one, can you look at me and tell me that you don't love me anymore?"

The sweet nearness of her filled him with a surge of hope. He'd offered her complete freedom from him, and she'd refused. She had said that Simon was not a consideration. Chauvin had been wrong. Joy and triumph beat through him.

"Gabrielle," he began.

But now a loud outcry from the street nearby checked his words. Angry shouting came on the wind, and they could hear Simon's loud voice arguing with someone. "Now what?" Neill exclaimed.

He strode down the garden path toward the noise, and though Gabrielle lifted her wide, hooped skirts to keep pace with him, he left her swiftly behind. As he turned the corner of the Colonel's house, he saw that Simon was standing in the middle of the street, blocking the passage of a horse-drawn cart. The angry driver was flourishing his whip and cursing loudly, and the noise had attracted a fair-sized crowd.

"Get out of my way, then," he was bellowing. "What right yer got to block an honest man's way?"

Simon replied in his slightly accented English. "You swine, you call yourself honest? It was you who drove us to the English ships. Get down from your cart or I'll pull you off myself."

The crowd around Simon and the cart's driver increased, and a few yells against Acadian Frenchies were heard. To counter them, French-accented voices shouted against English repression. "Christ," Neill growled, "that young fool is inciting a riot."

A few long strides took him to Simon's side. There he caught the enraged youth by the arms and hustled him to the side of the road. Simon glared up at the big Englishman. "That man was the cart driver who would have taken us to Yorktown. I've a score to settle with him."

"Have done." Neill gave Simon an ungentle shake. "You damned idiot," he went on bitterly, "don't you ever learn? How would your sister feel if you ended in jail—again—for raising hell in the Williamsburg streets? And have you considered how it would embarrass your host?"

Simon's color was high, but he spoke more loudly than before. "I don't care. Kittery is an Englishman—and so are you. In a few weeks I'll wipe English earth from my shoes forever and so will my sister."

About to shake some sense into the boy, Neill saw that Gabrielle had caught up with them. Her eyes were wide as they took in the scene, her hands clenched to her sides.

"Simon—not again," she exclaimed, and as she did so some bystander raised his voice in a shout.

"Damned French," Gabrielle heard the hoarse voice yell. "Why the hell don't they keep out of our colonies?"

Above Simon's head her eyes met Neill's, and in his expression she read anger and disgust. For Simon—and perhaps for her. He was right, she thought in despair. They did belong to different worlds. In these colonies she would always be a liability to him. Even if she dared to let her impulsive, often foolish brother go to France alone, she would bring no credit to Neill. She would always be "that damned Frenchwoman."

She felt her heart grow cold and empty, and when she spoke her voice was also chill. "You are right, Neill. We belong to different worlds."

And as she turned and walked toward the house away from him, Neill seemed to hear the cold mockery of Chauvin's taunt. He had lost after all.

Chapter Twenty

"YOU ARE SO LUCKY, MY CHILDREN, SO VERY fortunate," Father Maboeuf chuckled. "To return to *la belle France,* to live in happiness and honor. Is this not the greatest fortune in the world?"

Gabrielle was silent, but Simon replied enthusiastically for both of them. "Yes, we're very lucky, Father. And as soon as we claim our inheritance, I'll keep my promise and send enough money to you to help our people and even to build a church."

The old priest's nod was happy. He had insisted on accompanying the de Montfleuris to Yorktown, where they were to board the Baron de Sandoville's private ship this early morning, so that he could bless the voyage that would take them to New Orleans and then on to France. "A church would be a blessing indeed, my son," he told Simon, and then he couldn't help reminiscing. "So much has happened since that day when the English came marching into Laforet, but everything is known to *le bon Dieu*. He has been with us through all our troubles."

Because Father Maboeuf was looking at her, Gabrielle said, "I, too, can't wait to leave."

It was true. She was on fire to be gone, to cut the past away from her forever. Each moment away from Neill hurt, in this country where the sights they had seen together haunted her constantly. Even this dock was full of memories.

She turned to seek relief in the ships in the harbor, but here, too, there were remembered sights. In the dawn light they all seemed to be resting together: shore boats and hulks, ships that were being fitted and some that were being repaired, bumboats and heavy-bowed merchantmen. Suddenly, it was as if the early spring morning was no more. Instead, she was transported back to the deck of *The Cameroon*. She had just said goodbye to Neill, but he had come to her . . .

The hand that fell on her shoulder shattered her memories and robbed her of breath. The harbor scene disappeared in the wild, joyous leap of her heart, and she thought he had come after all. But when she turned, she saw only Simon.

"It's time to go," Simon said. Then, blinking at the expression on her face, he added, "Gabrielle, what's the matter with you?"

"It's you," she stammered. "I thought . . ." She bit off the rest of the words and fought for control against true despair. Of course it wasn't Neill, she told herself. Why should it be? She hadn't seen him since that day at Major Kittery's house, when he had told her they belonged to different worlds. By now, he was probably making plans to return to Boston—to *his* world.

"It's time to leave," Simon was repeating. "The Captain wants to catch the tide." He began to walk toward the Baron's ship, and as she followed him, a wind sprang up that carried with it the scent of salt, the mewing of soaring gulls and the clip-clop of carriage horses' hooves in the distance. It was still too early for much activity on the dock, and she was glad. Just now, she couldn't face the usual cheerful harborside clamor.

"Come on, Gabrielle, hurry." Simon paused for Father Maboeuf's blessing, then strode up the gangway. As Gabrielle hugged the old man and followed her brother, he frowned at her.

"Why are you crying?" She shook her head in denial, but his eyes widened and he exclaimed, "*Sacré nom*, is it because of—Craddock?"

Gabrielle remained silent, and Simon leaned close to his sister. "You thought that I was Neill Craddock back there, didn't you? Look, Gabrielle, he's English. You'll find a fine man in France—an aristocrat. You'll be married and live happily with him."

For a moment she allowed herself to think of another man in her life. She could cook for another man, might even spin clothing for him, if indeed fine ladies spun in France, but there the possibilities ended. To be touched, held, loved by another man was horror unthinkable.

"No," she whispered.

Her brother was frowning. "You said you

wanted to come to France with me," he accused. "But you were lying, weren't you?" She didn't answer. "You want to stay here with him."

"Don't be foolish—" she began, but he cut her short.

"You never cared anything about the inheritance—you're coming because you're worried about me. Gabrielle, I wish you'd been honest with me."

Dropping all pretense, she spoke in a low voice. "Neill's feelings have changed since he learned about our inheritance. He feels that we belong to different countries, and that the differences between us can't be bridged. We both agreed it was for the best for us to part." She tried to speak decisively as she added, "Having an Acadian wife would be an embarrassment to him and—there would be no place for him in our life in France."

But Simon was shaking his head. "You really don't know much about men, Gabrielle. Neill Craddock may be English, but he's a gentleman, and he must love you a lot to let you go like this."

"You're wrong." But her eyes were searching the dock as she spoke, and what she saw confirmed her own words. Nowhere was there sight of a tall man with tawny hair and broad shoulders. Even Father Maboeuf had gone. She turned away from the dock and looked blindly into the horizon as Simon spoke again.

"Gabrielle, if I'm the cause of your unhappiness, I'll never forgive myself. And—and it's not fair to me, either. You should have trusted me enough to tell me how you really felt about Neill. I'm no longer a child, after all."

Touched by his obvious sincerity, she leaned against his shoulder. "You're right. I wish now that I'd been frank with you. But what could it have changed? My telling you wouldn't have changed Neill's feelings."

He answered heatedly, "You still can't see it, can you? He's left you for your peace of mind, ninny! He thinks you *want* to go with me. Plus, of course, he's thinking that he couldn't keep you from your inheritance." He added earnestly, "Perhaps you can still go to him, Sister. Talk to him."

Two sea gulls, following so close to each other as to seem to blur into one, sped by the ship. Their whiteness dazzled in the bright sunlight, and Gabrielle suddenly recalled the story of the Indian lovers. To live, to die together—she envied those lovers from the bottom of her heavy heart as she shook her head.

"It's too late," she told Simon quietly, and as if to underscore her words, the Captain of the Baron's ship now gave orders to raise anchor. "Whatever his reasons, Neill and I have said goodbye and there's nothing else for us to discuss. He's gone and we're going. It's over."

The ship, Neill realized, was readying itself to sail with the dawn tide. He was yet too far to see much more than the ship itself, but he knew that the Baron's personal sailors were busy on deck, that the passengers were getting ready to board.

Why, he asked himself, had he come to Yorktown? Both he and his horse were flecked with mud and sweat from their long ride out of

304

Williamsburg. He hadn't intended to come. He'd purposefully stayed away from the de Montfleuris during the days she remained in Williamsburg, and had conducted C. and C. business in various parts of Virginia instead.

When he had returned to town late last night and learned that Gabrielle and Simon were leaving for New Orleans, he had even felt relief. He had intended to let her go, and yet the need to see her again had drawn him like a magnet, and he had ridden to Yorktown through the night like a man possessed. Now he sat on his horse, unwilling to continue on to the docks and yet unable to stay back.

"Monsieur Neill—my son!"

He turned as he heard the breathless voice calling his name and saw Father Maboeuf hurrying toward him. For a moment he was surprised, and then he realized that the old man had also come to bid the de Montfleuris goodbye. Panting from the unaccustomed effort of running, the old priest was saying, "I have a favor to ask of you. You must go to Gabrielle."

"Isn't she well?" If he had ever pretended to himself that he didn't care, the painful rush of emotion he now felt gave him the lie. The old priest shook his head, and Neill leaned down from his horse to demand, "What's wrong with her?"

"She is sick at heart." Father Maboeuf had managed to get his breath now. "She should be happy to leave for *la belle France,* but she isn't. She does not want to leave you, my son."

"That's idiocy." With effort, he softened the hard note in his voice. "You're wrong."

The old man spoke earnestly. "For many years I have known Gabrielle, and I tell you that in her heart she cries for you. At the docks I saw Simon put his hand on her shoulder, saw her turn to him with such a look of hope and joy in her eyes that tears came to my eyes." There were tears in his eyes now as he added, "She thought that you had come to her—as indeed you have."

"I only came to see them on their way." But in spite of himself, his eyes went to the ship again.

Father Maboeuf saw that look and gave the horse's reins a shake. "Go and say goodbye to her," he urged. "What harm can there be in that?"

Neill couldn't think of any good reason to deny the old man's request, but as he spurred his horse forward and guided it closer to the harbor, he knew that Father Maboeuf was wrong. No matter what the priest said, he told himself, there was no need to go nearer. He drew rein in the concealing shadow of some warehouses and from this vantage point looked toward the ship again.

Now he could see the de Montfleuris. Simon stood against the ship's rail, gesturing excitedly, no doubt painting a bright picture of the life they'd lead in France. Beside him Gabrielle stood with her back to the shore. At first he was almost grateful that he couldn't see her face, but the lack was only momentary, for his treacherous memory furnished details of dark eyes and tender mouth framed by a waterfall of sable hair.

He'd been right to tell her what he had, he told

himself around the ache in his heart. She would not have left for France otherwise, and she would have sacrificed not only her fortune but her brother as well. If she had stayed, what could he have offered her? Though by no means a poor man, he could not give her what Chauvin had so cruelly said she deserved: recognition as an aristocrat's daughter, the glittering court of France and the de Montfleuris' untold wealth. This way, she was free to start anew and be happy.

And he'd be free, too. He thought of the challenge of turning the C. and C. into a powerful force through the Americas, thought of travel and adventure. But all these images, once so intriguing, paled to empty pleasure. With painful clarity, he knew that without Gabrielle there could be no real happiness, no full savoring of life for him. When she sailed, she would take a part of him with her.

There was no point in staying here to tear out his heart, and he wouldn't hurt her by letting her see him. Abruptly, he turned his horse and applied the spurs to its flanks.

"Wait—please wait!"

Her voice hit him like a blow to the heart, and he twisted around in his saddle and sawed hard at the reins. His horse reared and plunged, and as he fought to control it, he saw her running toward him.

She had been wearing a fashionable hat, which now hung by broad ribbons to her neck, and her upswept hair had come loose and was tumbling about her eager face. She held her dress away from her hoops as she ran, but she nearly stumbled twice in her hurry to get to him. "Neill," he heard her calling, "don't go."

He didn't answer, and she saw him hesitate, saw the emotions war in his eyes. Catching her breath, she ran as swiftly as she had done as a girl in Laforet, and caught at his hands. "Neill . . ."

She had breath to say no more but lifted her pleading face to him. He himself felt breathless as he saw the unmistakable blaze of love in it. It was the face that had filled his dreams and haunted each waking moment and yet he forced himself to hold back.

"I came to say goodbye," he began, but she shook her head so that the black silk of her hair flew like a triumphant banner in the wind.

"You are lying to me again," she panted. "Enough lies, even if they are lies of love." Then she added, "We have already said goodbye, so if you came it was because I have prayed you would come. Because we can't live apart from each other."

"Gabrielle—" But now he couldn't keep the yearning from his voice and when she tugged at his hands, he swung her upward. She put her foot on his, and then she was in the saddle in front of him and they clung to each other. Mindless of curious eyes, heedless of anything and anyone but her, he kissed her hair, her forehead, her lips. "I'm starved for you," he whispered, and then his voice changed. "But—Simon?"

With her cheek pressed against his shoulder, she replied, "It was Simon who saw you, he who sent me to you. He knows how I feel for you, and he told me that he could never have another happy day if he came between us."

"And you believe him? You can let him go on alone?" he persisted.

She met his questioning eyes frankly. "He promised me to stay in New Orleans for some time with the Baron de Sandoville before going on to France. There he'll have a chance to learn more about our father. I will not lie to you and say that it is easy to let him go alone, but Simon has grown up, Neill. He has finally started to think of someone other than himself. So we need not worry about my brother—only about ourselves."

Her lips were soft and inviting. His mouth brushed hers, caressed it, then took the willing, waiting lips captive with his own. She felt all his yearning, all his adoration in that kiss, and she whispered his name in triumph against his mouth. "My Neill, my golden tiger, my dear one."

The horse snorted beneath them, and realizing where they were, he held her tenderly against him as he turned his mount toward a more secluded part of the docks. Here he dismounted and then lifted her from the saddle to stand within the circle of his arms. Sunlight danced about them and on the blue waves, and in the near distance the Baron's ship, its sails bellied with wind, glided away.

Gabrielle smiled through her tears as she waved to the departing ship. "Simon must seek his own destiny," she said softly and lifted her face to his again. But this time, instead of kissing the inviting lips, he spoke seriously.

"Gabrielle, I didn't stay away only because of the de Montfleuri fortune or because of what you felt was your duty to Simon. France is your country, and in spite of its war with England, you'd have been safe there. I'm not so sure about the colonies. You know as well as I do that there's growing unrest, and in a few years, the time may come when I'll be forced to take sides against English rule."

Her eyes were also grave. "Don't you think I know this? And do you for a moment think that such a consideration would keep me away?" Then, speaking quietly as she might in prayer, she added, "No matter what comes, all I ask from *le bon Dieu* is that we live together and for each other for all our lives."

He kissed her again, even more fervently than before. Holding her close to him and tasting the wine of her lips, he was filled with deep happiness. "It's been so long since you and I were together," he told her. "I want to show you how much I've loved you and missed you. But there's something I have to do that's even more important."

Her eyebrows rose in surprise, and her dark eyes held a glint of mischief. "More important even than this?"

"Infinitely more important. We have to walk down to the docks and persuade Father Maboeuf to marry us. I think we'll have no trouble on that score." Bending to kiss her again, he spoke against the willing warmth of her lips. "You had your chance to be free, my lovely lady of the forest. Now you belong to me."

To his surprise, she shook her head and her

mischievous, happy laughter bubbled into the bright spring morning. "But that is not true," she told him softly, and when his eyes questioned hers, she leaned happily against him. "Don't you know that we have always belonged to each other?"

Tapestry

HISTORICAL ROMANCES

POCKET BOOKS

If you've enjoyed the love, passion and adventure of this Tapestry™ historical romance…be sure to enjoy them all, FREE for 15 days with convenient home delivery!

Now that you've read a Tapestry™ historical romance, we're sure you'll want to enjoy more of them. Because in each book you'll find love, intrigue and historical touches that really make the stories come alive!

You'll meet Aric of Holmsbu, a daring Viking nobleman…courageous Jeremiah Fox, an American undercover agent in Paris…Clint McCarren, an Australian adventurer of a century ago…and more. And on each journey back in time, you'll experience tender romance and searing passion…and learn about the way people lived and loved in earlier times.

Now that you're acquainted with Tapestry romances, you won't want to miss a single one! We'd like to send you 2 books each month as soon as they are published, through our Tapestry Home Subscription Service℠ Look them over for 15 days, free. If not delighted, simply return them and owe nothing. But if you enjoy them as much as we think you will, pay the invoice enclosed.

There's never any additional charge for this convenient service—we pay all postage and handling costs.

To begin your subscription to Tapestry historical romances, fill out the coupon below and mail it to us today. You're on your way to all the love, passion and adventure of times gone by!

HISTORICAL *Tapestry* ROMANCES